LEADING LADY

LEADING LADY

HEYWOOD GOULD

FIVE STAR
A part of Gale, Cengage Learning

GALE
CENGAGE Learning™

Detroit • New York • San Francisco • New Haven, Conn • Waterville, Maine • London

GALE
CENGAGE Learning

LIBRARY OF CONGRESS CATALOGING-IN-PUBLICATION DATA

Gould, Heywood.
  Leading lady / Heywood Gould. — 1st ed.
    p. cm.
  ISBN-13: 978-1-59414-648-0 (alk. paper)
  ISBN-10: 1-59414-648-9 (alk. paper)
  1. Burglars—Fiction. I. Title.
PS3557.086L43 2008
813'.54—dc22   2007037896

First Edition. First Printing: February 2008.

Published in 2008 in conjunction with Tekno Books and Ed Gorman.

TO PATTIE

AUGUST 2006
"JERRY LOVES GLORIA."

Lang traced it with his fingernail on the cool, silken curve of Gloria's behind.

"Guess what I wrote," he said.

She yawned. "I can't."

"You can too." He slid his nail across the small of her back. She shivered and tried to suppress a moan. After all these years she still had to be seduced and he loved her for it.

He traced "Gloria loves Jerry" on the other cheek. "Guess."

She turned over. Stretching languidly, she grasped the bed-post. "Gloria loves . . . pizza. I'm hungry, Jerry."

He nuzzled the fragrant stubble on her thighs. Her essence rose in a cloud around him. "I can never get you to say the L word."

"I say it and you'll be gone in the morning."

"After five years you still don't trust me."

She raised her belly off the bed and arched her back. "Can't trust anybody who makes me feel like this."

The sun slanted through the blinds, but stopped discreetly short of the bed. Her body glowed like a pearl in the gloom. It was so quiet it seemed time had stopped.

He always wanted to make love on the afternoon of a score. He told her it relaxed him, but it was really his way of saying good-bye. In case the thing went south that night and he got caught he wanted to make sure he had her smell in his nose and on his fingertips, her taste on his tongue, so he would have the memory that much longer until it faded. But he never told her that.

"Nervous?" he asked.

"Edgy," she said.

He explored the places on her body where one part ended and another began. The secret spot where her ass flowed into her legs. The downy trail to her navel, the smooth hollow of her belly and above it the hard ridge of her ribs that led to a meadow of soft flesh beneath her breasts. He kissed the warm pulse on her neck just under her ear. Her lips parted and she put her finger in her mouth as if she had forgotten something. Eyes squinty shut . . . Waiting . . .

Gloria, Gloria, Gloria . . .

"What Are We Stealin'?"

Gloria asked.

"*Self Portrait* by Isaac Levitan."

He showed her a photo of the drawing. The head of a long-haired young man with a trim goatee and an amused expression like he was laughing at a secret joke.

She stared at it, shaking her head. "This thing is worth millions? You can get a guy on Sixth Avenue to do it for fifteen bucks . . ."

"Aintcha got no culture, bitch?"

He read her the description he had taken off the Internet. "The work of Isaac Levitan belongs to the highest achievements of Russian culture," it said, and went on about how Levitan had been friends with "the cream of the Russian intelligentsia and had been adopted by Anton Chekhov." He hadn't painted that many pictures in his short life. Most of his work was already in museums, so what was in private hands was priceless.

"What's the fat Albanian gonna do with this priceless work of art?" she asked.

"Hanif won't do nothin'. He got the contract from Tony Rasso, who probably got it from Joe Di, who probably got it from some crooked art dealer. He pays us forty-five and gets a hundred from the dealer who's probably got a buyer lined up for a coupla mil. Everybody makes more goin' up the food chain. We're on the bottom. We do all the heavy liftin' and we get the least . . ."

"How do we go up to the next level?"

"Get different parents."

Lang had jogged past the building for a quick look. It was what they called "prewar," which meant built in the '20s with ledges and overhangs and flying buttresses that made climbing easy in case you had to get out fast. It had big picture windows overlooking Central Park. Fourteen floors with a penthouse, one duplex to a floor. Small lobby, one elevator, no operators. The elevators opened onto the apartments so all you had to do was push the floor button, pick the lock on the elevator door, and you were in. There was probably a silent alarm that rang at the security office. Not a problem. He'd be long gone by the time the cops showed up.

He had rented two rooms at the Orsini, a tourist trap across from Lincoln Center, for the drop. One room was down the hall from the other. The plan was for Gloria to get there early and watch through the peephole to make sure Hanif wasn't sending guys to rip them off.

She laughed at his precautions. "Look at all the money Hanif makes on you. He wouldn't hurt a hair on your head."

"Ever hear the story of the scorpion and the frog?" he asked. "The scorpion says, 'Gimme a ride across the pond on your back.' The frog says, 'If I do you'll sting me.' The scorpion says, 'No I won't 'cause I'll drown.' Off they go. But in the middle of the pond the scorpion stings the frog. As they're dyin' the frog says, 'Why'd you do this?' The scorpion says, 'I'm a scorpion, it's my nature.' Hanif's a crook. It's his nature to screw people even if he screws himself in the bargain."

Gloria winced. "I've had enough of this world, and the shmucks in it."

"Don't worry," he said. "After this you won't have nothin' to do with them."

She was still warm and flushed from the shower, a towel

wrapped like a turban around her head. Lang nibbled a tiny hair curling out of one of her baby pink nipples. "How come you always look so good? You never do anything but smoke weed and drink champagne . . ."

"When I hit thirty it'll all start saggin'."

"What'll you do then, get surgery?"

"You kiddin', I can't wait to get fat and ugly. Maybe men will leave me alone."

She put on a simple black cocktail dress and threw a distressed leather jacket over it for that "I could care less" touch. He wore the tuxedo with the black silk shirt and the red string tie with the diamond steer's head clasp that he'd bought in Houston. Put his tools in a Mark Cross envelope.

At seven thirty they took a cab to Fifty-ninth and Fifth and walked along the park side. A line of gleaming limos was in front of the building. A young crowd, sleek and sexy, was streaming in. The paparazzi were making a commotion taking pictures at the entrance. It was a high-profile party, Security checking invitations at the door.

"This is a pretty stupid time to hit the building," she said.

"It's the only window we have," he said. "Act impatient. Rich people don't like to be kept waiting."

She gave him a shove. "Take a walk around the block, coach. I know what to do."

The wisecracks gave him a pang. Her attitude had fooled him for years. After going through three leading ladies who had broken down at crucial moments he thought he had finally found a cool customer. But after they became lovers, after he got through to her softness, he realized that the wisecracks were just a cover. She was scared stiff. But she always stepped up.

A light rain began to fall. Chauffeurs opened beach umbrellas to escort their clients to the door. Lights blazed on the seventh floor where the party was, but almost every other window was dark.

Lang hid in the horde of autograph hounds and celebrity groupies clustered at the curb. A security guy checking invitations gave Gloria that look of disbelief guys got when they saw her. A paparazzo tried to take her picture and the security guy shoved him away. Then he escorted Gloria into the entrance. Lang could see she was getting a good look at the guest list. He walked to the door and heard her say, "There's my husband." She ran out and grabbed his arm. "Here you are . . ." And whispered: "We're Fred and Molly Hutchinson. You came straight from work and forgot the invitation." As they neared the entrance she went into her peevish rich wife act. ". . . And this photographer jumped up in my face—that creep over there—and wouldn't leave me alone until this nice man chased him . . ."

The security guy blushed. "No problem . . ."

"Did you bring the invitation?" Gloria asked.

Lang slapped at his pockets. "Oh jeez, I must have left it in my suit at the office. Should I go back?"

"No, it'll be all over by then." Gloria turned pleadingly to the security guy. "Could you trust us, please. Fred and Molly Hutchinson."

The security guy checked the list. "Where do you live?"

"Eight Seventy Third Avenue."

He gave her a keen look. "That the building on the corner of Eighty-eighth?"

"That's it," she said with a secret "call me" smile.

Lang played the clueless husband. "Thanks man."

They squeezed into the elevator with some giddy gay guys, who checked Gloria out, memorizing her style, while they talked about what was hot at the silent auction.

The elevator groaned and wobbled like the Ferris wheel at Coney Island.

"That's New York for you," Lang said. "Ten million-dollar apartments and they still have the original elevator."

The door opened onto a gala scene. Everything was black and gold and bubbly. Guests did the room with the precise choreography of hardened party people.

"What if the real Fred and Molly show up?" Gloria asked.

"They'll give their tickets to the other security guy," he said.

"What if they don't?"

"They will," he said. "God protects drunks and cat burglars . . ."

Gloria grimaced in annoyance. "Can I get a straight answer?"

"Do one turn around the room and leave," he said. "Your work is done."

As soon as she hit the vestibule he could see heads turning. A waiter came up to offer her a cocktail.

The door closed and he pushed twelve. The elevator got to the floor and stopped. The lock was rudimentary, the same one they used on the mailboxes. He had a thin metal pick in his case. A push and a twist and the door slid open. A narrow foyer led to a large living room. Lang played his pencil flash across the room. If there was a motion sensor it had already picked him up. Worst case he'd have at least a minute. He took a deep breath and walked quickly into the living room, panning the flash. There was a lot of art on the walls, paintings with lights hanging over them. No simple pen, ink, and watercolor drawings. Could be in the study or the master bedroom.

He walked to the end of a long hallway.

The master bedroom was large and hexagonal. There was a round bed with black silk sheets under a round canopy. The smell of weed hung in the air. Bottle of cognac on the night table; big-screen TV with a pile of porno discs; Jacuzzi, douche, and a steam shower in the master bath: the room read "player," a guy whose money had come fast and shady.

Lang spotted the drawing in a short hall that led to the library. No light over it, a cheap lacquered frame. Hung in an obscure spot like it had been put up to cover an empty space on the wall.

He broke the frame and slid the drawing out. He rolled it up in plastic laundry wrap and put the package in a Bergdorf's shopping bag.

In the elevator, he turned the key, relocking the floor. He heard a blast of gaiety when he passed the seventh floor. Downstairs, guests were streaming in. The security guy didn't even see him leave.

In the cab he called Gloria at the Orsini. "Everything cool?"

"I'm watching *Horny Housewives* on Spectravision."

"Hold that thought, I'll be right over."

He called Hanif.

"Done?" Hanif asked.

"We'll be at the Orsini Hotel, room three eleven."

"Where you find this place, Hicksville?" Hanif loved his American slang.

"Look in the Yellow Pages."

Tour buses were double parked outside the Orsini. The lobby was full of anxious foreigners sitting on their luggage. Lang always got a room on a low floor so they could make a quick getaway. A red-cheeked family clutching theater tickets pushed their way onto the elevator as he got off.

He went to 321 and put the Bergdorf's shopping bag on the bed. He called room service and ordered champagne for 311. Piper Heidsieck was the best they had. As he walked down the hall he heard parental voices raised, toddlers screeching behind the doors. He knocked softly.

The door opened. A big guy with a blonde buzz cut and rimless glasses stepped out of the darkness. "We got your girl," he said. He shined a flashlight beam on the back wall. It caught

Gloria standing in the corner. A shadowy figure was behind her. A thick hand with a ruby pinky ring was over her mouth.

Hanif set me up, he thought.

Another guy came out from behind Buzz Cut with a big gun, maybe a .45. He put the barrel to Lang's forehead, while Buzz Cut frisked him.

"Give it up," Buzz Cut said.

"Look, we're all professionals here," Lang said. "Let's talk this over."

Buzz Cut shifted his weight. Lang knew what was coming and steeled himself. A big fist crashed into the side of his jaw. He staggered and tried to stay on his feet, but the floor came up and cracked him in the head. He heard a muffled shriek. It sounded like Gloria, crying. "Jerry . . ."

"You don't have to roughhouse the girl," he said.

Somebody kicked him in the ribs. The breath flew out of him. "Three twenty-one," he gasped. "Card key's in my pocket."

Buzz Cut stuck out his foot and rolled him over. Snatched the card out of his pocket. "Take the girl," he ordered.

Lang could hear Gloria cursing behind that thick hand. There was a scuffle as they dragged her out.

Buzz Cut stepped hard on the back of his neck. "If it's not there, she's dead."

"It's there. Why would I lie?"

The door opened. The light flooded in. The door closed. It was dark.

Lang tried to get up, then stopped. In the silence the air screamed like a million sirens. Someone was in the room. A chair squeaked. Lang focused on a spot at the corner of the bed. A foot appeared. He grabbed an ankle and pulled.

A shot cracked, the bullet crashing into the rug next to him. He twisted the ankle and raised it off the floor. He could feel the guy fall back and fight for balance. Lang pulled harder. The guy went down with a thud that shook the room.

Lang scrambled over a thick, squirming body. He found the gun hand and twisted the wrist. Grabbed a clump of hair. Slammed a face into the floor once . . . twice . . . three times. The gun came loose.

Gotta get Gloria.

The guy rolled over pinning him against the bed. Lang slammed him in the head with the gun, but the guy kept coming, arms and legs churning.

Gotta get outta here.

Lang pulled the trigger. The gun jumped, the acrid smell of cordite biting into his nose. The arm went limp.

Lang crawled over the body.

"Gloria!"

He opened the door and stumbled out, blinking in the harsh light.

"Freeze! Police officers."

The hallway was full of guns all pointed at him.

Cops. How did they get here?

"Turn around or you're dead."

People rushed by him into the room. Somebody yanked the gun out of his hand.

"Major Hartung, get in here," somebody yelled. "Donofrio's down."

"Sonofabitch!"

Buzz Cut came at him. Then he was falling. Eyes closed, clawing at the air. Falling, falling, wind roaring in his ears.

Calling . . .

Gloria . . .

"The Russian is Angry,"

the Voice said.

Major Cliff Hartung, Delta Force on temporary assignment to Special Ops Domestic wanted to throw that stupid red phone against the wall. It had been an impossible operation from the get-go and now he was going to take the heat for its failure.

"I don't know what happened, sir. Last I saw Lang was out cold on the floor."

"Well he got up, didn't he?" the Voice said. "The Russian is calling all over town. He's spoken to my bosses and to their bosses. He wants to know what happened."

"I put him down hard, sir. All Donofrio had to do was to shoot him."

"You should have had two men in the room."

"With two men it would have been tougher to justify killing him while he was unarmed."

"Easier than trying to resolve the problem now that he is alive," the Voice said. "You should have picked a better man."

"Donofrio was the only reliable person we could get."

The Voice snapped. "The Army is like baseball, Major. Three alibis and you're out."

"Sorry sir."

"Do you know who the Russian is?"

"Yes sir, I recruited him," Hartung said, but he knew that wouldn't stop the lecture.

"He's our connection to all the big oil brokers in Central Asia."

"Yes sir, I know that."

"He's our best source of information in that area."

"I know."

"He makes a lot of money for a lot of important people."

"Yes sir, I surmised that."

"A word from him can make or break both of our careers. Do you understand that, Major?"

"Yes sir."

"We promised we would take that individual out of his life."

"I know, sir."

"Do you have any ideas on how to proceed going forward?"

"Not yet."

"Well, get some."

"Yes sir."

"TAKE THE DEAL,"

Lang's lawyer said.

"But it's a cover-up."

"It doesn't matter. You shot a cop . . ."

"I didn't know he was a cop."

"It doesn't matter. He's in a wheelchair with a tube in his dick. You could get fifteen to twenty-five for attempted murder of a law enforcement officer, tack on another three to seven for burglary. But they're willing to give you seven to twelve for assault with a deadly weapon."

"You know why? Because they stole the painting."

"They say you stole the painting and hid it. It's the official version. Nobody's going to believe your story."

"What about this Major Hartung?"

"There was no cop named Hartung on the team that arrested you."

"I didn't say he was a cop. He was a major. Maybe State Police. Maybe Army."

"For chrissake, there was no Major Hartung, okay? You were delirious. You had just shot a cop . . ."

"I shot him because he was trying to kill me."

"You can't plead self-defense. You shot a decorated police officer in the performance of his duty."

"But they killed Gloria."

"No one at the hotel remembers a woman of Gloria Pavlich's description."

"It was the cops, don't you understand?"

"It doesn't matter, don't YOU understand? You're a degenerate criminal who stole a work of art and paralyzed a heroic public servant for life. Take the deal."

A Cell is a Good Place

to remember. At dawn when the noise had finally subsided and there was only the murmur of the radios and the occasional squawk of a guard's walkie, Lang would console himself with the memories of Gloria and their time together.

In those days he was going through two or three leading ladies a year. One had gotten knocked up, another couldn't stay away from the blow. He had dumped the latest because she couldn't get over in upscale restaurants and hotels. You could teach a grifter anything but class.

And then he found her.

His fence, Hanif, had a strip joint called the Casbah in the wholesale meat district. He walked in there one night with nothing but a few cocktails and a trashy stripper on his mind. A leggy blonde with a turned-up nose was working it on stage. She was sexy and unattainable. Your best friend's little sister. Your brother's girlfriend. The butchers were climbing over each other to shove twenties in her garters.

She was the one.

Hanif was getting two hundred for a lap dance with her plus two fifty for an eight-dollar bottle of Korbel. Lang threw five hundreds across the bar.

They sent him to a room in the back. The blonde came in and turned an hourglass upside down. Took the Marlboro from between his lips. "Dirty habit . . ." She had a smooth contralto voice, which was a key asset. Those screechy sopranos broke the spell as soon as they opened their mouths.

"You're special," he said.

"You don't have to grease me, baby," she said. "I'm yours 'til the sand runs out."

"I know you do well here," he said, "but I can put you next to some real money."

"You gonna make me a star, lover. Gee, I've never heard that before."

"I got a cleaner job for you," he said.

"Hanif won't let me go. I'm sort of under contract to him."

"That's okay. Hanif's sort of under contract to me."

Later that night he made Hanif an offer. "I wanna buy the blonde. Three Gs against the commission on our next score."

Hanif was a middleman for Tony Rasso, who ran robbery crews for Joe Di Corso, a Gigante captain in the Village. He was a chunky guy with a livid scar down his shaven head. He wore a driving glove on his left hand to cover the three ugly stubs where someone had cut off his fingers. Lang called him "Mittens," when he got too cocky.

"I don't know, Jerry, she's a big earner for me."

"I wouldn't want her if she was a dud, Mittens. I'm bein' nice. I could pull her outta here."

"Yeah, but then she'd be in a fire and wouldn't look so good. Five Gs flat."

After hours she came to his apartment. She was wearing four-inch spikes and a red leather mini skirt.

He shook his head. "All wrong. I need class."

"Class needs money," she said.

"Hanif tell you who I am?"

"He told me I could do well with you."

"I need a stall. Someone to distract the mark while I do my thing."

"They tell me I can be very distracting," she said.

"I gotta warn you. Hang with me and there's a felony in your future."

"At least I'll have a future." She looked him up and down. "Anything else I have to do?"

"That'll be up to you."

She took the cigarette out of his mouth. "You're gonna be easy . . ."

And he was. Five years and he never looked at another woman. They went all over. Everything was smooth, no arrests, only a few close calls. She got better and smarter with every move. No place was off limits. She had the kind of sex appeal that made men go weak in the knees and worry if they could measure up. But women never resented her because she had the assets they really admired, thick hair, flawless skin, great taste . . .

They made middle-class money, low six figures. Lang was careful and only took the easy scores. He had spent a year in Rikers and never wanted to go back. Gloria had never been inside at all. He had promised her that he would always take the heat if they ever were busted, but as the years went by she was getting nervous.

"Our luck won't last forever," she said.

"It wouldn't if it was luck."

"It is luck," she said, her voice going up, "and it won't last forever."

A woman will buy your story for years, but one day she decides she's had it and then it's time to come up with something different.

He took her to Hana, on Maui. They walked on the beach, the warm rain splattering in the sand. At night the surf roared and the waves crashed against the rocks, while she slept with her head on his chest.

They drove into a small town on the winding road along the

coast. There were motels, restaurants, souvenir stands. It looked like any other tourist spot, but then Lang ran into Sam Ruben, an old-time weed dealer from Coney Island. It turned out that the whole town was peopled by retired marijuana desperados, the smart ones who had cashed out before the cops or the Colombians showed up at their door. They were the dour merchants in the flowered shirts selling leis and pina coladas.

It was a town full of people who minded their own business and never asked questions. After a week he told her, "I've never felt so peaceful in my life."

"So let's stay," she said. "We could open a little snack bar or something."

"You wanna wear cutoffs and flip burgers for a buncha whiny kids?"

"I wanna get high and hang on the beach. Eat pineapple and coconut and fresh fish. I wanna relax and not keep lookin' over my shoulder."

Lang did a quick audit. He had taken twenty Gs out of the safe deposit box for the vacation. That left a hundred and eleven thousand, plus seventy-eight thousand in the Schwab account.

"The idea is to build up the portfolio slowly, so we can look like smart investors. We quit when we have a million clean money."

"That'll take years. Who says we won't get killed or busted before that and the state gets it all?"

"They'll never catch us," he said. "We're too good."

She gave him a weary look. "You'll never quit. You love stealing. For you it's like sex, probably better. Well, it's not as much fun for me. I got wrinkles I shouldn't have. The paranoia is making me old before my time."

A woman stops buying your story and then tells you she's getting old because of you, you've got a problem. "Okay," he had said. "Next job is our last."

"Promise?"

"I promise."

She looked at him, dubiously. "Don't lie about this."

"Have I ever lied to you?"

"You never had to."

Back in the city Gloria checked their voice mail. "The Albanian called seventeen times."

Lang got him on the phone. "Hey, Hanif . . ."

"I thought you were dead."

"I was on vacation."

"So you don't send a postcard? I'm sittin' on big money for you."

"This our last job?" she asked when he hung up.

"Last job," he said. And he meant it.

"Joe Di has a guy inside Tiffany's at the Bellagio in Vegas," Hanif said. "He says a Russian is coming to town with a load of uncut diamonds to sell."

It was probably swag, but uncut jewels were untraceable. And in the jewelry business nobody looked a gift horse in the mouth.

"He's asking a million and a half," Hanif said, "which probably means it's worth four or five mil wholesale. Joe Di will pay twenty-five Gs plus expenses for you to steal it."

"Why doesn't he just give some thug a thousand bucks to hit the guy on the head?"

"Joe don't wanna blow his Tiffany guy's cover. He wants you to make it look like the Russian was scammed by hotel hustlers."

Three days later they checked into the Bellagio. There was an envelope waiting for Lang with a passkey from Housekeeping that opened all the rooms. "Go to Petrossians, the caviar joint in the lobby," Hanif had told them. "There'll be a white-haired guy in a dark suit with an American flag in his lapel drinking

Cristal. The guy he's with is the mooch."

And there they were. The white-haired guy was desperately amiable. "Overplaying," Lang said. The mooch was wearing a Sean John jumpsuit, flashing gold, laughing a lot, and throwing twenties at the waitress.

"Party animal," Gloria said. She watched the mooch flirt with the waitress. "I won't have to convince this clown he's irresistible, he already thinks he's God's gift."

That night she put on a pair of black slacks and a white silk blouse that hung loose, but you could see her breasts stirring every time she moved. Her blonde hair was pulled back from her forehead, framing the perfect oval of her face. Her untroubled baby blues looked like they saw no evil.

In the casino they spotted the mooch at the hundred-dollar blackjack table. Gloria took a seat across from him. Lang went to the lounge for a drink. When he came back they were sitting together and the mooch was teaching her how to double up.

Lang went to twenty-dollar video poker machines. He was already down four hundred when she walked by without looking at him and said: "Room twenty-two eleven. We're going to the Picasso . . ."

It was a fancy joint off the lobby, a three-hour meal. He'd have plenty of time in the room.

There was a security guy by the elevator. Lang flashed his room key. The guy smiled and let him pass. They're gonna have to close that loophole, Lang thought. Just 'cause you're stayin' in one room don't mean you can't break into another.

He used the passkey to get into 2211. Another loophole. They got a computer that tells them somebody's in the room, but they don't know who. Pretty soon they'll have a fingerprint reader by the door, so they can make sure the right person is in the right room, but I'll be clippin' coupons on Maui by then.

The closet safe was like opening a can of tuna, but it was empty. Lang searched all the obvious places, drawers, mattress, suitcase, clothes, air conditioner. In the bathroom he checked the shower drain, the vents. The guy had a mini salon of moisturizers, cremes, conditioners. He checked the blow dryer, found a big black dildo and took that apart . . . Nothing . . . Found a vial with about fifty blue pills. Viagra, don't leave home without it. If he thinks he's gonna get lucky with Gloria, he'll run up and pop one so he can hit the ground running.

Lang stepped out of the room. On the way down the hall the mooch hurried by, fumbling for his key. Lang smiled—Gloria had him all lathered up. In the elevator he remembered: the guy was wearing fancy casual but had a beat-up old Nike fanny pack around his waist. That was it. The safest place to keep the diamonds was right on him in that fanny pack. He'd only take it off to go to bed.

Lang walked through the lobby to Picasso. Gloria was alone at a table, staring into a goblet of red wine.

"I think he's got the goods in that fanny pack," Lang said. "You'll have to make him take it off. Did you bring that stuff they give alcoholics to stop 'em from drinking?"

"Antabuse, my secret weapon. But that'll just make him puke."

"So hold his head and put him to bed. Then when he's out, take the pack. I'll get you a substitute in case he wakes up."

"I'm doing all the work on this thing."

"Sometimes it be's that way."

Lang went down the street to Caesar's Forum Shops and bought a fanny pack at the Nike store. Gambling bored him, but he knew Security was watching on closed circuit screens and would get suspicious of a guy just sashaying around, so he went back to the Bellagio and fed the video poker machine.

After an hour his pager went off. On the twenty-second floor,

Gloria was sitting on the bench by the elevator, holding the fanny pack.

"The diamonds are in here just like you said."

"Bow down in the presence of genius."

He gave her the dummy fanny pack. "Won't need it," she said. "He'll be out for the night . . ."

They were checked out in a half hour. Lang had rented a car so they wouldn't have to sweat airport security. As they drove into the desert, Gloria opened the fanny pack. The uncut, unpolished jewels didn't look like much, but they caught the light in their jagged edges and they seemed to fill the car with their presence.

"Tell me about it," he said.

"You men are a trip," Gloria said. "You'll do anything for five minutes of fun."

"Did you ever watch guppies screw? It's over in a second and then the female eats her hubby. You'd think the male guppies would turn queer or go into the priesthood . . ."

She looked out of the window. She wasn't in the mood for his jokes.

"That Antabuse usually has them on their knees in a minute, but Sasha was strong," she said.

"Sasha, huh? Got pretty friendly."

"I know he felt it comin', but he was so horny he wanted to get it on with me before he got sick. In the elevator he was all over me. 'You're so beautiful, he says . . . So classy.' "

"You look like royalty next to these Vegas sluts," Lang said.

"We got into the room and he threw the fanny pack on the floor. Poor guy, he was so anxious he just doubled over. I took him in the bathroom and he puked his guts out. After a while it was nothin' but water. Then he got the dry heaves, and he didn't even have enough fluid to break a sweat. He was white as a sheet. He reminded me of Carl."

"Your junkie ex?"

"Carl used to scream and roll on the floor. Sometimes I'd have to put him in a cold shower. He'd turn so white you could see his veins right through his skin. So while I was in there I was thinkin': Here I am back where I started, cleanin' puke again."

"Only this time it's for a bag full of diamonds," Lang said. "Did you tuck little Sasha in?"

"Yeah. Put a cold towel on his head. He kissed my hand. 'You are an angel,' he says."

"Love at first sight. Too bad we can't come back and nail him again."

"Told me he was a big shot in New York."

"Who isn't?"

"Said he could do a lot for me."

"He just did."

She didn't laugh. When he brought champagne into the motel room later that night to celebrate the score, she was asleep. He stood over her, but she burrowed deep into the pillow in that don't-wake-me mode.

In the morning, she turned him away.

"Don't you want to celebrate our final score?" he asked.

"I'll believe it when I see it."

She had lasted longer than most of his other ladies, but the pressure was getting to her.

This was one leading lady he didn't want to lose.

"Pick out a nice spot," he said. "As soon as I collect we'll go on a long vacation. Then we'll figure out what we're gonna do with the rest of our lives."

Lang didn't trust Hanif. He would pick an out-of-the-way place for the drop and give Hanif an hour and a half to get there. He would show up early and case the area to make sure Hanif didn't have guys ready to rip him off. This time he chose a Howard Johnson's off the Sunrise Highway in Queens. He rented a white commercial-looking van and sat in the parking lot for an hour. This really is the paranoia that makes you old, he thought.

Right on time, Hanif showed up in his gold Mercedes with his cousin Malik. They were sitting in the last booth in the empty dining room eating hot fudge sundaes, fat guys getting fatter and not caring. Lang had put the diamonds in a FedEx envelope. Hanif handed him the payoff in a paper bag.

Lang counted two hundred and forty-eight hundreds under the table.

"You're two bills short."

"Somebody's gotta lick the envelope," Hanif said, but he gave up the two hundred.

"I always catch you. Why do you keep doin' it?"

Hanif shrugged. "I'm a thief . . ." He slipped a piece of paper across the table. It was a printout of a drawing. "Your next job. Am I good or what?"

No point in telling Hanif he was retiring. Lang read the artist's name.

"Isaac Levitan," he said. "Sounds like a furrier."

"We gotta have it by Friday," Hanif said.

"What's the hurry?"

"The owner is lending the drawing to a museum in Dallas for a traveling show. It'll be away for months."

The address and apartment number were on the back of the sheet. Central Park South, twelfth floor. No number meant one apartment to a floor. That meant very rich people with a lot of stuff to steal. "Doorman building, I assume," Lang said.

"Doorman and security . . ."

"They got off-duty cops working in those buildings now. Think I'll take a rain check."

"Joe Di wants you."

"There's other guys."

"Not for this one. See, there's gonna be an AIDS benefit in the building on Thursday night. Big party. It'll take somebody who looks good in a tuxedo. Somebody with a nice lookin' broad on his arm."

"It'll also take somebody with an invitation," Lang said.

"Thirty-five Gs," Hanif said.

That was ten more than he'd ever gotten.

"Fifty," he said.

Hanif nodded sourly. "I knew that was comin'. They played it wrong uppin' you ten. You woulda done it for the same money."

"Maybe not. Then they lose their big payday. You tell them cheese benders I won't do it for less than fifty."

"I'll tell 'em you called 'em cheese benders, too."

Hanif had phoned ten times by the time he got home. "When you gonna give me your cell number?"

"Never, I hope."

"I mean mobile number, wiseass, you know what I mean. They're pissed about the money, but I told 'em you were the only man for the job."

"You're my new best friend," Lang said.

"They had a big discussion about it," Hanif said. "They'll go forty-five . . ."

"They got elevator operators in the building?"

"How should I know, I don't live there."

"Where's the drawing?"

"In the apartment like I told you."

"What is it, a studio?"

"You want me to tell you what room it's in, whether they got elevator men. Want me to steal it for you too?"

Gloria had gone out to Brooklyn to visit her mother. She'd

had it tough growing up strict Catholic and then hitting the streets when she was fifteen. The old lady had disavowed her and now she was trying to get back in her good graces with handbags and costume jewelry, nothing too gaudy. She had made up a phony cover story that she was working as a legal secretary and going out with a young associate in the firm. She dyed her hair back to its natural brown before every visit, dressed in sensible business clothes, and spent a few hours getting her story straight because she knew the old lady would grill her looking for lies. It never went well. She'd come back cranky, vowing never to see "the old bitch" again. It was always the best time to sell her on another score.

She knew as soon as she walked in. "You look like a dog who just pissed on the rug . . ."

"I gotta break my promise," he said.

She didn't look surprised.

"I know I told you Vegas was the last one, but this one is too good to turn down."

She hardly listened as he laid it out. He knew she was still replaying her day with Mom.

"I'll do this one, Jerry, but then I'm done. I'm not kiddin'."

"This is the last one. I swear," he said. "Forty-five Gs will get us a nice long vacation on Maui . . ."

Her sigh broke his heart.

"Let's go to Fiji," she had said. "I wanna be as far away from Brooklyn as I can get."

A grifter always pulls one score too many. A week later she was dead.

"Not good enough. I want the burglar dead."

Hartung reported to the Voice.

"You know the burglar, you know when he's going to do it," the Voice said. "Should be easy."

But it had turned out to be a nightmare. In the Army there were soldiers known as "survivors." No matter what happened they came out alive. You always wanted to be in their units, hoping they might drag you through with them.

Lang, this little lowlife burglar, was a survivor. He had emerged unscathed from Hartung's brilliant ambush. Now he was safe behind bars, but the Russian still wanted him dead.

"Think of it as a training exercise," the Voice said.

Hartung kept his tone level. "We've never trained to break into a prison and kill a man, sir," he said. "We have no operational precedent."

"The ability to improvise is the sign of a good officer," the Voice said.

A junior officer never refused an order. But you were allowed to use logic to show that a course of action would not yield the desired result.

"Yes sir, but it seems to me that the consequences of failure far outweigh the reward of success."

There was a pause. It was like when you hit a guy and he was stunned for a second before he came at you.

"What's your point, Major?" the Voice asked.

"Well sir if we fail, the whole Domestic Ops unit will be exposed."

"That's true every time we embark on any operation."

"Yes sir, but this operation has such a low probability of success that it is putting the whole mission in considerable jeopardy."

"You don't show a lot of confidence, Major."

"I make a probability assessment of every operation I

undertake, sir. I feel it's my duty to tell you that this one is not looking good."

The Voice got clenched. "A very important asset has made a personal request that this guy be dealt with, Major."

"With all due respect, sir, our primary responsibility is to track terrorists and prevent attacks on our soil. Jerry Lang is a small-time criminal. Now that he is in jail I don't see how he can be considered a threat to national security."

"He has been so designated, Major. 'Ours not to question why. Ours just to do or die.' Our mission is to make sure he doesn't get out of jail alive. Any further questions, Major?"

"No sir."

NOVEMBER 2006
THEY TRIED TO KILL LANG

in Dannemora.

A Mexican gangbanger who was doing life for shooting three kids in a drive-by flipped a firebomb made of cleaning fluid and floor wax through his cell door during cleanup. In a heartbeat, the eight-by-ten space was an inferno. The guards sprayed him with a fire extinguisher while they waited for the first aid team. In the thirteen seconds it took to put the fire out he got second-degree burns over most of his body. The wet towel he managed to drape over his head scalded the skin off his face.

They put a twenty-four-hour guard on him in the hospital.

"You got a problem with the Mexican Mafia?" they asked.

He tried to shrug, but the slightest movement sent waves of fire through him. The vibration from his whisper rattled the charred skin of his throat. "Must have been a mistake. I get along with everybody."

They transferred him to Greenhaven. In the library an old lifer came up behind him and jammed a handful of sharpened pencils into his neck. He kept stabbing at Lang like a man possessed until guards pulled him off. Two of the pencils penetrated an inch and a half, almost piercing his jugular. Lang developed lead poisoning with such a high fever that he was on IV antibiotics for three days. In his delirium he saw Gloria snarling and flailing as they dragged her out of the hotel room. That last look of terror in her eyes was frozen in his memory.

When the fever subsided and the fog cleared he asked himself:

who's trying to kill me? There was only one answer—Hanif. He was giving out jailhouse contracts on him. But why?

The warden came to visit.

"This old man hasn't raised his voice in twenty-three years in here," he said. "What'd you do to him?"

"I don't even know the guy," he said.

"What's with the code of silence, Jerry?"

"It's a mistake. I'm not in any cliques, I'm not into any rackets. I get along with everybody."

They moved him to Elmira and put him in the protection unit with the fruits and the snitches. He was in isolation, alone in his cell twenty-three hours a day, surrounded by guards everywhere he went. But he knew Hanif had reached out for somebody. It was just a matter of time.

A guy named Joe Comparelli moved in next door. A "one-hit wonder," who had only broken the law once, killing his partner and burying him in the grease pit of their body shop.

He showed Lang pictures of his kids and cried over the mess he'd made of his life. He was just a football player with a bad temper, who didn't know his own strength, he said.

After a few weeks, the guards let them work out together. After a few more weeks, Lang noticed they weren't even coming into the exercise area when the two of them were there.

One day it was raining in the yard. He and Comparelli took shelter under a ledge. The guards were patrolling above and couldn't see them. The surveillance cameras would show them as blurry silhouettes. Lang knew he would have at least thirty seconds. He grabbed Comparelli's arm.

"Who's payin' you to kill me, Joe? Who's pickin' up your kids' college tuition?"

Comparelli blinked. "What?" His free hand strayed toward his back pocket. Lang clawed his face and slammed his head against the wall. Jammed his thumbs into Comparelli's eye sockets.

"You got one chance before I make you a blind man," he said.

Comparelli tried to shake his head. Lang pressed harder.

"Don't waste time, Joe."

Comparelli gasped . . . "Okay . . ." But before he could talk, Lang heard footsteps and felt a shock.

They tased him, pepper sprayed him, whacked him with clubs, kicked him in the back. A guard stepped up like a batter at the plate and slammed him in the head. The hot lights went on. Then everything went black and cold. He was in a coffin so narrow his arms were stuck to his sides. He panicked and tried to kick his way out. He couldn't move.

He woke up in the prison hospital. He had gone into taser shock, kicking and screaming so hard they had to put him in restraint. He had a broken cheekbone, a fractured skull, and cracked vertebrae.

They gave him an Ambien. As he was drifting off, the Captain of the Guards showed up at his bed.

"I thought you and Comparelli were friends, Jerry?"

"He had a shank in his back pocket," Lang said. "He was gonna kill me."

"You got him first, Jerry," the captain said. "You gouged one of his eyeballs right out of his head."

"Good," Lang said and fell asleep.

He dreamt that Gloria was walking through the lobby of the Waldorf Astoria in a black off-the-shoulder dress with the pearl necklace and the diamond earrings. Heads turned, talk stopped. As she passed she flashed him that secret smile, which said, "I've hooked every man in the room. Which one should I reel in?"

When he was better they brought him to the local DA's office. The warden was there and some guys who looked like Feds.

"Give us a hand, Jerry," the warden said. "We're trying to save your ass."

"And doin' a piss poor job," he said. "You guys need a snitch to tell you your names. There's more rats in this joint than on a sinking ship and you can't even catch a rumor . . ."

They finally decided they couldn't protect him in the state system so they shipped him to Allenwood, a federal minimum-security facility in Pennsylvania. They put him in a dormitory with tax cheaters, insider traders, mail fraudsters, mellow crooks who were doing easy time and waiting to get back to their hustles. No killers in the population, not even a bully. The guards were like valets, doing little favors, phoning brokers, bringing bagels and the Sunday papers. The inmates lavished money and gifts on them, custom shirts, Eagles tickets.

Lang worked himself up to a thousand push-ups and two thousand sit-ups a day. The other inmates called him "Animal," and vied to get him on their flag football teams. Even the guards tried to reassure him. "The only thing you have to worry about in here is a bad stock tip."

After a few months the easy routine of the place began to get to him. He started dreaming about Gloria again. She was in the motel room, waiting for him in bed. He came in with the goods and pulled the covers off. She held her arms out to him and shivered as he laid a handful of cool diamonds on her body.

A new guy named Breen came in, a cop who had been caught shaking down Ecstasy dealers in Pittsburgh. He was a buck-toothed Irish guy with squinty blue eyes and thick, mottled fists. He looked with scorn at the other inmates like he was still a cop and better than they were.

A week later the bus brought another new guy, Hassan, an ex-Marine, who had been busted getting hashish sent to him

HARTUNG HAD BEEN ALL STATE

quarterback three years in a row. But the college recruiters said he was too slow and would never stand up under a Big Ten pass rush. That was seventeen years ago and he was still pissed off about it.

He didn't have the grades or the boards for a D2 school so he joined the Army. As an enlisted man there was only one way to rise through the ranks: volunteer for the elite units. He got into the Special Forces just in time for Gulf One. They sent him on high-risk recon missions three weeks before the invasion. He hang glided over the desert to check Iraqi positions. Buried himself in a berm out of sight of the Iraqi patrols and watched the portly old men and frightened boys of the notorious Republican Guard dig trenches around the perimeter of Kuwait city. Then, a few weeks later, he flew over the battle zone in a Blackhawk as Hussein's "crack" troops were overwhelmed in one day by tanks and Bradleys. He watched bulldozers bury thousands of men in tons of sand, while Cobras and A-10s with their thunderous ordnance swooped down to pick off the ones who tried to retreat. "Operation Fish in the Barrel," the pilot said, and they all laughed.

After the Berlin Wall the Pentagon had decided it needed a unit that was capable of gathering intelligence and deploying small groups for assassination and sabotage in the former Soviet Union, just in case some of the Reds didn't want to go quietly. Hartung volunteered. They promoted him to lieutenant and sent him to language school in Monterey for an eight-week course in German. When he passed that they gave him eight weeks of Russian and he aced that. They sent him to Fort Bragg for a six-week course in intelligence gathering and psychological warfare. Then they stationed him at the embassy in Berlin. His cover was military attaché. He recruited agents and went on assassination missions in Kosovo and Croatia. In '93 after the first attack on the World Trade Center he had parachuted into Afghanistan and lived in a cave for three months trying to locate Osama.

After 9/11 they bumped him up to captain and sent him undercover to Iraq. He used his knowledge of German and his blonde Nordic looks to pose as a Swiss arms dealer. He went to every police and army post from the Basra right up the highway to Baghdad before the invasion, taking photos on his cell phone and e-mailing them back to Command and Control in Kuwait. They made him a major for that. He was a three-R man, "Ribbons, Ranks and Raises." As a major he averaged around sixty-six K a year with combat pay and allotments. Garbagemen made more than he did. But after twenty years he might be able to parlay his medals and war stories into a big-time security job. That is, if he stayed alive and didn't mess up.

In seventeen years his missions had been clear, which made his orders easy to execute. The key to success in the military was acceptance and obedience. When they woke him up and said he had been chosen for a top secret mission he packed his bag.

They flew him to an old ABM base in South Dakota. The briefing was held in an underground war room, the kind they had built in case of Soviet attack.

The men were escorted separately into cubicles so they couldn't see anyone else in the room. Each cubicle had a terminal. A civilian, his face obscured, his voice altered, appeared on the screen and gave the briefing. Hartung assumed he was a civilian because of his smartass way of talking.

"Most top secret missions are voluntary," he said. "But this is one is so sensitive we knew we wouldn't get any takers, so we volunteered for you.

"The Pentagon is responsible for the war on terror," he said, offering another clue that he was a civilian because a military man never even used the word Pentagon. It was always "the suits."

"But we are not satisfied with the intelligence we are getting from our most crucial theater of operation, the U.S.," he said. "So it has been decided to expand our activities in this area. We are launching a unit called Special Ops Domestic to collect information on terrorist activity and to take action when necessary to prevent an attack.

"Although the military is forbidden by law to engage in any intelligence activity on American soil, the Secretary has gotten written authority from the White House and the relevant congressional oversight committees. We will be allowed to operate, to develop sources, to spy on our enemies, and to take action when we feel our national security is threatened."

"Aren't we overlapping the FBI on this?" someone asked.

"Maybe, if they were doing their job in the first place," the civilian said.

Hartung heard feet stirring, chairs creaking, throats clearing in the other cubicles. It was clear now that this operation was directed against the rival agencies as much as it was against spies and terrorists.

"The level of secrecy in this program is unprecedented," the civilian said. "Officially, you will not have a change of assignment. Your checks will still be drawn on the Department of the Army. You will not know any of the other station chiefs in the program. Nor will you know your commander. He—or she—

will be an altered voice on a red phone. You will have an office and a squad working under you. Your job will be to keep tabs on the informers, defectors, suspected spies and terrorists in your area and to take whatever action we deem necessary to prevent another attack on American soil."

After the briefing Hartung had gotten his orders in a sealed envelope. They flew him back to DC and he drove down to Fayetteville, North Carolina, the small city that had grown up outside of Fort Bragg. He lived in a complex of town houses, the "officer's club," the locals called it, a comfortable community of retired and active military. The houses were of solid red brick. There were vans and jeeps, basketball hoops in the driveways, gas grills in the back yards.

When Hartung got home his kids were in the kitchen eating DeGiorno pizza and his wife, Beverly, was on the back porch with a cigarette and a glass of chardonnay.

He bent to kiss her on the back of the neck. "Guess what," he said. "We're going to New York."

That had been eight months ago. They put him in an office with a cover business, Executive Airline Leasing Inc. He had passed the time pleasantly enough, following Arabs and minor diplomats. The only hard part was ducking the FBI and Secret Service and DHS guys who were working on the same targets.

Then they dropped the Russian on him and he learned the real purpose of his mission: to babysit this priceless asset. Pick up his dry cleaning, drive him around when his chauffeur was otherwise engaged, get his Chinese takeout. He was a valet, a personal secretary, and then, suddenly, an avenger.

One day the Russian took him into the alcove off his bedroom. He showed him a little ink and watercolor drawing of a bearded young man.

"Somebody is planning to steal this from me," he said.

"So call the police," Hartung said.

"Not good enough. I want the burglar dead."

Hartung reported to the Voice.

"You know the burglar, you know when he's going to do it," the Voice said. "Should be easy."

But it had turned out to be a nightmare. In the Army there were soldiers known as "survivors." No matter what happened they came out alive. You always wanted to be in their units, hoping they might drag you through with them.

Lang, this little lowlife burglar, was a survivor. He had emerged unscathed from Hartung's brilliant ambush. Now he was safe behind bars, but the Russian still wanted him dead.

"Think of it as a training exercise," the Voice said.

Hartung kept his tone level. "We've never trained to break into a prison and kill a man, sir," he said. "We have no operational precedent."

"The ability to improvise is the sign of a good officer," the Voice said.

A junior officer never refused an order. But you were allowed to use logic to show that a course of action would not yield the desired result.

"Yes sir, but it seems to me that the consequences of failure far outweigh the reward of success."

There was a pause. It was like when you hit a guy and he was stunned for a second before he came at you.

"What's your point, Major?" the Voice asked.

"Well sir if we fail, the whole Domestic Ops unit will be exposed."

"That's true every time we embark on any operation."

"Yes sir, but this operation has such a low probability of success that it is putting the whole mission in considerable jeopardy."

"You don't show a lot of confidence, Major."

"I make a probability assessment of every operation I

undertake, sir. I feel it's my duty to tell you that this one is not looking good."

The Voice got clenched. "A very important asset has made a personal request that this guy be dealt with, Major."

"With all due respect, sir, our primary responsibility is to track terrorists and prevent attacks on our soil. Jerry Lang is a small-time criminal. Now that he is in jail I don't see how he can be considered a threat to national security."

"He has been so designated, Major. 'Ours not to question why. Ours just to do or die.' Our mission is to make sure he doesn't get out of jail alive. Any further questions, Major?"

"No sir."

November 2006
They Tried to Kill Lang

in Dannemora.

A Mexican gangbanger who was doing life for shooting three kids in a drive-by flipped a firebomb made of cleaning fluid and floor wax through his cell door during cleanup. In a heartbeat, the eight-by-ten space was an inferno. The guards sprayed him with a fire extinguisher while they waited for the first aid team. In the thirteen seconds it took to put the fire out he got second-degree burns over most of his body. The wet towel he managed to drape over his head scalded the skin off his face.

They put a twenty-four-hour guard on him in the hospital.

"You got a problem with the Mexican Mafia?" they asked.

He tried to shrug, but the slightest movement sent waves of fire through him. The vibration from his whisper rattled the charred skin of his throat. "Must have been a mistake. I get along with everybody."

They transferred him to Greenhaven. In the library an old lifer came up behind him and jammed a handful of sharpened pencils into his neck. He kept stabbing at Lang like a man possessed until guards pulled him off. Two of the pencils penetrated an inch and a half, almost piercing his jugular. Lang developed lead poisoning with such a high fever that he was on IV antibiotics for three days. In his delirium he saw Gloria snarling and flailing as they dragged her out of the hotel room. That last look of terror in her eyes was frozen in his memory.

When the fever subsided and the fog cleared he asked himself:

who's trying to kill me? There was only one answer—Hanif. He was giving out jailhouse contracts on him. But why?

The warden came to visit.

"This old man hasn't raised his voice in twenty-three years in here," he said. "What'd you do to him?"

"I don't even know the guy," he said.

"What's with the code of silence, Jerry?"

"It's a mistake. I'm not in any cliques, I'm not into any rackets. I get along with everybody."

They moved him to Elmira and put him in the protection unit with the fruits and the snitches. He was in isolation, alone in his cell twenty-three hours a day, surrounded by guards everywhere he went. But he knew Hanif had reached out for somebody. It was just a matter of time.

A guy named Joe Comparelli moved in next door. A "one-hit wonder," who had only broken the law once, killing his partner and burying him in the grease pit of their body shop.

He showed Lang pictures of his kids and cried over the mess he'd made of his life. He was just a football player with a bad temper, who didn't know his own strength, he said.

After a few weeks, the guards let them work out together. After a few more weeks, Lang noticed they weren't even coming into the exercise area when the two of them were there.

One day it was raining in the yard. He and Comparelli took shelter under a ledge. The guards were patrolling above and couldn't see them. The surveillance cameras would show them as blurry silhouettes. Lang knew he would have at least thirty seconds. He grabbed Comparelli's arm.

"Who's payin' you to kill me, Joe? Who's pickin' up your kids' college tuition?"

Comparelli blinked. "What?" His free hand strayed toward his back pocket. Lang clawed his face and slammed his head

from Iraq. A wiry black dude, he was neat and quiet and taped porno shots around his bunk, so nobody would get the wrong idea. He and Breen circled each other for a few days like they were going to do battle for Alpha Dog.

But Lang knew it was an act. They were the ones. They were picking their spot.

He asked for a transfer. Said he couldn't sleep because he was under constant fear of attack. They showed him the closed circuit cameras that monitored the dorm 24/7. He asked to be allowed to exercise alone. "This place is a menace," he told the warden. "You got pool cues, free weights, baseball bats . . . Lethal weapons . . ."

The warden laughed. "This isn't a prison, Jerry, it's a time-out for spoiled rich kids. We haven't even had a fist fight in four years."

"Send me to one of the Air Force bases where I can have my own room," Lang said.

"C'mon Jerry, we can't treat you that good. After all you shot a cop."

Late one rainy autumn afternoon, he was doing squats, 275 pounds, in the twilight. Across the yard he saw two silhouettes on the wall come together briefly, then melt away. In a second it was dark and the yard was empty.

People were watching the news in the rec room. There was a shuffling footstep. A shadow fell across his path. He spun like a discus thrower and threw the barbell at a clump in the darkness. There was a crash and a grunt. He stumbled, trying to regain his balance, and crashed headfirst through the picture window.

The inmates scattered in a panic. He lay dazed in the broken glass, blood pouring off his face.

"They were going to kill me," he told the guards.

"Who?"

"Them," he said pointing to Breen and Hassan, who had just walked in.

The inmates were spooked. They insisted Lang be taken out of the barracks. Felons they might be, but some of them still had influential friends.

The warden came to see him in the infirmary.

"You're outta here, Jerry," he said. "Mattewan . . ."

"That's a psycho ward," Lang said. "You gonna punish me because you can't protect me?"

"You had a paranoid episode, Jerry. You could be a danger to yourself and the other inmates. We're doing this for your own good."

They were writing him off, getting him out of the system. When it finally happened they would blame him. "How were we supposed to help the guy when he wouldn't cooperate?"

He'd be an easy target in the hospital. People coming and going, doctors, nurses, patients, visitors. There were a hundred ways to kill him. Poison his food, pin him down and shoot him full of adrenaline, drown him in the bathroom and blame one of the psychos.

They gave him two Atavan. He palmed the pills—this was no time to be groggy. He heard voices and feigned sleep. The guards wheeled in Elliot Straubing, a cold calling con man who sold phony annuities to senior citizens, wiping out their life savings.

"Hey, Jerry, wake up, you got a roommate."

Lang rolled over and rubbed his eyes. "What happened to him?"

"He was watching the news. Suddenly he jumps up. 'Lies,' he yells, 'all lies,' and goes over like a tree."

"Can you imagine, a guy strokes out over somethin' on TV?"

"I gotta lay here with a stiff all night?" Lang said.

"Don't worry, they're sending an ambulance to move him."

After they left Lang pulled back the sheet and looked down

at Straubing. He was still warm, still looked aggrieved.

It was a long shot, but he had nothing to lose. He sneaked into the examining room and found a pair of scissors. Then he lifted Straubing onto his bed, turning his still petulant face to the wall. He tied Straubing's toe tag around his own big toe, got into Straubing's bed, put the sheet over his face and waited.

It took hours for the ambulance attendants to show. They were grumbling about hitting traffic into New York and why didn't they get a freezer to store these guys . . . who ever heard of a jail without a morgue?

They zipped a body bag around the sheet with him in it and dropped it so hard onto the gurney that he flinched. But they didn't notice, and wheeled him down the corridor, bouncing him down the steps and throwing him into the ambulance. They didn't bother to lock the wheels so the gurney flew around the back, slamming into walls. On a short stop it banged so hard into the back door that the body bag fell onto the floor with a thump and Lang had to bite his lip to keep from yelling.

"That's gonna leave a nasty bruise," one of them said and they laughed like it was the funniest thing they ever saw.

Soon Lang caught a whiff of marijuana smoke. They were blasting the radio, still laughing about the bouncing body. He got the scissors out and cut a hole in the body bag, enough to reach the zipper. He started to ease out of the bag. Slowly, slowly, hoping they wouldn't turn.

But then it came to him. Two stoned-out dudes. They'd freak when they saw a zombie walking. He stood up and stretched out his arms like Frankenstein. The driver caught sight of him in the rearview.

"Wha!"

His partner jumped and shrieked.

Lang jammed the scissors against the driver's neck.

"This'll teach you to disrespect the dead."

HARTUNG HAD A
TWELVE-INCH

Meatball Marinara, extra cheese, from Subway and a new *Golf Digest*. Then the red phone rang. It was the Voice.

"Jerry Lang is out."

"Finally," Hartung said.

"Not out of your life. Out of jail."

Hartung put down his meatball. "Escaped?"

"It was kind of ingenious, really. He switched places with an inmate who had dropped dead. Got into the body bag. Overpowered the ambulance attendants, tied them up, and dumped them in the woods along the Jersey Turnpike. He took their ATM cards, hit 'em for the max in Fort Lee and then hit another machine in Manhattan, so he's got walking around money. Your boys Breen and Hassan missed him by a mile. Put them on the next plane back to Baghdad."

"Cops'll get him," Hartung said.

"Maybe not. He had a three-hour head start. We assume he's in the city."

"I guess I should alert my friend on Central Park South."

"What you should do is find Jerry Lang. You have a file on the case. Cover every place he would go, everybody he would see."

"I'll have to take Osler and Stewart off the Iranian."

"Do it."

"What should I do when I find him?"

"Make sure he doesn't hurt our friend."

"Turn him over to the cops?"

"It's probably better just to finish this once and for all."

Hartung thought that if he repeated the order the Voice would see how crazy it was.

"Finish it? On the streets of New York? Without blowing my cover?"

"That's what we pay you the big bucks for," the Voice said. And hung up.

Hartung called the Central Park South number. A woman picked up. "Hello, Major Hartung."

"You're not supposed to answer this phone," Hartung said.

There was a second as the phone passed from pillow to pillow.

"Good morning, Major," the Russian said.

"Morning, Colonel. Your friend has escaped." In the silence Hartung could see the man reaching for one of those stupid Russian cigarettes with the big filter. Then replying in that irritating, pedantic way.

"Once again we are faced with the enigma of America. How has the most powerful country in the history of the world been created by such a bunch of incompetent boobs?"

"You're safe," Hartung said. "I'll protect you with my life."

"Your children's lives as well," the Russian said and hung up.

was the Casbah. He told the cab driver Little West Twelfth, but when he got there he thought the guy had taken him to the wrong place.

Only two years before there had been trucks clogging the streets, butchers carrying bloody sides of beef, hairy pigs, and prim white lambs swinging from meat hooks. Seven o'clock in the morning the Casbah would be jammed with beefy guys in blood-spattered white coats, chugging Buds and pounding the bar. Now all those empty storefronts where the homeless camped out had been turned into boutiques and bistros. There was a steel and glass hotel where there had been a garage and an SRO.

It was one of those late fall days when the light turned blue early and you could feel the knife of winter in the air. Lang opened the door and a shaft of sunlight shot into the bar, falling on a lady bartender in a leather vest. She blinked irritably and stepped back into the gloom. There were only two customers, a Hasidic Jew chewing his beard and an old white-haired Irish guy with a drink in his hand.

Lang closed the door, restoring the consoling darkness. He was wearing the ambulance driver's uniform, shirt unbuttoned, cap on backward, the perfect wiseass civil servant.

The bouncer was sitting on a stool by the door, reading a Greek newspaper. He had three chins, two of them shaven, and bright, beady snowman eyes.

"Nobody called an ambulance," he said.

"Hope not," Lang, said. "Hanif around?"

The bouncer shook his head. "No Hanif here."

"He don't own the joint no more?"

"No Hanif here," the bouncer said.

In the old days, the Casbah was so packed that between the smoke and the body heat you could break a sweat. Now it was as cold as a subway toilet. On the bar a dancer stood splay-legged over the Hasid while he fumbled through his bills trying to find a dollar to put in her G-string.

"Hurry up rabbi, I'm freezing."

"I'm looking, I'm looking . . ."

She was tall with broad shoulders and big hands. Her breasts drooped softly over muscled abs. Pelvic bones lurked like sharp stakes over the smooth flesh of her hips. Her hair was short and dyed white blonde. Slashes of aqua eye shadow highlighted her green eyes. She was dancing to New Age music, whale moans, castanets, and waterfalls.

The bartender slid a coaster in front of Lang and folded her tattooed arms. She reminded him of those bodybuilders in the can who couldn't make up their minds what team they were on so they alternated between giving blow jobs in the shower and beating the crap out of guys in the yard. Everybody in the bar reminded him of a jailhouse character. The bouncer was like one of those thickheaded thugs who had done one small time crime after another until they finally got locked up for stupidity. The old Irish guy was like a befuddled lifer. Even the Hasid looked like those guys who were in for swindling Medicaid or killing oldsters in crooked nursing homes. Only the dancer was different. He hadn't seen anybody like her in jail, although a few of the guys had given it a good try.

"Hanif around?"

"Nobody of that name around here."

Lang took out a pack of Marlboros.

The bartender flexed her tris with an ominous look. "No smokin'."

"Who says?"

"Mayor Bloomberg. Where you been?"

He thought fast. "Baghdad for fifteen months."

"They got newspapers there."

The old Irish guy came to his defense. "Leave the kid alone, Maxine, he's fightin' your battles for you. What are you drinkin', pal?"

"Stoli rocks." Good thing it was dark. They would have taken one look at his "jail pale" and realized he hadn't spent much time under the desert sun.

"I was in the Merchant Marine," the old guy said. "Torpedoed twice in the Atlantic . . ."

Maxine gave Lang a short shot. A real "drop dead, get outta my joint" drink. But it was the first booze he'd had in two years and it went right to his head. He clutched the bar while a top spun in his brain. When it slowed down he caught the dancer's eye. He thought he saw the story of her life in that one brief glance. He wanted to yell up to her: "They always try to trample the beautiful souls." He closed his eyes and breathed through his nose. Calm down, the booze is blowing your fuses. The ardor subsided. But as she walked offstage he got panicky like he was never going to see her again.

"Hey, where you goin'?" he called.

"Show's over," Maxine said.

"Can I get a lap dance?"

"They're called privates now and we don't do them in the morning."

The bouncer showed up next to him. "Your ambulance is double parked, my friend."

He was a big guy, but light on his feet, and wouldn't go down easy. "No smokin', short shots, no lap dances," Lang said. "How do people have fun in here?"

The bouncer put a heavy hand on his shoulder. "People do. You don't."

Lang flashed a roll of twenties. "Boss wouldn't like it if you let me walk outta here with all this money, would he, Maxine?"

She looked at the bouncer. He shrugged.

"A hundred bucks for the dance. A hundred and fifty for the champagne," she said.

"The champagne costs more than the girl? What's this world coming to?"

"Sit at that table in the corner. She'll be right there."

"Hurry up, I'm afraid of the dark."

The dancer squatted on stage squinting over at him as Maxine gave her the rundown. The bouncer went back to the door and peered over his paper, a flicker of interest in his dead eyes.

The dancer came through the darkness carrying a bucket and a bottle of champagne.

"You want me to pop your cork, lover?"

"I'm counting on it." He watched as she wrestled with the bottle. "You're new to this."

"Yeah."

"Actress?"

"Not lately."

"Taking class. Waitressing, temping. Some dude you thought was your friend recruited you. Said you could make more money as an exotic dancer. You didn't know what that really meant."

"I knew . . ." She spread his knees and moved between his legs, undulating slowly. He got lost in the whiteness of her skin. Breathed her perfume. It had been a while since he had smelled a woman. You forgot . . .

She put a cool hand on his forehead and pushed him back. "No touching, lover, you know the rules."

"You have cat's eyes. Anybody ever tell you that?"

"Every day."

"Cats are proud. They say, 'Here's my beauty. You don't see it, your loss.' "

She bent closer, teasing him with her warm breath. Her breasts swayed hypnotically.

"You see most strippers have a dog's mentality," he said. "A dog says, 'Love me please. I'll lick you, I'll roll over. Anything, just love me.' "

"You're a talker," she said.

"Talk stops time. As long you're talking you're okay."

She fondled herself, gazed adoringly at his crotch.

"What's your name?" he asked.

"Letitia."

"Letitia. Nice name. Your mother had high hopes for you, givin' you a name like that. Boy, if she could see you now."

"I think we can leave my mother out of this."

She turned. Bending slowly she wrapped her arms around her knees until her behind was staring him in the face. The whale moans got louder, Chinese cymbals crashed.

"Does Mittens still own this place?" he asked.

"Who?"

"Chunky Albanian guy. They call him 'Mittens' because somebody cut off the fingers of his left hand with a chainsaw."

She straightened up suddenly and took a closer look. "What are you up to?"

"You ever go out with the customers?"

"I'm not a hooker."

"Too bad, it's an easy life. You sit in a warm apartment, watch soaps and wait for the phone to ring . . ." Lang showed her a fistful of twenties. "Thousand bucks . . . ?"

She smiled and kissed him lightly on the forehead.

"I'll be right back," she said.

moved through the darkness, head down, hoping she could get past the bar to the liquor room where she dressed.

CiCi, a skinny Salvadoran girl with no ass and huge boobs was on stage, shaking and jiggling. "Check 'em out, dudes, they're real."

Letitia didn't know who this guy was, but his eyes were gray like rain clouds. If he had a problem with Hanif she didn't want to be in the middle. She'd grab her clothes, slip out the back exit, and never return.

Spiro, the bouncer stepped out and grabbed her arm.

"Hanif wants you."

The hallway was lined with photos of strippers. Spiro punched out a code and opened the door on a windowless office filled with smoke. Hanif was wearing a leather jacket with a driving glove over his mutilated fingers and talking quietly on the phone. His cousins, Archie and Malik, two dark guys in car coats and ski caps, were eating bagels out of grease-stained bags.

Hanif's bloodshot eyes bored into her. "What'd he want, that Mick?"

"Wanted me to go out. Offered me a thousand bucks . . ."

"It's a come-on, he don't have ten cents. He's gonna stiff ya or rob ya or worse. He could even be a psycho pervert." Hanif looked indignantly at his cousins. "You believe these sick bastards think they can come in here and victimize our girls?"

"Unbelievable," Archie said. "I don't believe it." He made every "v" sound like a "w" and every "w" sound like a "v."

"We gotta teach this guy a lesson," Hanif said.

"Send a message," Malik said.

"Where you live, baby?" Hanif asked.

"Forty-fourth and Tenth."

Hanif took a long drag as if he were trying to suck all the smoke out of the cigarette. "Schmooze this guy. Take him to your place."

"I'm just a dancer here."

Hanif nodded reasonably. "I know. Do it as a personal favor to me."

When Hanif asked for a favor you did it. The nicer he was the bigger the threat. Letitia had heard stories about girls who wouldn't go home with him or do lesbian shows for his friends. They were beaten up and gang raped in back of a van in a Bronx garage. And they never worked in any strip bar on the East Coast again.

She had been so careful to stay out of trouble in New York. There had been a girl in her scene study class who had gotten drunk at a loft party, fell down an elevator shaft, and lay there for hours with a broken leg, screaming and fighting off the rats. Letitia had been careful about drinking after that. She had been careful about men after a guy she didn't even like drained her ATM card. She was wary of agents who promised big modeling jobs, girls who wanted to stay at her place for a few days because they always stole her makeup. After two years in New York she thought she had it covered, but careful wasn't good enough. You had to be lucky and she wasn't.

"Do I have to screw him?" she asked.

Hanif squinted at her through a cloud of smoke. "Nah, we'll screw him for you."

I Can't Believe

I'm falling in love, Lang thought.

It would be funny if it weren't so pathetic.

He watched Letitia walk toward him, hips swinging, totally on the hustle. She was just a dayshift stripper, a semipro, who was about to have sex for money with a guy she thought was a jerk.

So why am I making a poem out of her?

He was getting Gloria vibes all over again. It was horny plus some other feeling that he couldn't locate in his body or mind. It went deeper than looks or attitude. Back to the caveman days where you picked your mate by smell. Smell never lied, smell never changed, smell hooked you for life.

She had changed into a Mets jacket and a pair of jeans.

"This how you go on a date?" he asked.

"I don't like being hassled on the subway."

"Flaunt it. Short skirts, tarty makeup. Men will be intimidated. And leave you alone."

"You an expert on male psychology?"

"Most men are petrified of sexy women. They know they're in a battle they can't win."

"What about you?"

"I always give up without a fight. I can get a room."

"I'd rather go to my place."

Lang opened the door and breathed in the bright, brittle air.

He was a little off schedule, but it didn't matter. He'd hang with this girl until dark, then slip away to fight another day. A chilly gust blew off the Hudson. Letitia shivered in the skimpy windbreaker and he put his arm around her. She seemed to melt right into him.

"Don't worry," he said. "It won't be so bad."

HARTUNG'S OPS HAD AN
IRANIAN

in their sights.

He was a slow-moving old guy named Farraj, who had spied on the mullahs for the Americans. When the Ayatollah took over he grew a beard, took off his tie, and spied on Americans for the mullahs. His cover was commercial attaché to the Iranian American business community. The Iranians thought he was an effective sleeper, but from day one Hartung had been onto him.

Hartung had sponsored Osler and Stewart, two Delta Force vets, for his unit. It had been a struggle. The Voice called them "Frankensteins" because all they could do was kill. But Hartung argued that what they lacked in finesse they made up in balls.

He gave Farraj the code name "Smoothie" for his calm, unhurried MO. "Sit on this guy," he told his boys. "Everywhere he goes, everyone he sees." Osler and Stewart followed Smoothie for seven months while he visited businesses and made speeches about investment opportunities in Iran. He hadn't spotted them, which was big points right there when you were dealing with a professional. Now he had made his move, contacted his American connection, the manager of a Yemenite restaurant on Atlantic Avenue. They would meet on the subway or in noisy restaurants. The next day the Yemenite would go to a dead drop where he would pick up a plain white envelope. Maybe Smoothie was passing him money or coded instructions or dirty pictures. It didn't matter; it was big and they had it all on video.

They had gotten a court order to bug the Yemenite, his friends, and family.

But Hartung had called them in early that morning. "Flag on the play."

He showed them mug shots of Lang. "Guy's a cat burglar. Shot a cop. Escaped from Allenwood last night."

"Not for nothin', boss, but we're about to catch Smoothie with his dick in his hand," Osler said.

"I hate that expression 'not for nothin',' " Hartung said. "This guy Lang could be a threat to a very important asset of ours. It's about a nine million to one shot that he'll get near him, but we have to be proactive." He gave them a list of Lang's former addresses and hangouts. "Last seen in an ambulance," Hartung said. "Probably wearing an ambulance driver's uniform."

"What if we find this guy?"

"Watch him and report back to me."

"I don't understand," Osler said. "Why pull us off Smoothie for a tail job?"

"You never know," Hartung said. "I may need your special skills."

LETITIA LIVED

on the second floor of a three story walk up on Tenth Avenue and Forty-fourth Street.

"Hell's Kitchen they used to call this neighborhood," Lang said. "To us it was the West Side."

I'm pathetic, he thought. I'm trying to impress a hooker.

Her door was between Hunan Taste and Mundo Viajes, a travel agency.

"Viajes al America del Sud," Lang read. "Sounds like a love song, don't it?"

I'm tryin' to make a hooker laugh.

They walked up a steep, dark stairway.

"The toughest people in the world lived in this neighborhood," he said. "Shanty Irish, they called 'em. No hope but a lotta imagination. When you have imagination but no hope you can be a very dangerous person."

I'm tryin' to be profound.

She had a door lock, a top lock, a dead bolt. "Forget the hardware," he said. "Get yourself a pit bull."

She finally got the door open. He moved in close, admiring the soft downy curve of her neck. Sunlight was seeping through the slats in the blinds. Then something moved and blocked the light. Someone was in there waiting for him.

This bitch is setting me up.

He grabbed her at the door. "Gimme a preview, baby." He jammed his lips against hers, slipping the surgical scissors out

59

of his pocket.

She tried to push him away. "Wait a second . . ." He twisted the collar of the Mets jacket under her neck, shoved her around the door, and stepped in behind her.

A man was flattened against the wall, a tire iron raised over his head. Lang stabbed backhanded, catching him in the forehead. Then caught him in the cheek. The tire iron came down over his shoulder. He stabbed blindly, once . . . twice. The man sagged.

There's always two.

A shape rose from behind the couch. Something glittered. Lang lunged for it, flailing with the scissors. Hot blood spurted onto his face. The shape turned into a man, hands clasped around the scissors in his throat. He staggered and tried to talk, but spat blood instead of words. His legs buckled and he fell, clawing at the air.

In the silence, the ceiling creaked. The upstairs neighbor was moving around. A TV went on. Lang felt along the wall for the switch.

Letitia was crawling on her belly toward the door. She froze when the light went on. The man at her feet wriggled like a sleeper trying to get comfortable. Blood seeped out from under him.

She turned away, jamming her fist into her mouth.

"You know this guy?"

She nodded and whimpered. "Archie . . ."

Lang picked her by the elbows and dragged her to the couch. The other man was lying with one leg bent under him, the scissors jammed in his neck, blood bubbling around it.

"Him?"

"Malik . . ."

"They're Hanif's cousins, ain't they?" He dug his fingers into her shoulders and shook her hard. She went limp, and her eyes rolled up in her head, but he kept shaking. "Go ahead, say it. 'Hanif, I don't know no Hanif.' "

She gagged into her hand, hot bile running through her fingers.

He walked her into the bathroom and held her head in the toilet while she vomited. Then left her to lay face down on the cool tile. He fished a cigarette out of the bloody pack and tried to calm down.

He'd been inside for four years. Lost his edge. Hanif had been in the Casbah after all. The bouncer, the bartender, and this bitch had all lied to him and he hadn't picked it up.

Hanif knew Lang's weakness. He had always laughed at the way Gloria treated him, contradicting him in front of other people, ordering him around.

"You're scared of a woman, Jerry."

"Yeah, but I ain't scared of you . . . Mittens . . ."

Hanif knew that he dropped his guard around women. He had sent this bitch out to sandbag him. And it had almost worked.

Lang found a roll of Bounty and covered the men's faces. He went back into the bathroom. Letitia sat up and looked at him, her eyes big with fear.

Some women cry when they're scared. Some beg. Some just look at you with big eyes. Lang's mind was swirling with memories. All that time sitting alone in a cell. One thing would remind you of another and another . . .

Edie, his first leading lady, had looked at him with big eyes like that. She was a redhead with freckles and an overbite, fourteen and built like twenty-five. He was fifteen, stealing hubcaps and side mirrors off parked cars and taking them down to the basement under the Horse Shoe Grill on Eighth Avenue. Walter, an old man with a boxer's messed up face, sat on a pile of beer cases buying swag, a deuce a mirror, eight bucks for a set of caps. Lang was fast and had big, strong hands for his size. "Gonna play for the Knicks, kid?" Walter said.

They made Lang a "trunk buster." Taught him how to spring the trunk lock of any car with a simple screwdriver in ten seconds. He steered clear of the luxury models—rich people never left anything in their cars—and concentrated on the beatup old sedans. The Puerto Ricans kept their tools in the trunks, special wrenches and screwdrivers for auto repair; Stanleys and Black and Decker toolboxes, which went for three, four hundred bucks; hack saws and drill sets with fifteen different bits. You could get fifty bucks for a set, but you could also get killed. The PR's set up a trap one night and caught this kid Tommy Haynes popping a trunk. They threw him down the basement steps and split his head with a lug wrench. After that, Jerry looked around for another grift. "You a music lover?" Walter asked him. He gave him a trench coat with deep pockets cut into both sides. "LPs, kid. I'll take as many as you can get." They were in the last days of vinyl. Collectors were scrambling for records and the wiseguys were trying to corner the market. Lang didn't know that, of course. He was just a kid, stealing for the fun of it.

Edie was his girl. She had taken him under the stairs by the garbage bags for his first time. She liked to kiss a lot. Wouldn't do anything until he had kissed her a bunch of times.

Lang dolled her up in cut offs, clogs, and a halter top with kewpie doll make up. They went into Macy's record department at closing because the sales people were halfway out the door and weren't paying attention. She'd wander up and down the aisles and pull every eyeball on the floor. Meanwhile, he'd be grabbing twelve, fifteen albums at a time with both hands and stuffing them into the pockets. They'd walk out with a hundred, sometimes more. Walter gave him a quarter an album.

They hit every store in Manhattan and downtown Brooklyn. Then winter ended and he couldn't use the coat gag anymore. Edie faded out of his life. A few years later he was playing Hold 'em on Twenty-eighth when somebody said, "There's that skank again," and it was Edie. She was eighteen, tops, but she was over. Hunched and smeared, a roll of fat jiggling over the mini skirt, teetering on spiked heels, she had turned into a street trick. "Gentlemen," Edie said. "Can I blow on your cards? Can I blow on anything?" Then she saw him. "Hey Jerry." A hug and he smelled desperate sweat. "Here's the guy who started me on my life of crime . . ." The other guys griped. "Get her outta here, she's chasin' the luck."

She drew him aside. "Jerry, can I talk to you a second." In a corner, it spilled out fast and slurry. "I'm in trouble, Jerry. I hooked up with Ronnie Henry . . ." She said it like he was supposed to know who Ronnie Henry was. Pimps were the biggest things in the universe to these girls so they thought everybody knew them. She showed him the punctures in her toes, the busted veins in the back of her knees and her thighs. "Every trick he takes half for himself and then another taste for my meds. If I don't bring in my quota he holds out on me. I get so sick. I didn't know you could be so sick and still be livin'. Just gimme a coupla hundred, Jerry. Enough so I can split on him. I'll get myself straight and then maybe go on Methadone . . ."

The pimp came in. Ronnie, a fat black dude in a leather jacket and a White Sox cap. He grabbed her. "What'd I tell you about comin' in here?"

She twisted away and whispered urgently. "He'll beat the shit outta me, Jerry. Lemme stay with you, please."

Lang wasn't scared. Ronnie had no back up, pimps didn't cover each other. But she was too far gone to save. She'd be back on the streets in no time.

Couldn't give her a stake because Ronnie would take it all. Couldn't do anything but watch as he dragged her out. The farther away she got the bigger her eyes became. At the door she laughed crazily. "Bye Jerry . . ." And he never saw her again . . .

This girl on the bathroom floor was looking at him with the same big eyes of fear.

"Get up and go into the living room," he said.

She kept the place clean. There were books, theater posters. No family photos, graduation shots, no snaps of her and the boyfriend on some beach. No prom photos, spring break photos. If she had memories she was trying to forget them.

She stood in the center of the living room, trying not to look down at the bodies.

"You deserve to die, you know," he said.

"Hanif made me do it," she said.

"You could have said no . . ."

"You don't say no to Hanif."

"You could have just walked out the door and never come back."

"I tried that, they caught me. Hanif said he was going to teach you a lesson. I thought they were going to push you around, scare you a little."

It sounded true. Anyway, he thought, who am I kidding? I'm not gonna hurt this girl.

"They were gonna kill me. Kill you, too."

"Why me? I didn't do anything to them."

"Neither did I."

He put the bloody scissors to her throat. "Scared?"

Her eyes clouded over. She tried to say "please," but her lips were trembling.

Lang ran the scissors blade up her cheek. He scooped up a

tear and held it, glistening, on the point. "This is your lucky tear drop."

Lang Stood Over Letitia.

"I got blood all over me," he said. "Let me give you your options so I can take a shower without tyin' you to the toilet."

She was sitting at the counter of her kitchenette. He had put a cup of instant coffee in front of her, but she couldn't drink it. She had shapely arms, long tapering fingers.

"Are you going to kill me?" she asked like someone who had already resigned herself to dying.

He had the answer. "Not if you do what I tell you . . ." It would scare her, keep her in line. But he didn't have the heart to use it.

"I'm not gonna kill you."

"Can I get out of here?"

"Not yet. We got stuff to do."

"We . . . ?"

"Lemme give you your options and why none of them will work, okay."

"I'll do anything you say," she said dully.

"I know, but it won't be any good unless you wanna do it. So, Option One. You swear you'll be a good girl, but you call the cops as soon I step in the shower. They show up and grab me, but they arrest you as an accomplice. You make a deal and testify against me and Hanif. There's no Witness Protection in a state rap so they dump you and you're on your own. Hanif puts out an open contract on you. Whoever gets you cuts off your head to prove you're dead."

66

She put her fingers to her nose. "What's that smell?"

"One of them must have crapped his pants." Lang lit a cigarette and handed it to her. "This'll cut it."

She held the cigarette gingerly between her thumb and fore-finger.

"Option Two," Lang said. "You run back to Hanif. Not that you're dumb enough to do that, but let's cover the base anyway. You tell him what happened. He kills you on the spot. They never find your body."

"Hanif got me into this in the first place. Why would I run to him?"

"I'm goin' over all this because I know you're thinkin' of ways to survive and I don't want you to make the wrong move, okay?"

"Just tell me what you want me to do."

"Lemme explain what you shouldn't do first. You shouldn't scam me. Think I'm just another geek with a dick who wants to be told how great he is. You know why?"

"You don't have to go over this . . ."

"Because if I wake up and you're gone, then I leave and there's no proof that anybody else was ever in this apartment. Then when these guys start to stink the cops'll be lookin' for you and only you."

"They would never think that I could kill two men," she said.

"Two stiffs in an apartment, the tenant is on the lam, they won't have to think and they like it that way. Which brings me to Option Three, killin' me."

She shook her head. "I could never do it."

"Give yourself a coupla days of this craziness and you can do anything. You pick up a kitchen knife while I'm sleepin'. Even a nail file will do it, or a sharp pencil. Close your eyes, grit your teeth. Gets easier after the first few stabs. But it wouldn't solve your problem . . ."

"I'd be back to square one."

"Thank you. Now let me tell you what you should do."

"What?"

"Help me."

She looked at him in amazement.

"I've got a crazy story," he said. "The only part you have to know is that I'm a thief. Hanif used to find me things to steal, he was kinda my manager. He plugged me and my partner into a high end burglary, but when we went to get paid, there were some bad guys waiting. They took the thing we stole and killed my partner. They were gonna kill me, but I fought back and shot a guy who turned out to be a cop. They threw me in jail and Hanif's been tryin' to kill me ever since . . . That's the story right up to today."

Her eyes got bigger. "What can I do?"

"I wanna get even with the people who killed my partner."

"You want to kill Hanif?"

"I want him to lead me to the people he was working for."

"How about your partner? Didn't he have any friends who could help you?"

"She," he said.

Her eyes widened even more. "She . . . ?"

"My partner was a woman. I was her only friend for five years. She loved me, trusted me, and I got her killed."

He crouched by Archie's body. The movement blew the paper towel off his face. Letitia turned away from the bloody gashes.

"He looks like he wants to say something."

Lang went through Archie's pockets. "Dead people can't hurt you. That is unless you believe in ghosts and what kinda world would it be if God let a prick like this come back to haunt you?"

He took out a cell phone and a wallet. "Okay, I'm makin' a little plan. If it works, somebody'll come and take our two friends like they were never here and you'll be outta the woods. Plus I'll make a nice score and I'll give you some of it. That is, if you help me. Got something to write on?"

She handed him her Con Ed bill.

"Catch." He flipped her Archie's phone. "Look on his contact list for Hanif."

There was a crust of dried blood on the phone.

"The number will come up on Hanif's call list, so he'll think Archie gave you his phone," Lang said. "And if he wants to call Archie to check he knows you have his phone so that's why Archie isn't answering. Also, obviously, we don't want a record of any call from your number to the Casbah." He tapped his forehead. "It's like a chess game. You gotta be a coupla moves ahead . . ."

She found the number and called. Hanif grabbed it on the first ring. "Archie . . . ?"

"This is Letitia," she said. Lang handed her the paper and she read what he had written. "The house is cleaned. Archie told me to tell you he's taking out the garbage."

Hanif's voice tightened. "You okay, honey?"

"I'm okay, Malik's not feeling too well," she read. "He needs a doctor. Archie told me to stay with him until he got back . . ."

"Yeah, yeah, okay, I understand," Hanif said. "Tell Archie I'm coming right up."

Lang scribbled on the bill and handed it to her.

"Archie says you should bring a car for Malik. He says . . ."

"Not on the phone, honey," Hanif said quickly. "I'll be right up and we'll straighten everything out. Wait for me. Don't go nowhere."

"I won't."

Lang grabbed the phone away from her. "Good acting job." He looked past her with a smile as if he were seeing something in the distance. "I'm gonna take a shower. Can I trust you to

69

stay? Remember your options and tell me I can trust you."

I'm going to die today, she thought.

"You can trust me," she said.

HANIF'S NAME

was on everybody's database. He'd been a wheel in the Albanian secret police under Hoxha, the Communist dictator. He was in charge of counter espionage, which meant that everybody he couldn't shake down he framed as an American spy. But when Russia started to crumble he could see his days were numbered. The smart guys were getting into smuggling to make the dollars to sweeten their exile. Hanif smuggled women. It was easier than drugs, more lucrative than soft contraband like cigarettes or electronics. In a poor country you could promise girls jobs as housekeepers, waitresses, factory workers, and they would accept, no questions asked. Hanif fixed up phony visas and shipped the girls to the brothels of Western Europe where they found themselves starving and stateless and at the mercy of the local pimps. He got paid by the girls at one end, the pimps at the other. Sometimes he worked a deal with families where they could redeem their wives, sisters, and daughters out of servitude, so he got paid a third time.

The CIA had a file on every Albanian cop they thought they could corrupt and Hanif was in the top ten. The plan was to blackmail him into cooperating. But when they approached him he said, "I've been waiting for you." He gave them names and bios on every official in the bureaucracy, planted bugs, and even fingered his friends for them. In return they let him run his little racket on the side.

When the Soviet Union finally collapsed the house of cards

71

toppled over in Albania. Most of the old regime segued smoothly into the new and got even richer. But in a Muslim country a guy who turned sisters and daughters into whores couldn't be rehabilitated. Hanif appealed to his CIA bosses. They didn't like him, but if you don't protect your assets word gets around and you can't recruit new ones. They found him a distant relative in the Bronx to be his sponsor. He got out of Albania a few days ahead of the death squad.

Once in the States the CIA lost contact. He would have been the FBI's problem if the FBI knew about him. But the agencies didn't share their information so Hanif was free to live his dream.

He started small with a few strip clubs in the Bronx. Then he got lucky when the janitors and doormen in the luxury buildings in Manhattan went on strike. He rounded up all the Albanians he could find and rented them out as scabs to the landlords. They were a surly lot. They didn't hail cabs or carry packages, but they swept the sidewalk and ran the elevators.

When the strikers tried to keep Hanif's Albanians from crossing their picket lines they got their heads busted. The union settled quickly and the Albanians got some of the credit. They also got a reputation for being efficiently brutal. Powerful people who need occasional violence were impressed. Soon Hanif was selling bouncers, collectors, security guys, and drivers. His biggest customer was the Bronx Mob, its ranks depleted by death and desertion. He became known as a creative assassin. Years of extra judicial murders had made him an expert in staging accidents. He could arrange a car crash or a short circuit fire, a lethal flight of icy subway steps or an unfortunate collision with an exposed power cable.

Hanif's janitors had access to luxury apartments. They had spotted paintings, jewelry, safes, furs. He had people working in the hotels, who clocked the wealthy guests. He collected from the burglars and the fences. He loved taking a cut at both ends.

Then one night he was spotted by a Kosovar whose sister had paid for an au pair job in Stockholm and ended up in a Genoese brothel. On his way to his gold Mercedes he was waylaid and taken to a basement in Queens. They kept him there for three days, burning him with cigarettes, plunging his head into a bucket of freezing water, banging the soles of his feet until he passed out. Then they began cutting his fingers off. They were going to do his fingers and toes, then work on every other detachable part of his body.

He offered them fifty Gs . . . a hundred . . . a hundred and fifty. When the sum got ridiculous they demanded proof. So he had Archie and Malik show up with a satchel full of cash. This was America after all. In the face of all that money, the culture of bloody revenge for insults to family honor seemed very far away. They took the money.

A month later, Archie and Malik showed up and shot every man, woman, and child in the house. They sprinkled a few grains of cocaine on the floor and the police called the killings drug related.

After that Hanif put in alarms and closed circuit systems. He never went anywhere without his cousins.

Osler and Stewart had seen Hanif's name on Lang's contact list. They ran him through their data bank and saw enough to make them decide to visit him first. When they arrived outside the Casbah they saw the ambulance Lang had hijacked parked outside. They called Hartung.

"He's here," Osler said. "It's a strip bar. You want us to go in?"

"Just sit on the ambulance," Hartung said.

At that moment Spiro emerged from the Casbah. A second later, Hanif peeked out. Spiro walked him to his gold Mercedes.

Then got into a Caddy CTS-V.

"It's Hanif Gallega, and he's in a hurry," Osler said.

"Okay, okay," Hartung said. He flipped a coin in his head. "Follow him."

"CREATION AND DESTRUCTION

are the laws of the artist's universe," Letitia's acting teacher had said. "The artist creates and then to restore the cosmic equilibrium he destroys . . . And what he usually destroys is himself."

Letitia sat in the living room, looking out of the window for Hanif, while Lang took a shower. I've destroyed myself, she thought. And I never even had a chance to create.

Her teacher's name was Jamie Robertson and he was a legend. "I've worked with and taught the very best," he told the class, "and I will release that wellspring of talent within you"—he raised a cautioning finger—"if it is there." For that you would go through three auditions, pay an outrageous tuition, endure his withering sarcasm, and risk his ultimate verdict that you were "empty" and should get a day job forthwith.

He had a mane of white hair over a pinched, shrunken face. His speech was measured as if he loved to hear the sound of his "instrument." But there were nights when his words rushed out, tumbling over one another. When he would recite with relish the litany of the great artists and their tragic ends. The Deans and Clifts and Monroes and Garfields . . . The booze, the drugs, the loneliness, the rejection, the "early bloomers and the flameouts that you never heard of . . ." That was when he would sway, hands on hips, and say to them: "That is the fate that awaits some of you, the ones who are good."

She spent a year financing his class with waitressing jobs. When that wasn't enough she applied to temp agencies and registered with services that supplied mother's helpers to working moms. But day jobs conflicted with Robertson's famous scene study class, which began at four in the afternoon.

She was working at Ben's Famous Deli in midtown, selling chunks of cheesecake the size of cement blocks to oohahing tourists for meager tips. She was running out of money, panicking that she would have to drop her classes. She pleaded with Skenda the night manager for a weekend shift. He was a young Albanian studying accounting at Baruch College and had already sold the shifts to other girls for ten percent of their tips. He looked her up and down. "Did you ever do exotic dancing?" he asked. He gave her a card for the Casbah. "My cousin's place," he said. "You can make two, three hundred a day. I'll tell him you're coming."

The Casbah's neon marquee stuck out like a sore thumb, the last dive among the designer stores and hot restaurants in the newly trendy Wholesale Meat District. It was spooky, music blasting, a girl gyrating on the small stage above the bar, the customers, gray shapes, shifting in the darkness.

Spiro brought her into Hanif's office. He was scary with his scarred head and mutilated hand. His cousins, Archie and Malik leered. Maxine squeezed into the room behind her.

"You know my cousin from college?" Hanif asked.

"From Ben's deli."

"Okay, college girl, take off your clothes," he said.

"Here?"

"When you buy a car you kick the tires, no?"

Archie and Malik laughed . . . "That's good."

Maxine leaned against the door, arms folded.

Letitia stripped down to her panties, but kept her tee shirt on.

"Everything, darling," Hanif said.

"But I'm not wearing bra."

"Neither am I," he said.

Archie and Malik roared. "Neither are you . . ."

She pulled her tee shirt off over her head. The room got quiet. She shivered. Hanif stared at her, nodding.

"You hate me," he said. "You feel abused. But now you will be able to walk around naked in front of anybody without caring. You'll be proud of your body. And then you will thank me."

They gave her the morning shift, a hundred and fifty a day, twenty percent of every bottle of champagne she sold and twenty percent of all the privates she gave. After four months she sensed more men in the room, especially around lunch, but she hadn't sold a bottle or done a dance.

"They're afraid of you," Hanif said. But he didn't seem to mind and Maxine gave her a hundred-dollar bill and a fifty after every shift. "Hanif isn't that into the business," she said. "He has other interests."

Letitia would dance until two, then run into the drafty dressing room and rub off her makeup before taking the bus uptown to class.

This is performing, she told herself. It is making me a better actress.

But Jamie Robertson didn't seem to agree. After a year he barely acknowledged her, except to summarily interrupt in the middle of a monologue to tell her she had it all wrong and to "reprepare." One day she was doing a scene from *A Streetcar Named Desire* with Eloy, a scholarship kid from Washington Heights. Robertson stopped them: "Enough. It'll never work. No chemistry."

After a rebuke students were expected to take their seats, but she stood there, heart pounding, fighting tears. "I love this play and this part. I pay you to tell me how to do it right."

The class held its breath waiting for the explosion. You never discussed money in this temple of art. Robertson got up from behind his desk, relishing the drama. "Pause until you feel the focus," he always said. So he paused and then began:

"During rehearsals for the original production of *Streetcar*, Elia Kazan couldn't get a performance out of Brando and Kim Hunter. No chemistry. So he invited them to his house for dinner. When they showed up he wasn't there and the table was set for two. Both actors realized what he wanted them to do. And they did it. And suddenly the sparks were flying. And the rest was history."

He's daring me to screw this guy, Letitia thought.

"I thought acting was technique," she said. "If you have to experience everything before you can express it, what's the point of studying?"

"The method we teach can only recall a sensation you've had," Robertson said. "If you never had it you can't recall it. You're a repressed New England girl . . ."

She wanted to scream, "This repressed New England girl is dancing naked in front of a roomful of perverts every day just to pay for your fucking class."

"You're a repressed New England girl," he repeated as if he liked the sound of it. "You can't know what it's like to have great sex with a person you don't particularly like."

After class, Eloy asked her out. The rumor was that "Jamie" (that's what everybody called him) who was famous as an aggressive homosexual, had his own way of deciding who got in for free. Eloy was his star pupil so you could draw your own conclusions. He was short, at least two inches shorter than she, but with his shiny black hair, fluttery lashes, and smooth, brown arms, he had cut a swath through the females and some of the males in the class.

She was sure that Jamie had put Eloy up to it. That he would go back and tell him everything that had happened and they would have a good laugh about how he liberated the repressed New England girl.

She'd show them both. As Ceci, the stripper, said to the sickos at the Casbah, "The fuck stops here . . ."

After a few beers and a joint Eloy suggested they go back to her apartment to rehearse. His cologne made her dizzy. She couldn't wait for him to make a smarmy move so she could see his look of total shock when she deflated him. But when he grabbed her shoulders and stuck his tongue into her mouth she was energized. His violence gave her license. She dug her nails into his biceps and felt him wince. She wrapped her thighs around his back and squeezed the ribs through his thin chest. She exulted when he groaned and tried to ease free.

In the morning he strutted, convinced that her vehemence had been passion for him. She remembered her friends having contests to see who gave the biggest hickeys to their boyfriends. Then giggling about how proud the boys were of those purple marks as if they were a sign of passion. Never knowing that the girls were using their necks as playing fields.

"Jamie" was wrong. Sex with someone you didn't like was demeaning, she had already learned that. Still, she realized that news of her affair would raise her stock. He liked excess and decadence. Maybe he would believe in her talent now that she had degraded herself. Maybe he would be convinced that she knew how to express Stella Kowalski's self-destructive sexuality. Eloy had served his purpose. Destruction would lead back to Creation. Curtain down. No need for an encore.

But she couldn't get him out of her life. After the first night their tussles were joyless, pure theater on her part, but she didn't end it. Just like Stella in *Streetcar*. She gave him a key, she didn't know why. He came and went at all hours, "borrowed" money and never repaid it, brought his friends up and acted like it was his house, bossing her around. And she took it. Went off to bed and lay there listening to the raucous laughter in the living room, feeling somehow it was directed at her. Later, he'd slip in to bed, smelling of rum and cocaine, limp, and desperate to get it on.

He would take her uptown to salsa clubs where she sat in booths with sullen girls in spiked heels and short skirts, each vying to show more skin, dance crazier, and complain more bitterly about their boyfriends. Never calling them by name, always "he." They were full of contempt for the men, but they followed them dutifully onto the dance floor, threw their hair back and danced like wild women . . .

One night, her head spinning from tequila shooters, she suddenly recalled being awakened by muffled screams from her mother's bedroom and thinking, "Daddy's hurting Mom." But Daddy was away on sea duty and when she peeked through the slit in the bedroom door she saw that Mom was with Mr. Wilner, their next door neighbor. It looked like they were play fighting. He had his hand over her mouth and was whispering, while she writhed and groaned under him. It was funny because Mom hated Mr. Wilner. Said he was fat and vain and didn't know how much his wife loathed him. Made vicious fun of him in his shorts. "Look at those stubby little legs . . . And he thinks he's so sexy."

When Daddy came home, Mom had her roots done and made a chocolate cake. They went down to the ship to meet him with the other families. There was a feeling of forced gaiety, cameras clicking, toddlers shrieking in panic as their dads, who were just strange men to them, lifted them high in the air.

Daddy always looked so clean and sparkly in his CPO uniform. She waited as he kissed Mom, then turned to her. "Hello young lady . . ." Knelt and looked deeply into her eyes.

"Did you take good care of Mom?" And she reached out and hugged him to hide her face.

It all came back to her that night. Her mom, who would always promise the "wrath of God" if she disobeyed, who had predicted doom and degradation if she went to New York. She was like those girls in the club, trapped in compulsive sexuality, hating herself and her partner but unable to break away. Like Stella Kowlaski.

Letitia found she could conjure up Stella from Mom and those girls in the salsa club every time she played the scene. Jamie never complimented her, but never gave Stella to any other girl in class. He sat in the back of the room and watched her do it with different partners and when it was over would take a pause to pull focus and say "no adjustments." After class one night he invited her for a drink. His apartment was crammed with posters and plaques and photos of him with everybody who was anybody. A smiling pink faced man who spoke in whispers, made a pitcher of martinis, and bowed out. Jamie sat on a couch that had been part of the set of *My Fair Lady*, and told theater stories for hours. When the martinis were gone, he took her hand and his eyes moistened. "Did you go with Eloy because I wanted you to?" he asked.

"Yes," she said. "I knew you wanted me to."

He sighed. "Actors will do anything to be loved. It's so sad." Then he lay back and passed out on his throw pillows. As if on cue, the smiling pink faced man appeared and took him to bed.

Letitia went home to the apartment that was just starting to accumulate programs and mementos of the few shows she'd been in. What a strange life I've chosen for myself, she thought.

Then she got up to go to work. A few hours later Lang walked into the Casbah . . .

LANG HAD SHAVED WITH
LETITIA'S RAZOR

and the scrapes looked like clown makeup on his white face. Without the beard he could almost be an altar boy, except for those quiet gray eyes.

"See anything?" he asked, wrapping a towel around his waist.

"No fancy cars," she said.

"Got any clothes here?"

"No . . ."

"Your boyfriend never even left a pair of pants?"

"My boyfriend is a taker, not leaver."

"Okay." Lang put the ambulance pants on under the towel. He saw her looking. "Where I've been it's not a good idea to show your ass."

He patted a paper napkin over Malik's face and went through his pockets. Took out a card case, a phone, and roll of bills. Pulled off his shoes—"These guys always carry case money in their socks"—and found a couple of hundreds rolled tightly in a rubber band. He turned the body over and showed Letitia a pearl handled automatic. "This is for close work, like in the back seat of a car or an elevator or across a table in a restaurant where you don't wanna get a back splash . . ."

"I get it," she said.

"I'm not tryin' to gross you out. Just wanna show he deserved what he got."

Letitia turned back to the window. "There's a gold Mercedes," she said.

Lang came to the window and watched as the Mercedes nosed to the curb followed by a white Cadillac with a black vinyl top.

"Let's play this by ear," Lang said.

He took Letitia out into the hallway onto the landing facing the apartment. "These stairs lead to the roof?"

"Yeah."

"Go on the roof. Don't move until I call you. If I don't call you, it means I'm dead and you're on your own."

The downstairs door opened. A shaft of gray daylight shot up the stairs. Letitia squinted over the banister and saw Hanif and Spiro checking the mailbox. Lang shoved her and mouthed . . . "Go . . ."

Spiro came up the stairs, hand in his pocket, shielding Hanif with his bulk. Letitia saw Lang tense and raise the gun. They knocked softly at her door. Nobody answered. "It's open," Spiro said.

"Go see," Hanif said. He lit a cigarette.

Lang eased back along the banister. The steps creaked. Hanif turned toward the noise and Lang jumped down at him. He slammed Hanif's face into the wall and jammed Malik's gun against his head.

"No trouble, Mittens."

Hanif nodded quickly. "No trouble, Jerry."

Spiro came out . . .

"Tell Fatso to take his hand out of his pocket, Mittens."

"Take it easy, Jerry," Hanif said. "You heard him, Spiro."

Spiro took his hand out of his pocket.

The door across the hall opened a crack, then closed quickly. "That's what I like about this neighborhood," Lang said. "Everybody's an accomplice . . . Letitia . . ."

She came downstairs.

"That's a gun in Spiro's pocket, Letitia," Lang said, "he's

definitely not glad to see you. Right pants pocket. Get it out."

She had always thought a gun would be cold and heavy. This one felt like a plastic toy.

Lang took it out of her hand. "Glock, yeah. Better than that peashooter Malik was usin'."

"I can help you, Jerry," Hanif said.

"I'm counting on it," Lang said. He hooked his thumb into Hanif's ear and pulled his head back. "Let's go inside. We've got a lot of catchin' up to do. Tell Fatso to go in first and not to try to slam the door or do anything cute."

"He won't, Jerry."

Spiro went in. Lang pushed Hanif through the door and turned back to Letitia. "Lock it on the chain."

Hanif stumbled over Archie's body. He jumped back.

"I know what you're thinkin', Jerry," he said.

Lang bent to pick up the tire iron that Archie had dropped. "Hey Spiro . . ."

Spiro turned and Lang clubbed him, the tire iron ringing off the side of his head. Spiro staggered, blood oozing out of a gash in his temple. Lang poked him gently in the chest with the tire iron. He fell back against the wall and slid down with a bewildered look. "Don't be a hero, Spiro," Lang said. "Tell him to be a good boy, Mittens."

Hanif growled a few guttural foreign words.

"English, Mittens," Lang said.

"I was just tellin' him to do what you said . . ."

Lang took a casual, backhanded swipe. The tire iron hit Hanif's kneecap with a sickening crunch.

"Ah," Hanif said. "Ah . . ." He clutched his knee. "Jeez Jerry . . . Ah . . ." He fell over on his back, holding his knee. "Jerry . . . Ah . . ." He wheezed and tried to catch his breath. "Inhaler in my pocket."

Lang found it and stuck it in Hanif's mouth. Hanif grasped it with both hands and took gulping breaths.

"Isn't that cute, he looks like a little baby," Lang said.

Hanif talked through the inhaler. "I got asthma, you believe that? All those years in smoky joints."

"Too much stress in your life," Lang said.

"I didn't know it was you, Jerry," Hanif said. "These perverts have been harassing my girls . . ."

Lang took a golf swing. There was a crack as the tire iron met the shinbone. Hanif screamed. The inhaler shot out of his mouth.

"You saw me on your hidden camera," Lang said. "Called somebody and made a deal to whack me. Who'd you call, Mittens?"

"You got this wrong, Jerry . . ."

Lang jammed the Glock against Hanif's knee. He screamed . . . "No, Jerry!"

Letitia touched Lang's arm. "Don't . . ."

He pushed her back. "What are you, a liberal? He was gonna kill you, too."

"Jerry, I swear on my mother's grave . . ."

Lang twisted the barrel of the Glock into Hanif's knee. "Look on the bright side, Mittens. If I blow your knee off you'll be a double cripple. They'll let you on the bus half price. You'll be able to use the big toilets at the airport."

"Jerry, lemme talk . . ."

"Who's got the Levitan, Mittens?"

"The what?"

"The drawing I stole."

"Oh yeah. I forgot the name. Look Jerry, we had a good run, we made a lotta money together."

"So?"

"So you can give me five minutes to explain."

Lang took the Glock off Hanif's knee.

Hanif tried to sit up. "I think you broke my leg, Jerry."

"Clock's ticking, Mittens."

Hanif talked fast. "You know what ruined my culture, Jerry? You know what held Muslims back for eight hundred years?"

"Camel shit?"

"Revenge, Jerry. Revenge is like bangin' a fat girl. It's somethin' you gotta do, but when it's over you don't remember why."

Lang shoved the Glock against Hanif's knee. "What's that, an old Albanian proverb, Mittens?"

Hanif winced and took a breath and the desperate words tumbled out. "I mean here you are making money and having a good life and some hick from another village pinches your baby sister's ass. So now you have to drop everything to get even. You have now a feud with his clan that lasts a hundred years. Their sons are getting even and your grandsons are getting even. For what? You don't even remember anymore."

Lang jammed the Glock back into his knee. "So you're sayin' somebody clips my partner, who also happens to be the only person in the world I care about it, and I should just forget about it."

"Revenge is dealin' with the past instead of plannin' for the future," Hanif said, his voice becoming more confident. "You have to look ahead. You need money. A place to go . . ."

"And you're gonna get it all for me."

"Anything you want. I'll get you anyplace you wanna go with a pocketful of money so you get red carpet treatment."

Lang stood up with a thoughtful look. "You know how much that Levitan was worth?"

"It's been five years."

"C'mon, you remember every score you ever made."

"Okay, Jerry. I think I remember a million."

"Five million was what the papers said. What's five percent?"

"Two fifty."

"Two fifty by close of business today."

"You got it, Jerry."

"And a passport."

"Passport, driver's license, credit cards with good numbers . . ."

"Airline tickets . . ."

"Where you wanna go? Sao Paulo? Dubrovnik? Pristina? Macao? Any place on the Gulf? No Wahabis in those countries, you live like a king."

"You got contacts in those places?"

"Everywhere. There's a big market for a guy like you, Jerry. I got people all over who can hook you into good things."

A fly buzzed through the room. It circled, then landed on one of Archie's bare feet. It took off again and landed in one of the bloody wounds in his face.

Hanif was watching Lang carefully. *He thinks he's getting over,* Lang thought. "You gonna tell me you didn't see me on that camera?" he said.

"All I seen was a pervert hasslin' one of my girls, Jerry," Hanif said. "I thought you were in jail."

"Okay, okay, so maybe I believe you," Lang said. "I still gotta do one thing." He patted Hanif down and found a phone. "Do me a favor. Call Tony Rasso. Tell him you got a friend in from Boca with a jewelry score."

Hanif sat up, painfully. "This opens a new can of worms, Jerry." But he punched the number. "It's me," he said into the phone. "A good friend of mine is in from Boca with a jewelry proposition . . . Okay . . ." He disconnected. "Cornelia Street in an hour . . ."

"Those guys still stay in that club?" Lang said. "You'd think the FBI would have the whole street wired by now."

"You meet there and they take you some place else."

"Oh so the FBI can tail you to the new place. Mob security

precaution. No wonder they're dyin' out." He smiled up at Letitia. "Seem like I'm babblin'? Don't worry, I got a plan. Letitia's my new leading lady, Mittens. What do you think?"

Hanif squirmed, trying to find a painless place for his leg. "She's a smart girl. College girl, right?"

"Wrong," she said.

Lang stood next to her. "I think she's too tall for me."

"So she can wear flats . . ."

"Gotta wear heels in this business. Gotta look sexy. But I don't wanna look like a shrimp standin' next to her. Gloria was just the right height. Remember Gloria, Mittens?"

"I didn't have nothin' to do with what happened to her," Hanif said in a choked voice. "I swear on my mother's grave . . ."

"Your mother's busy," Lang said. "Try your grandmother . . . Spiro the hero, how ya doin'?"

Spiro was on his hands and knees, watching his blood drip onto the floor. He looked up, dumbly pleading.

"Say thank you Mr. Lang for letting me live," Lang said.

Spiro sobbed. "Thank you, Mr. Lang, for letting me live."

"You're welcome, Spiro. Now after we leave you go back to the Casbah and wait for Mittens to call. Say 'I understand, Mr. Lang.' "

Spiro nodded obediently. "I understand, Mr. Lang."

"Okay, let's go." Lang yanked Hanif up onto his feet. Hanif's leg buckled. "Ah, Jerry. Please . . ."

"I ain't gonna carry you, Mittens. If you won't walk I'll throw you down the stairs."

Hanif stretched his arms like a man on a tightrope.

"I'll walk, Jerry, I'll walk."

OSLER PULLED THE
UNMARKED VAN

past the building. It was a dusty old Ford Econoline, corroded with body cancer and looked like a homeless guy was living in it, but it was state of the art. It had video cameras that projected into the rearview and both side mirrors. GPS so you could track a subject without even tailing him. The windows were treated to look like soot and dirt had made them opaque. They could follow somebody all day, then get out and sit next to him in a bar and he'd never spot them.

The girl came out first. Then Hanif Gallega, hopping and dragging his foot. Then a guy in an ambulance uniform. Stewart pulled up the mug shot on his laptop, while Osler got Hartung on the phone.

"What do we get for a double bingo?"

"I can tell you what you get for an attitude," Hartung said. He was in no mood for jokes. He was on watch until this thing was over and had already called home and told Beverly he might be gone for days. His daughter Amy's soccer team was in the playoffs and the coach had benched her for coming late to practice. He had promised to drive her there yesterday and speak to the coach about her missing a few practices for choir rehearsal, but then eleven new consular officers arrived at the Syrian Embassy and he couldn't take off. When they sent a big group over like that there was usually a spook or two in the crowd. He'd been in the office until midnight cross checking them against the other databases and creating new files for Spec

89

Ops Domestic. Beverly had taken her, but they got stuck in traffic and were late and the coach had sent her home in tears. That morning he had rescheduled with the coach and had promised to take Amy for shoes today, but then this bozo, Lang, broke jail and he was stuck again. He could imagine the scene when he finally got home: his little Amy crying; his son, Warren, who went from the TV to the Internet all day, in his room on some weird chat room. He'd been away a lot since 9/11 and after every mission it was harder to reconnect. Beverly was bitter. "Dad's making America safe for the oil companies," was her new line. She had joined a gym and worked out more than he did. Said it gave her something to do, but he wondered if she were staying in shape to be sexy for somebody. After he got back from Kabul he had caught her looking at his dick like she was trying to measure it against someone else's.

"We got the subject," Osler said. "He's with Hanif Gallega and some girl in a Mets jacket. Gallega's limpin' real bad."

"Are they helping him?" Hartung asked.

"No."

"Okay, so it's not a friendly trio . . ."

"We can take him out," Osler said.

"We're not even allowed to operate domestically, and you want shoot a guy on the street?"

"We could grab him. Hand him to the cops."

"Too many questions."

"We can call in an anonymous tip," Stewart said. "Tell them where to find him."

"We could do that," Hartung said, "but we'd still leave a fingerprint. As of now our mission is to keep this guy away from our asset. And he's nowhere near him so we're cool. What are they doing now?"

"Getting into a gold Mercedes. Lang shoved Gallega into the back seat and got in with him. The girl's driving."

"Sounds like a snatch," Hartung said. "If it is any interven tion by us could get violent. Meanwhile, the cops and the FBI are after Lang plus Gallega's people. They'll catch up to him pretty soon."

"They're pulling out," Osler said. "What do we do?

"Follow them and watch the fun."

"Letitia Feels Sorry For You

Mittens," Lang said. "Nice people always feel sorry for the underdog, even if he's a rat."

Hanif was lying on his stomach on the floor of the back seat. Lang sat over him, Spiro's Glock dangling between his fingers. "What's he's got in the glove compartment, Letitia?"

She looked. "An owner's manual, a roll of duct tape, a box cutter . . ."

"Roll of tape and a box cutter, huh. Think he's usin' that for flat tires, Letitia? Pass 'em back."

"How can I get the money for you, Jerry, and all the other things you need if I'm tied up like this?"

Lang wound the tape several times around his ankles. "Any Army Navy stores around here, Letitia?"

"I know one on Lafayette Street."

"That's on our way." He pointed gleefully out the window. "Hey, an old fashioned donut shop. Pull in here. Chocolate donut was the first thing I ever stole, you know that, Mittens . . ."

"Could you at least do me the favor of not callin' me that name," Hanif said.

Lang searched Hanif's pockets. "Let's see what you got, Mittens . . ." He pulled out a money clip. "Nice . . . Solid gold." He snapped off a hundred and gave it to Letitia. "Go and get a coupla dark coffees and a half dozen donuts, jelly, chocolate, glazed, a bear claw, an apple fritter . . ."

Letitia opened the door and started out, but Lang grabbed her arm. "Remember, half of everything is yours if you come back. Plus I get rid of your Albanian guests . . . If you run away you're on your own."

"I'll remember," she said.

When she had first gotten to the city she would walk the streets looking at the buildings, wondering what dramas were playing behind all those windows. Now she was in one.

An angry bark snapped her out of her daze. A terrier with a curly white coat was on its hind legs, straining at its leash trying to get to her. Its owner, a tiny blonde lady, tried to pull it away. "Fritzy, Fritzy calm down," she said in a French accent. "I don't know what he's doing," she said to Letitia. "He's never like this . . ."

That's a lie, Letitia thought. He's a Jack Russell. He's a killer. She remembered those crisp March mornings when the "Jack Russell man" would come to her grandfather's farm to kill the rats. Birds sang and the sun sparkled through the awakening trees as they walked through the woods to the old barn he used for storage. Three little Jack Russells trotted at their master's heel, muzzled to keep from going after each other. They would snarl and pull on their leashes as they picked up the scent. Grandpa would open the barn door and the hundreds of rats that had taken shelter during the winter would turn, tails raised, beady red eyes staring in alarm. At the sight of their prey the dogs charged into the shed, dispersing like trained soldiers. There was a blur of thrashing bodies, a din of barks and squeals. Some of the rats escaped, running through her legs, but most of them were caught, their necks broken with one bite, then flipped away. When it was over the Jack Russells trotted out, their shanks streaked with the blood of their victims, their fury hardly appeased.

She had been appalled at the carnage. "Why do you do this, Grandpa?"

"It's cleaner than poison," he said. "It's nature's way."

In the store a bent Vietnamese with a burn scar on the back of his neck threw donuts in a bag. In a small town you know everybody, but in a city you look at people and you wonder: what is their story?

Killers became victims and suddenly you felt sorry for them. Rats in a barn. Archie, the cold one, who ignored the girls as if they were whores, beneath contempt. Malik, who told bad jokes, but you had to laugh, who waited outside and pushed open the door of his car and you had to get in.

She opened the door of the Mercedes. In the back seat Lang smiled. "Welcome back." He kicked Hanif in the ribs. "Mittens and I were just talkin' about you. He said you wouldn't come back. Let's go to that Army Navy store."

Letitia slid behind the wheel and watched in the rearview mirror as he pressed an apple fritter to his nose. "Oh yeah . . . Simple pleasures. Can't get nothin' like this in the can."

"Can I have a little sip of that coffee, Jerry," Hanif said. "I'm really dry."

"You'll be okay."

Hanif coughed so hard it sounded like someone was plucking strings in his chest. His face was ashen. Droplets of sweat coursed down his neck.

"I'm chokin' to death, Jerry."

"Nah, you're a survivor," Lang said. "Hold on a coupla hours, I'll get my money and you'll be back in the Casbah like nothin' ever happened. What size coat you wear, Mittens?"

"Forty-eight extra large." His voice trembled. "Why you wanna know?"

"Well, I won't be around for Christmas, so I figured I get you your present now . . ." He leaned over the front seat to Letitia.

"See, I'm not such a bad guy after all."

She watched him go into the Army Navy surplus store. He had a plan. For the first time she was curious to see what it was.

"Distract, Don't Disguise."

That was Mickey Quigley's motto. Mickey was a toothless old stick up guy, famous in his day, but burnt out after nineteen years in Attica for shooting a security guard in the Central Savings Bank robbery. He held court from the end stool at Rudy's Bar at Eighth and Forty-eighth. He had adopted Lang as a protégé, told him war stories and gave him advice.

"A disguise is somethin' you gotta put on and take off. A distraction is just an everyday thing like a scar or a funny hat. People won't think twice when they see it, but it's all they'll remember about you."

Thinking of Mickey, Lang looked around the store until he found a bright green down jacket.

"Goin' huntin'," he told the saleslady.

"Good for you, sir," she said. She was a heavy Indian lady with silver streaks in her glossy black hair.

To hear Mickey tell it, he would have gotten away with every heist if it weren't for the snitches. "It's not the cops who get you, it's the rats," he said. "You do somethin' with a guy. Next day he gets popped for killin' his wife or rapin' a six year old. First thing he does is give you up to make a deal. If I clipped every snitch I ever knew there'd be so many bodies in the river you could walk to Hoboken."

After all those years in jail Mickey had a body crawling with tattoos, and a taste for young men. He'd go to the joints around the Port Authority where the desperate junkies stayed, spot a kid and invite him up to his ratty room. "The booze is cheaper and you can see the TV better . . ." Once Lang asked him: "Aren't you scared some guy'll beat you up?" Mickey shook his head. "I know who to hit on." One night he invited Lang up. "This ain't a come-on, don't worry. I don't like to talk in public." But after a few drinks he took out his dentures and tried to unzip Lang's fly. "Let's see what you got, kid." Lang pushed him away. "I thought you knew who to hit on." Mickey got a bitchy look. "Well, you didn't come up here for the river view." Lang had to laugh, looking at this smelly old drunk with his gray stubble and toothless jaw. "With all due respect, Mickey, what human being in his right mind would wanna get it on with you?" Mickey drew himself up. "I could name names, believe me." And you could see the preening queer behind the tough old con . . .

Lang found an orange Mets ski cap.

"Perfect," the saleslady said.

In those days Lang was a "flyer" with a burglary crew in Brooklyn. They did the fur district, supermarket safes, jewelry stores. His job was to find a way in and bypass the alarms. He scaled roofs, dropped through skylights, or got in a few floors above the score and worked his way down. At the end of the night he got an envelope with the same fifteen hundred whether they had stolen a Costco payroll or a tray full of rare coins. The crew boss was a two-time loser and real careful about setting up scores. Lang went weeks between jobs. He was risking serious jail time and not doing much better than a UPS driver.

One night, at Rudy's, Mickey tapped him on the shoulder. "Old friend of yours in the back. Wants to say hello."

It was Jimmy McAdams, a kid he'd fought in the St. Aloysius

schoolyard every day for the whole eighth grade. Jimmy was the rotten apple in a family of cops. His father and two brothers were cops, even his kid sister was a parole officer, but he'd been a bad guy from day one, shaking down kids, then later mugging drunks and hookers by the Lincoln Tunnel.

He was in the back booth drinking Absolut Vanilla. "I got the perfect score, Jerry," he said.

"That's nice . . ."

"A dealer down in Tribeca on Warren Street. Coke and meth to the Euro trash, the supermodels. He's got shitloads of money layin' around."

"Why you tellin' me?" Lang asked.

"I can't do this thing with the usual suspects," Jimmy said. "Mickey tells me you're good people."

"I don't do rip offs," Lang said.

"The guy's a stoned out little bitch, Jerry," Jimmy said. "He's got one bodyguard, fat drunk, gotta be at least fifty. This is a no lose."

"No such thing."

"There is here." He moved in even closer, dropping his voice. "Look, my brother Eddie, you know him."

"The cop?"

"Yeah. He's with Manhattan South Anti Crime. A stool gave him and his partners this dealer. The guy's new, nobody knows about him. They wanna hit him now before he goes on the map and gets the Task Force on his ass. If this goes good they can set us up with walkovers like this all over the city."

Lang didn't like the idea of working for crooked cops. Jimmy saw his dubious look and started selling. "This is easy. You put a gun to the dude's head, he does what you want."

"I could never shoot nobody."

"That'll be your little secret. Look, my brother says the guy's got at least a hundred and fifty Gs stashed. Half of that is seventy-five. Your end comes to thirty-seven five for low. More than you make in a year of sneak thievin'."

Every instinct told Lang to walk away. But he couldn't say no to that kind of money. "Okay."

They set it for Tuesday night when the downtown bars were slow and there wouldn't be a lot of street action.

Lang remembered Mickey's advice and looked for a distraction. He found a leg brace with rods and straps, a real contraption.

Tuesday night a light rain was falling, just enough to make the streets stink. Jimmy met him outside a bar on Spring Street. "He's in the back. Take a look."

The dealer was a wispy little guy with a scraggly beard and a whiny voice that sounded like he was saying something snotty even when he was just making small talk. He was drinking vintage port. A guy with a big gut and purple glasses was standing behind him. Lang limped by them to the bathroom. They checked out his brace, nobody looked in his face. Just like Mickey had said.

Lang waited across the street in a storefront. Closing time they came out with two giggly girls. He was relieved when they whistled down a cab and put the girls in it. He followed them to their building. Jimmy crossed the street, and caught them just as they got to the door. He jammed a big .45 into the little guy's back. "Don't turn around." Lang shoved the barrel of a Beretta nine into the big guy's neck.

"Okay?"

"Okay," the big guy said.

Lang took a .380 out of his belt and walked him into the building.

They got into one of those old fashioned freight elevators left over from when the million dollar lofts were sweatshops. The elevator creaked to the fourth floor.

"I just want you to know I'm covered in this neighborhood," the guy said. "I'm hooked up with Tony Rasso."

"Good guy to know," Jimmy said.

The elevator opened onto a spacious loft. The guy had all the toys, big screen TV, Bose speakers hanging all over the place, a bar, special game screens, Coke machine, old pinballs . . .

"Anybody else in here?" Jimmy asked.

"Nobody," the little guy said.

Jimmy walked them into the middle of the space. Made them drop to their knees, hands behind their heads. He kept it calm and businesslike. "You know what we're here for."

"Under the black couch," the little guy said. "There's a loose floor board."

"You been hangin' with the Rastas? That's where they stash their money. Go get it, Jerry."

Lang was surprised Jimmy used his name. He pried up the board and found five double wrapped cellophane bags full of twenties.

"Where else?" Jimmy asked.

"That's it."

"You can always make more money, pal," Jimmy said, loose and friendly, "but you can't make yourself a new dick after I shoot this one off."

"In the table by the bed. There's a false bottom in the drawer."

Lang pulled the bottom out and found another cellophane bag, this one filled with hundreds.

Jimmy laughed. "Look at all that cash. How come you wrap it up like that, pal?"

"Roaches like to eat money," the little guy said.

"They know what's good. Okay, like the dentist says, we're almost done. Go into the bathroom, Jerry. Look for a tile with loose grouting."

The little guy looked up. "How'd you know about that?"

"I'm a mind reader. Go Jerry . . ."

Lang went around behind a partition. The bathroom had a big tub with a Jacuzzi and gold fixtures, but they'd kept the original floor, the chipped ceramic tile you saw in high school bathrooms. Lang moved the hamper and there was the loose tile, its grout crumbly from constant prying. Inside was another cellophane bag in the crawlspace between floors. A yard and a half of hundreds.

As he stepped out, his burglar's radar kicked in. Somebody was there. There was a pile of blouses on the floor by the bed. He kicked them aside and looked under the bed. Came eyeball to eyeball with a girl, maybe fifteen, whimpering.

"Stay put and shut up," he whispered. Then went out, limping hard so she'd remember.

"Find it?" Jimmy asked.

"Yeah . . ."

Jimmy threw Lang a roll of gaffer tape. "Tie 'em up . . ."

The big guy crossed his hands meekly, but the whiny guy got jittery.

"Somebody set me up."

"Get the elevator," Jimmy said.

"This is bullshit," the whiny guy said. "I take care of everybody in the neighborhood. I do the right thing and this is how I get paid back?"

Lang opened the elevator.

"You tell whoever sent you Tony Rasso's not gonna like this," the little guy said.

Jimmy crouched over the little guy and shot him in the back of the neck. The shot echoed in the big space. The fat bodyguard turned and said, "Listen man . . ." Jimmy shot him in the face. The bullet tore a bloody trail out of the back of his head. The little guy moaned and tried to roll over, but Jimmy put a foot on his back and shot him again. Then he walked calmly into the elevator. "Lady's lingerie please . . ."

They rode down in silence. Lang gulped back a wave of nausea. That girl under the bed had seen him. Should he tell Jimmy? If he did Jimmy would go back and finish her. Or would tell him to do it.

They went to an old Irish bar at Eighty-eighth and Third. Jimmy got hyper after a couple of drinks, face flushed, eyes spinning. Talking loud like he wanted to tell everybody, "Hey I'm bad, I just iced two guys."

Lang kept seeing the fat bodyguard's face. "Listen man," he had started to say, and it probably would have been something like "I'm not gonna give you up . . ." or "Listen man, he's got a million stashed in a safe deposit box . . ." He tried to drown the face in shots of Bacardi 151, but the scene got sharper, the voice louder. "Listen man . . ." Pretty soon the booze convinced him that they'd asked for it, shooting their mouths off about Tony Rasso.

"That little guy shoulda shut up and not made threats," he said to Jimmy.

"Didn't matter," Jimmy said. "He was dead no matter what. Part of the deal and we get a ten percent bonus for doin' it."

"You didn't tell me there was gonna be a hit."

"I must have forgot." Jimmy looked in the mirror and lowered his voice. "There's somebody I gotta talk to." He slipped Lang a tin foil package. "Go take a piss . . ."

In the bathroom, Lang flushed a pinch of the white powder down the toilet so it would look like he had taken a one and one. When he got back Jimmy was gone. The bartender called him down to the service end. "Jimmy said he had to go and you should talk tomorrow . . ."

Lang looked out of the bar window. A black Navigator was parked in front of a hydrant. There were two guys inside; he could see their cigarette tips glowing. Another guy was leaning over a parking meter a few cars down.

Maybe it was nothing, just three random guys in front of a bar. But anticrime teams worked in threes. Maybe when he comes out they shoot him and say he was resisting arrest. They plant Jimmy's gun on him and say he did the murders downtown. They're heroes and meanwhile they've ditched a witness and they're a hundred fifty Gs ahead.

Then again, maybe it was just street paranoia, but you had to go with the worst-case scenario.

Lang walked back toward the bathroom like everything was okay, then ducked into the kitchen and out a back door leading to a courtyard. There was no alley, just a big apartment building looming overhead. The bar was in one of those two story taxpayers that hadn't been torn down yet. He shinnied up the drainpipe, hoping the corroded tin wouldn't come loose. Ran to the edge of the roof and looked down. The Navigator was still parked. He hung over the lip of the roof and dropped onto a dry cleaner's awning. Slid down onto the street and hailed a cab.

He went straight to Mickey Quigley's room, lifted the lock, and waited in the dark. Around dawn, Mickey came in. "You're in deep shit, kid."

"What happened?"

"There was a girl in the loft. Saw the whole thing. Now it's a homicide with a witness. Jimmy's brother gonna try to take you out to make sure you don't give him up. It gets worse. This guy you clipped was kickin' back to Tony Rasso, so you took money outta the wrong pocket. Better take a slow boat to China."

Lang was on a bus to Vegas an hour later. He tried to sleep, but kept seeing those two guys on their knees. Two guys dead and nothing to show for it but bad dreams.

In Vegas he hooked up with a thief who was hitting hotel

rooms. It was a tight little crew. A clerk at the junket company spotted the high rollers. A Mexican kid picked up the passkeys from the cleaning ladies. Lang cleaned the rooms. Another guy fenced all the swag in LA. Fifty percent went back to the Vario family in Brooklyn.

Lang learned how to look classy in a tuxedo, how to play the high roller from LA or the oilman from Texas. He was so good they gave him a nickname, "Jerry the Actor."

The only trick was dodging Security. These guys had their eyes glued to the closed circuit TVs, looking for cheaters and petty thieves. He used distraction, a limp or a cast, a weird suit or a pair of fancy boots, anything to get their eyes off his face. The best dodge was to hire a flashy hooker, dress her up and walk behind her, and they'd never look at you. You could go back two, may be three times a year.

After a year, Lang heard rumors that the other Mafia families were angry that their protected spots got hit. There had been threats and sit-downs.

One night he was in the sports book at the Stardust when his boss came over. "There's been a shake-up back east. We got a new skipper." He brought him over to a redheaded geep bulging out of an Armani suit. "Jerry Lang, meet Tony Rasso. He's gonna take care of you from now on."

He remembered the little guy on the floor. "I'm hooked up with Tony Rasso," he had said before Jimmy shot him.

The wiseguys always start out real friendly. They draw their lips out over their teeth and call it a smile, they squeeze your fingers and call it a handshake, pat you on the back like you've been pals for years, but they're really looking for a soft place to stick the knife. "Jerry, the Actor, they call you, right?" Rasso said. "Nice to meet you, Jerry. You hungry?"

"Always hungry," Lang said.

Rasso's smile stopped at his eyes. "Me too, Jerry, but you

gotta give Vegas a breather. Go back east, we'll keep you busy."

"I got into a little jackpot in the city," Lang said.

"You're with us now, kid, everything's washed," Tony said.

In the city, Lang checked in at Rudy's. Mickey Quigley's stool was just another spot at the bar. They had found him tied face down on his bed, a bloody towel in his mouth, his little room ransacked in search of the cash everyone thought he was hoarding. Jimmy McAdams had been arrested for a series of bank robberies upstate. Somebody made bail for him the next day. He walked out of the Metropolitan Corrections facility and vanished without a trace. Jimmy knew too much. They had gotten him out of a warm cell into a cold grave.

Lang noticed that heads turned and voices dropped when he walked in. The word was out that he was "with" Tony Rasso.

In the time he'd been away his folks had gone downhill. After thirty-seven years of making sandwiches at the Smiler's on Fifty-fifth and Seventh, his dad had gotten emphysema. He had no union, no insurance. He was in Roosevelt Hospital and couldn't get a doctor to see him.

Maybe they'd said a hundred words to each other in all the years. The old man went from work to the bar to his bed. He worked six shifts. Wednesday, his day off, he sat in front of the TV in his work clothes, white shirt and black pants, waiting until it was respectable to start drinking. But he'd never hit his kids, never abused his wife. Once, when Lang was playing basketball at the Y, he looked out into the stands and there was the old man hiding in the top row. He never mentioned he'd been there.

His mom had worked as an usherette at the St. James Theater, a union job that had been passed to her by her mother. "Seventy years between us," she joked, "that's the longest run on Broadway." But they had cut the staff and forced her into retirement. Her union pension after thirty years was seventy-five dollars a month.

The hospital was seven hundred a day. The thoracic specialist wanted two grand in advance from all uninsured patients. His father stared at him bleakly from the coarse, gray hospital sheets. His mother, ashen and smelling of cigarettes, held his father's hand. It was the first time he had ever seen them touch.

Lang knew only one place to get money. He went down to the club on Cornelia Street and asked for Tony Rasso. They made him wait in a crowd at the curb. Rasso came out in a wedge of gavones. Some guys tried to talk to him and were shouldered aside, but he stopped briefly when he saw Lang.

"Go up to the Casbah on Little West Twelfth. Hanif will be taking care of you from now on."

Lang went to the Casbah and sat at the bar for an hour before they brought him into an office where a fat guy with a driving glove over a mangled hand flashed a gold toothed smile.

"You Jerry the Actor? I'm Hanif, your new agent . . ."

"JERRY TRUSTS WOMEN,"

Hanif said like it was the most ridiculous thing he had ever heard.

Letitia watched him thrash around in the back seat, trying to get loose. She could see Lang walking around the store trying on coats.

"Did he cuff you to the wheel?" Hanif asked.

"No," she said.

"You could walk outta this car right now. What's stoppin' you?"

"He promised me he'd get those men out of my apartment."

"What are you kiddin', he'll never go back to your place again. Think he's gonna take a chance for you? Only chance you have is to untie me and let us both get outta here."

She could tease him like a cat with a field mouse. Let him think he could get away, then pull him back. Just like Lang had done. "You were going to kill me once," she said. "How do I know you won't do it again?"

"Okay look, I got no time to argue. I stay on the floor here tied up like a turkey where I can't hurt you. You drive somewhere, anywhere. Walk away and leave me the way I am. Come to the club tonight and I'll give you twenty-five Gs."

"Oh sure, come to the Casbah so you can kill me there."

Hanif kicked the door in frustration. "Are you a college girl? Who's the killer here? Who killed two guys right in front of you?" His voice cracked. "Don't you understand, he don't care

107

about you. He just wants to get even for Gloria."

A man in a lime green bubble jacket with an orange ski cap walked toward the car. When reached for the back door she got frightened and started the motor. But it was Lang. "Wardrobe doesn't conceal identity, it creates character," Jamie Robertson always said.

"Like my new look?" Lang said, getting into the back seat. "I'm goin' for weekend hunter. Wear bright colors in the woods so my buddies won't take me for a deer. How you holdin' up, Mittens? Did he try to bribe you, Letitia? Did he swear on his mother's grave?"

"He says you won't let me live because I'm a witness," Letitia said.

"She's lying Jerry," Hanif said. "She just asked how much would I give her to let me go . . ."

Lang laughed. "And you said not a red cent because you wanted to help your pal Jerry Lang. You're in so deep you can't even make up a good story, Mittens."

They drove to a spot under the Williamsburg Bridge. A group of homeless guys scattered at the sight of the big Mercedes. They parked behind some junked cars.

"Check out time, Mittens," Lang said.

"Use your head, Jerry," Hanif said. "Two fifty gets you a long way. Killing me gets you nothing."

"It gets me even for Gloria."

"I didn't kill Gloria. Jesus Christ, Jerry, all the things I did, I gotta go down for something I didn't?"

"You know somethin' you sound so aggravated, I almost believe you. But you were gonna kill me, right?"

Hanif was quiet for a second too long. "I told you Jerry, I didn't know it was you."

"Pop the trunk, Letitia," Lang said.

"Three hundred Gs, Jerry. I can have it for you in an hour."

Lang's tone got sweetly persuasive. "Just tell the truth, Hanif," he said. "That'll clear the air and then we can do business."

Hanif was quiet for awhile. Then he sighed. "It was Tony Rasso, Jerry. He knew you had escaped. He told me twenty five-Gs if I did it today. You don't say no to these guys, Jerry, you know that. If I had my way . . ."

"If you had your way the price would have been fifty," Lang said. "But I never expected loyalty or friendship from you so that's okay. You do a few things for me now I'll let you live . . ."

"Anything Jerry," Hanif said.

"Okay, call Spiro and tell him to get your cousins outta Letitia's apartment."

Lang took Hanif's phone and found Casbah on speed dial. He held the phone to Hanif's ear.

"Spiro," Hanif said. He muttered in Albanian and looked up at Lang. "He's gonna call the moving men. It'll take a few hours."

"Speakin' Albanian, huh," Lang said. "I thought Spiro was Greek."

"He's a Macedonian. They all speak Albanian."

"They better, huh, Mittens . . . Hear that, Letitia, you're gonna get maid service. You know who the moving men are? Guys from the meatpacking district, who do a little butchering on the side. Next time you feel sorry for Mittens over here remember he was gonna have them cut you into little bitesized pieces of human sushi."

"Three hundred Gs Jerry," Hanif said

Lang opened the back door, yanked Hanif out by the shoulders, and dumped him on the ground. A few yards away, a pile of rags stirred. A man in a filthy pink baby blanket got up and scurried away.

Lang dragged Hanif like a sack of potatoes to the trunk.

"Three hundred Gs, Jerry," Hanif squealed. "Is killin' me worth three hundred Gs?"

"I'm not gonna kill you," Lang said. He horsed Hanif up by the collar and the belt and threw him with a thump into the trunk. Then took out a strip of duct tape. Hanif turned his head away. "No, Jerry. If I start coughin' I'll choke on my own puke." Lang clamped his hand on Hanif's forehead, held him down and stuck the tape over his mouth. "Remember you told me how you used to wrap guys up like mummies when you were jackin' oil trucks? So now you know how those guys felt."

He slammed the trunk door and got back in the car. Turned to Letitia with a smile.

"Now, let's go see Tony Rasso . . ."

As they pulled back onto Delancey the van swung in behind them. Osler was on the phone to Hartung. "He just threw Gallega in the trunk."

"He's acting like he's got a plan," Hartung said.

"This guy's pretty sharp. We'd better switch vehicles. You see this thing more than once it starts being conspicuous."

"Cab would be good," Stewart said. "Can't tell one from another."

"Stay with Lang," Hartung said. "I'll see what I can do."

"THE MOB'S LIKE A DYING SNAKE,"

Lang said. "It's still got one bite left."

They were going south on Lafayette Street. He was drinking coffee and eating a bear claw. "I can't finish this. Take the last bite."

"I've got two dead men in my apartment," Letitia said.

"Shit happens, but you still gotta eat."

"I think this is a little more than shit happens."

"Okay, imagine this. Twenty years after World War Two there were Japanese soldiers hidin' on them Pacific islands, who didn't know the war was over. Now, it's 1965. You're on vacation. You stretch out on a deserted beach. Before you know it some gook jumps out from behind a rock yellin' banzai and sticks a bayonet in you."

"I thought we were talking about snakes and bear claws," Letitia said. "Who's the Japanese soldier?"

"The mob, the Mafia, the Godfathers, the Sopranos, whatever. They used to be the worst scumbags in the world. Everybody wanted to take them down, but nobody could. In the end, you know what got 'em? Chinatown . . ." He pointed out the window at the markets and storefronts all with Chinese signs; the trucks with Chinese lettering on the panels; the bent old Chinese men, cigarettes dangling out of the corners of their mouths; the students with backpacks; toddlers staring out of strollers. "In the old days Chinatown stopped dead at Canal Street. Everything from here to Washington Square was Little

Italy. They owned everything and what they didn't own they shook down. You didn't sell a flounder on Fulton Street or a cantaloupe in the Washington Market, you didn't hang a lamb chop on a hook in the Meat District without givin' them their end. Open a restaurant, dig a foundation, start a newsstand, next day they'd come around with their hands out. If you bet a horse or played a number it was with them. Nobody had credit so if you needed money to pay for your daughter's wedding or your mother's operation you got it from them at six for five. Anything you stole, any scam you were working on, any cool idea you had, all of a sudden you had a partner. We used to sit around and try to figure out how much money they had, but it was hard because for every million dollar construction job they were scoring they were musclin' in on some nickel dime after hours in the Bronx."

Chinese signs on both sides of the street.

"All the rich Europeans and the Hollywood people have taken over this neighborhood," Letitia said.

"Those people are food," Lang said. "With all their money they're helpless, everybody takes a bite outta them. They're so fat they don't feel it." He pointed at an old man pushing a cart full of fabrics. "That's the real power . . . People . . . They flow in like water. Whatever you built just crumbles away. The wiseguys had an empire here, but the Chinese drowned 'em with people. Chinatown is overflowin' Canal Street like the Yangtze River. Chinese have their own gamblers and shylocks and shakedown artists. They got dim sum on Mulberry Street where the bocce courts used to be. Make a right on Broome."

They drove west on Broome. Lang pointed to a loft on the corner of Mercer. "There was a guy named Jackie George on the fifth floor. Everybody knew him. He sold swag suits, shoes, watches, jewelry right out in the open. The cops were in on it.

Guys on the beat got their pad, detectives got to pick Christmas presents for their wives. The captains put in orders for suits and TVs. Everybody was happy."

He pointed to an old stone garage with "1924" carved over the doors. "They used to kill guys all over the city, drive in here, dump 'em in one of the bays and pour lime on them. Then they'd go over to Vincent's for shrimp and hot sauce. Anything they did was an excuse to stuff their faces . . ."

"You should give a guided tour," Letitia said.

"Oh yeah I know them. They sit in the clubs, look at you like you're dirt. Buncha leeches, they never have an idea of their own. All they can do is live off other people's hard labor . . ."

She could sense him working himself up. If this were acting class, it would be preparation. Finding a memory, an association that would give you the right emotional level for the scene you were about to play.

They turned on Cornelia Street. "See how narrow it is. It was a mess when it snowed, all these cars buried and all. But they had so much juice they got the street plowed before Sutton Place . . . Pull in here. See they had this johnny pump put in front of the club so they could save the space for Chin Gigante. He died three years ago in jail, but nobody parks here out of respect. That's who they are. They rat out their own brothers, but they make a shrine out of ten feet of dirty gutter . . . Yeah . . ." He nodded as if someone had just spoken to him. "Gloria couldn't stand these guys. This was gonna be our last score. We were getting' out . . ."

They parked in front of a walk up. There was a store on the ground floor. The windows were blackened. A gray shade was drawn over the glass door. Inside, she could see the flicker of a TV.

Lang put Malik's pearl handled .25 in his left pocket and Spiro's Glock in his right. "You're not gonna believe this, but I never shot at nobody in my life," he said.

"Don't go then," Letitia said.

"Don't you want your money?"

"You can get it from Hanif."

"This way, you get twice as much."

"I won't get anything if they kill you."

"Smart girl. Can't win an argument with you." He zipped the green jacket up to his neck. Pulled the orange cap over his eyes and opened the door.

"Keep the motor running. I'll be back."

THE FIRST GUY WILL BE A FLUNKY

who won't know me, Lang thought as he walked to the door. He knocked at the splintered wooden frame. The shade flew up and a fat kid with a shaven head and an earring glared at him through the glass window.

"Hanif sent me," Lang said.

"Wait here," the kid said and pulled down the shade. Lang looked back at the Mercedes. If she takes off now that'll be okay, he thought. Anytime this thing ends is okay. A second later the shade flew up and the kid opened the door. Hunched over like he was cold, his hands in the parka pockets, clutching the guns, Lang entered a gloomy room with rickety bridge tables and a chipped wooden bar.

Nothing changes, he thought.

A few men in car coats were sitting at the bar watching stock quotes on CNBC. Tony Rasso, a little fatter, his crinkly red hair a little thinner, but still the careful dresser wearing a leather jacket and lighting a cigarette with a gold Dunhill came toward him. Lang kept his head down in mock humility.

"Whaddya got pal?"

"Jewelry," Lang whispered hoarsely.

Rasso stopped short. He recognizes me, Lang thought.

"Richie," Rasso said.

Lang turned. The fat kid was coming at him with a sawed off pool cue raised over his head. Lang let him get a step closer, then swiveled and fired the Glock. The blast was muffled as the

115

bullet tore through the pocket. The kid went down screaming, holding his groin.

A guy came up from behind the bar, bobbling a shotgun. Lang drew both guns and fired wildly around the room. Glass shattered; bottles flew off the bar. Guys dove off the stools and scuttled into the dark corners. Rasso hit the floor and tried to crawl away, but Lang kicked his legs out from under him. "Get up, Tony," he said, and announced to the room: "Don't nobody start nothin' or I'll kill the skipper."

Rasso snarled, trying to put up a front. "Who you think you're playin' with, Jerry?"

Lang smashed him so hard with the butt of the .25 that a piece of the pearl handle flew off. He grabbed the back of Rasso's jacket and ran him head first through the door. The glass shattered. Rasso screamed and clutched at his face, blood trickling through his fingers.

The Mercedes was still there. Lang opened the back door and threw Rasso onto the back seat. "Go," he shouted.

Letitia jumped on the pedal. The Mercedes lurched across the narrow street and slammed into a van double-parked on the other side. Rasso flopped like a rag doll, his forehead bouncing off the front seat.

In the van, Stewart dropped, arms over his head, while Osler ducked under the seat and called Hartung. "They hit us."

"Lang?"

"The girl . . . She's driving."

Hartung clicked on the "Lang" file that he had started that morning. "Surveillance 101," he said. "Never park close to the target."

Osler grimaced and shook his head. "Advanced Surveillance. On a crowded street be sure you maintain contact so you don't get stuck in traffic or behind double-parked cars. No way he knows we're on him. He just grabbed Tony Rasso and he's tryin' to get away."

The tires shrieked as the Mercedes peeled down the block.

"Stay with 'em."

"We can't tail 'em in the van now, they'll think we're chasin' 'em."

Hartung felt a stab of pain in his chest. "Somatizing," his doctor called it. He took a deep breath and visualized the eighth hole at the Kabul Officers Club golf course, a little gem of a par three. A nine iron got you over the bunker onto the green. He owned that hole. No matter how bad he was playing, he always parred that goddamn hole.

"No time to change cars, Mr. Osler," he said. "You have to maintain contact with the subject at all times. Use the incident as a pretext if you have to interact . . ."

In the Mercedes, Lang reached over and patted Letitia's arm. "Relax, we got the big pizza here. Nobody's gonna bother us." He grabbed Rasso by the hair and pulled his head back. "That rang your bell, huh Skip? When was the last time anybody ever dared take a poke at you?"

Bloody shards of glass glinted on Rasso's forehead. Blood trickled out of his nostrils. "Lemme put my head down, Jerry. I'm on cumatin and get a lotta nosebleeds . . ."

"See this, Letitia, all these guys got health problems. Is it advancing age or just the stress of bein' a connivin' rat bastard?"

Rasso put his head between his legs. "I got a piece of glass in my eye, Jerry."

"Yeah, I see," Lang said. "I wanna get paid for that Levitan score, Tony."

"You go through all of this for that? Why didn't you just say so?"

"I was gonna. But then Hanif put two gorillas on me . . ."

"What's that got to do with me?"

"He said you gave him the contract."

Rasso's neck reddened. "That's a lie. Why would I want you dead?"

"I earned for you, Tony," Lang said in an aggrieved tone.

Letitia looked at him in the mirror. He had a reproving expression on his face. He was acting, making Rasso think he could be manipulated. Then, just when Rasso thought he had the advantage, he would pull the rug out.

"Let's get your money," Rasso said, his voice pinched with pain. "What was it, I forget?"

"Forty-five."

"Joe Di wouldn't pay forty-five Gs for the Statue of Liberty," Rasso said. "But we'll call it forty-five, give you interest and make it fifty, how about that? Let's go back to the club, I'll have it for you in twenty minutes . . ."

"Fifty's not enough," Lang said.

Rasso groaned like he had known that was coming.

"The papers said the thing was worth five million," Lang said.

"They always hype the numbers."

Lang kept his tone deferential like he was trying to persuade a boss. "I looked this guy Levitan up, Tony. He was a big deal in Russia. He didn't paint that much so that makes his stuff worth more. Joe always paid five cents on the dollar."

Rasso gasped. "So what are you sayin'? Two fifty?"

"Don't blink, Tony," Lang said, "that glass will go deeper into your eye."

"Two fifty ain't petty cash, Jerry," Rasso said. "We don't have that kinda money layin' around like we used to."

"Okay Tony . . ." Lang sat back and took out a cigarette. "You wanna negotiate while you got a piece of glass in your eyeball that's your business."

Letitia could hear Rasso whimpering and breathing through his nose.

"I'll have to make some calls," he said.

"We have the technology," Lang said.

Rasso fumbled with a cell phone.

"Today Tony. I'm in a kind of a hurry."

"Yeah, yeah, I'm just tryin' to figure out who to call on such short notice."

Lang blew a trail of smoke rings into the front seat. "One more thing, Tony."

"One more thing? Whaddya mean one more thing?"

"I want the drawing, too."

"Ah . . . Shit . . ." Rasso dropped the phone and put his head down on the seat. "I gotta get to a doctor . . ."

"Doctor won't do you no good, Tony. You gotta get to a hospital right away before you lose an eye."

"I don't know where the drawing is."

"Joe Di stole it for somebody, right?"

"I don't know what he did. He don't keep me in his confidence . . ."

"Okay, don't get excited. We'll ask Joe Di about it."

"You can't talk to the old man, Jerry . . ."

Lang jammed the cigarette into Rasso's neck. He screamed and tried to pull away, but Lang held him down.

"Now you got a new nickname, Tony Ashtray," Lang said.

"He's senile, what do you want from me?" Rasso blubbered.

"Senile?" Lang brushed an ash off Rasso's neck with mock concern. "I go away for three years, everybody falls apart. This a dodge, Tony?"

"No it's real. He's in first stage Alzheimer's. He can tell you what Carlo Gambino had for breakfast forty years ago, but then he can't find his dick to pee."

"Okay, he's an old man. Makes sense. But we can still catch

him on a good day."

"He's not gonna remember what he did with a swag picture four years ago."

"He'd better for your sake," Lang said. He shook Rasso by the shoulder. "Talk to me Tony. Who's takin' care of the old man?"

"His sister."

"Anybody else? I don't want no surprises."

"I got a guy over there, Billy Dario, runs errands, drives him to the doctor. That's it."

"Where's he live?"

"Thirty-first between First and Second."

"Go up Sixth Avenue, Letitia," Lang said. "Make a right on Fourteenth . . ." He leaned over and touched her shoulder. His breath was warm and smelled of nicotine and pastry. A city smell.

"Havin' fun?" he asked.

"WE'RE IN A TIME WARP,"

Lang said.

Letitia had turned off First onto Thirty-first and suddenly they were on a tree-shaded street of row houses. Behind them on Second Avenue loomed the smudgy white towers of Kips Bay Plaza, but on this block you didn't even hear the traffic. They passed an elderly chauffeur in gray livery wiping down an old gray Continental. A nurse in a starched white uniform was watching a palsied bulldog urinate against a tree. Further up the street a bent, black janitor in a blue smock hosed down the sidewalk.

"Secret neighborhood," Lang said. "Lower Murray Hill. Quiet money. Old families livin' here for a hundred years, clippin' coupons. You hit one of these joints you need a ten-ton truck. Four floors and everything's worth stealin'. Paintings, jewelry, antique furniture, Deco, Nouveau or Early American, family jewelry, sterling flatware, two-hundred-year-old china. Open a hall closet and you find a Mason jar full of coins. Down at the bottom there's gold pieces from the 1890s. It's like the mummy's tomb, these old people."

"Jerry, please," Rasso pleaded.

"Where's Joe live, Tony?"

"Six seventeen. Middle of the block."

"How does a lowlife like him rate such a fancy address?"

Rasso could hardly speak. "He got the house off a guy who couldn't pay his Vegas tab."

"Jackals," Lang said. "Follow a wounded animal and wait'll it dies, then pick it apart. Take the car, the jewelry, the furniture, the clothes . . ."

There were jagged chunks in the stone steps. The varnish on the doorframe was peeling. Grayness lay behind the windows as if the rooms were empty.

"They gutted the house," Lang said. "Squeezed every last dollar out of it and walked away." He shoved Rasso onto the floor. "You guys . . . you kill everything you touch."

Letitia looked in the back mirror. "There's that van I hit."

Lang looked out of the window. "You got guys followin' me, Tony?"

Rasso snorted bitterly. "You kiddin' me, my warriors are still hidin' under the bar . . ."

The van pulled in front of them and stopped. A big black guy in an army jacket got out.

"It's a shake," Lang said. "They see the big Mercedes they want a payoff." He peeled three hundreds off Hanif's gold money clip and handed them to Letitia. "Go out and give 'em a hundred for starters."

Stewart watched the girl get out of the car. She was tall and slim. An easy smile, green eyes glittering.

"I guess I hit you," she said.

"Guess you did."

"I stepped on the gas instead of the brake."

"Happens," he said.

Now Lang, the target, got out of the car and gave him a friendly wave. "Sorry guy . . ."

"Guy." The patronizing word the brothers used to con white dudes. ("Be cool, guy.") A secret way of showing contempt. He didn't like it used on him.

"Look, I don't have any insurance," the girl said. She offered him a hundred. "Will this cover it?"

Stewart took the bill. "Yeah okay . . ." It would be nice to take her out. Throw her a hump she'd never forget. Then we'd see who the "guy" was. "You work in the Village?" he asked.

"Yeah."

"What's your name anyway?"

"Stella Kowalski," she said.

"Hi Stella, I'm Reggie Stewart. I work in the Village, too. Maybe we could go for a drink."

She laughed and pointed over her shoulder to Lang, who was helping the dude in the leather jacket up the steps. "My boyfriend wouldn't like that."

She was flirting. He was in.

"Some place I can reach you?" he asked.

"I'd better reach you."

This was the big no no in the sky, but he didn't care. He took her hand. Stroke the inside of the wrist, gives 'em chills. "Executive Air. Ask for Reggie . . ."

"Maybe I will," she said.

He watched her walk back to the car. Then got back into the van.

"What was that all about?" Osler asked.

"She's hot. I gave her my number."

"You crazy? What if she calls?"

"What do you mean what if?"

They made a left on Second Avenue. Hartung waved them down on the east side of Twenty-ninth Street.

"Had quite a little conversation with the lady, didn't you?" he said.

Stewart faltered. He didn't know Hartung had been watching.

"She asked him out," Osler said quickly, trying to cover him.

Hartung gave Stewart the fish eye. "That your story?"

Stewart stared back. "She came on to me. I had to play along."

"She came on to *you*. Okay guy, anything you say. I couldn't get a taxi on such short notice so I'm giving you my car. Black Tahoe across the street." He flipped Osler the keys. "Don't mess it up."

They watched Hartung climb in the van and drive away.

Stewart cursed. "Sonofabitch, disrespecting me like that."

"C'mon, he knew you were lyin' about the girl," Osler said.

"It's not that."

"Then what?"

"He called me 'guy,' " Stewart said.

RASSO STUMBLED AND GASPED.

"How many times I gotta tellya, the man don't even know his own name."

Lang pulled him up the steps by the back of his jacket. "Ring the bell, Tony."

A fat lady came down the steps and glared through the glass window.

"Who's this?" Lang asked.

Rasso turned with his good eye. "His sister, May."

The fat lady opened the door with a suspicious look. "Tony, what happened to you?"

"He had an accident, ma'am," Lang said politely. "Got hit in the eye. We were around the corner so he said let's come here and call a doctor . . ."

"Let us in May," Rasso said.

"Sure Tony."

She walked them through a large room, empty except for a few battered sofas and plasma TV.

"You new?" she asked Lang over her shoulder.

"Just got in from Miami," Lang said.

"Joe here, May?" Rasso asked.

"Where would he be?"

They followed her through another empty room. A hunting mural was peeling off the side wall. On the other walls you could see the bare spots where large paintings had hung.

In the kitchen a shrunken old man with a huge beak of a

nose in a terry cloth robe that hung off him like a tent was gumming oatmeal. A big hood, bulging out of a Hugo Boss suit, got up, wiping powdered sugar off his lapel.

Lang showed him the gun. "Hands over your head, partner."

The guy raised his hands. The jacket was so tight it hitched halfway up his chest. Lang couldn't miss the ruby pinky ring he had on his left hand, just like he hadn't missed it that night in the hotel room when the guy had that left hand over Gloria's mouth. Case closed, he thought. This day's gonna end right after all.

"If you dig long enough you get to China, you know what I mean, Tony?" he said. He bent down to the old man. "Hiya Joe."

The old man blinked and gave him an idiot grin. "Mr. Christmas Tree."

"Mr. Christmas Tree, huh. The green jacket and the orange cap. That's pretty good, Joe." He took the old man's bony arm. "Wanna go out on the town, Joe?"

The old man grabbed the sides of his chair with a stubborn look.

Rasso found a wet rag on the sink and jammed it into his eye. "Whaddya doin', Jerry?"

"Maybe if we give Joe a ride around the old neighborhood it might jog his memory a little," Lang said. "Hey Joe, wanna go for a ride?"

The old man shivered. "Cold."

"We got a nice warm car outside, Joe." Lang lifted the old man out of the chair by his scrawny neck. He squawked and struggled.

Rasso held up the bloody rag. "Look at this, Jerry, I'm on anticoagulants. I'll bleed to death . . ."

"What is it, one o'clock now? Seven thirty, that enough time to raise the two fifty, Tony?"

"I told ya I gotta make some calls."

The floor creaked. Lang turned and saw the fat lady coming at him with a kitchen knife. He grabbed her wrist and twisted it gently with his left hand until she dropped the knife. "Sorry Mama," he said, kicking it across the room.

The fat lady rubbed her wrist. "How can you do this to a sick old man?"

"With all due respect, Mama, this sick old man once shot a cook for putting too much cheese in the sauce. Know that parking area off the West Side Highway on One Fifty-eighth, Tony?"

"I'll find it," Rasso said.

"Put the money in a black garbage bag and dump it in the trash can in the lot. You got till seven thirty, Tony."

"Please Jerry," he pleaded. "I gotta make a lotta calls . . ."

"Just you and your flunky here. I see pizza boxes in the bushes I'll blow out what's left of Joe's brains . . . Let's go, Joe."

The old man squealed like a scared rabbit and shook his head violently. A gray green globule of spit the size of a golf ball flew out of his mouth.

"Good trick, Joe," Lang said. "Can you blow bubbles out your ass, too?"

The old man grabbed the refrigerator door. "No . . . No . . ." He went limp . . . "Mama . . ."

"We were gonna see Mama right now, Joe," Lang said. He dragged the old man along the kitchen floor like a stubborn puppy. "Mama's waitin' in the car and Papa, too . . ."

Stewart turned onto Thirty-first in Hartung's black Tahoe just in time to see Lang hustling a scrawny old man into the back seat of Mercedes. "Who's this now?"

Osler punched out Hartung's number. "He's got a new hostage," he said. "That old Mafia guy who walks around the

Village in his bathrobe . . ."

In the van Hartung logged onto the onboard computer and accessed Lang's file. He clicked on "Contacts" and found seven names. "Joe Di Corso," Hartung said. "Lang is probably holding him for ransom. So maybe he's just doing all this for getting away money and our asset is not on his agenda."

"So maybe we can go home," Osler said.

"Not yet," said Hartung.

In the Mercedes, Lang grabbed the back of Joe Di's neck. "C'mon Joe, talk to me."

Joe Di's head turned like a ventriloquist's dummy. His rheumy black eyes fixed on Letitia without comprehension. "Mama," he said.

"I don't think he's faking," Letitia said.

Lang turned Joe Di's head to him. "Feds are all over you, Joe. Won't let you die in bed. So you pull the nut act. Hold 'em up in court forever."

Joe Di screwed up his eyes and whimpered. "Mama . . ."

"Go east on Twenty-third to the FDR Drive," Lang said. "How about a swim, Joe?"

The old man's mouth flopped open like a fish and his eyes went up in his head. Lang laughed. "Another little trick, huh Joe? Nice . . ." And threw him against the back door so hard his head bounced off the window.

Letitia cringed. "Is there any point to this?"

"Don't feel sorry for your enemy because he's helpless," Lang said. "Rejoice because he's in your power . . ."

The old man jammed his thumb into his mouth and rocked back and forth making sucking sounds. "You gotta hand it to him," Lang said. "The screamin', the squealin', the babblin', the pukin' on cue, that's all good stuff. But you can't con a conner, Joe. What did you do this morning? Took a nice shave and a shower and then splashed on some cologne. Nuts don't worry about how they smell. My grandfather was a nut. Stank like a butcher's dumpster.

"And how about this bozo who works for you showin' up all dressed for a sit down. Think he'd squeeze his fat gut into a suit if he was babysittin' a feeb? No way, he'd come in Nike warm ups. But here's the dead giveaway: Tony Rasso's gonna raise the money to buy you back from me. Think he would kick in a nickel for a senile old man who was outta the loop?" He put his arm around the old man's skeletal shoulders. "He wouldn't lift a finger, would he Joe? Pull in here . . ."

Letitia turned off into a rest stop overlooking the East River. Lang opened the door. "Moment of truth, Joe. Pop the trunk, Letitia."

The old man clutched the back of the front seat with claw like fingers, staring right into Letitia's face. "Mama . . . Mama . . ." Lang grabbed his ankles. "C'mon Boss, you won't get no back up from her . . ." The old man's fingers slid off the seat. He fell face down on the ground. Lang dragged him, knees bouncing on the cobblestones up to the trunk. "Here's your new room mate, Joe."

Hanif was lying on his back, his forehead gray and prickled with sweat, his eyes bulging above the gag.

Lang grabbed the old man by the collar and held him over the trunk. "I got a math question for you, Joe," Lang said. "Say I put you in there with Mittens. Drive up to the country. Pull into the woods. I got one guy with asthma, one old man who's gotta have a bad heart after sixty years in the rackets. Question is: how many guys are dead when I open the trunk?"

Joe Di's eyes suddenly cleared. He cocked his head like a bird and smiled up at Lang. "Jerry the Actor. I ain't a bad actor either, huh Jerry?"

"I Thought You Were a Cop,

I swear to God," Joe Di said. He spoke in a hoarse, high pitched voice. A smile like a nervous tic played around the corners of his mouth. "The FBI is always runnin' guys in tryin' to catch me nappin'."

"They got a vendetta against you, Joe," Lang said.

"I'm givin' them the finger, kid. They put all the other old-timers away, but they can't get me . . ."

They were parked on a service road by the Grand Street projects, eating bagels as the cars whizzed by. Letitia watched them in the mirror and marveled. They were talking life and death in the most companionable terms.

"It must be tough, keepin' that act up all the time," Lang said.

"Gotta stay on your toes. I thought they sent you in to scare me into crackin'. But when I seen that Albanian in the trunk I knew, they wouldn't go that far." Joe Di nodded in admiration. "You got the jump on that fat fuck, huh?"

"Caught him by surprise."

Joe Di gave him an appraising look. "What'd you do to Tony?"

"Threw him through the door in the club."

Joe Di shook his head in disgust. "This guy is useless."

"He's supposed to protect you. Instead, he walks me right into your house."

Joe spat out a poppy seed. "You make 'em rich and they go soft. This guy's been around too long gettin' fat and doin'

130

nothin' like somebody's deadbeat brother-in-law. When this is over I gotta remind myself to give him the gold watch, you know what I mean?"

"He's raisin' the money to get you outta this jackpot," Lang said.

"Sure, 'cause every dollar he makes comes through me. If I go it's all up for grabs and he's scared he'll get shut out." He patted Lang on the arm. "I heard about you, Jerry the Actor. Tony came back from Vegas that time he signed you up. 'I got a real piece of talent,' he said. You made money with us, right?"

"A lot of money, Joe."

"You coulda made more. I had a lotta things you coulda done easy. You know, hard things that needed a guy who could get into a joint do the very hard thing and get out. But Tony said you wouldn't do hard things . . ."

"I'm not a tough guy," Lang said.

"Pretty tough today."

"If you set me up, kill my old lady, and then try to kill me, you'll make me tough."

"You lookin' at me for that?" Joe asked.

"Who else has the juice to reach into the jails to get a guy killed?"

"What's my reason?"

"Get the drawing for nothin'."

"That's for a one shot guy. I'm in business for years. Anyway, I was set to clear a hundred Gs on that thing."

"You remember it?" Lang asked, casually.

"I remember the banana I stole off a pushcart in 1954," Joe Di said. "It was a contract."

"Who for?"

Joe Di gave him an apologetic smile. "I don't like to name names, kid, you know?"

Lang shrugged with equal regret. "Everybody does things

they don't like some times, Joe. I'm not gonna like smackin' you to make you talk . . ."

Joe Di raised his hands in mock surrender. "Okay, okay, you don't gotta make threats . . . I got a guy, Herman Tessler, Stamps and Coins, little corner store on Fifth and Twenty-seventh. Thirty years I'm doin' business with this guy. Best fine arts fence in town. Deals with the Japs and the Arabs. Now he's got the Russians and the Chinks biddin' everything up. I'm tellin' you, Jerry, there's more money around now than there ever was. There's more opportunity for a smart guy than ever and nobody around to take advantage."

Lang dropped a cigarette in a container of coffee and watched it sizzle. "Tell me about Tessler, Joe."

"Most of the time I dealt to him, but once in a blue moon he'd have an order he wanted me to fill."

"So then somebody ordered this drawing from him, he gave you the contract to steal it and you hired me."

"That's right. Nice and simple. No reason to complicate it by killin' a valued employee like you."

Lang thought it over for a second. "There would be if you wanted to make it look like I had been pinched so you could keep the drawing for yourself."

"I'm the boss, kid. If I want somethin' that bad I take it."

Lang swirled the soggy cigarette in the coffee. For the first time Letitia could see doubt in his eyes.

"Mittens couldn't get crooked cops to do hits and rip offs. Only a guy with your power could do that . . ."

"You don't understand power, Jerry," Joe Di said. "A powerful guy don't have to make fancy plans. Hitler didn't say 'Let's kill the Jews and tell everybody they died from the flu.' If I want this thing so bad, who's gonna argue with me?"

Lang hung his head. "You're right, Joe."

Joe Di patted Lang's pocket. "What are you smokin', kid?"

Lang gave him a cigarette and lit it with Rasso's Dunhill.

"You know what the lawyers say. 'Never ask a question you can't answer.' You're fishin'. Tryin' to figure out who set you up. You got more important things to worry about."

"Like . . . ?"

"Like the future. Sittin' with a bag full of money is only half the battle. You gotta figure where you can go to enjoy it. Right?"

Lang gave him a sheepish look. "Right . . ."

The old man nodded shrewdly. Letitia could see he thought he was getting the upper hand. "You gimme a phone and I'll get you a clean car you can drive up to the Canadian border. I got a guy in Customs who'll walk you right across. You go see another friend of mine in Montreal. It'll cost you ten Gs, but you get a nice clean Canadian passport, airplane tickets, active credit cards. This time tomorrow you're on a plane anywhere you wanna go. Okay?"

"Okay Joe. Thanks . . ."

"But there's one condition, kid. I gotta be home safe in bed."

Lang shook his head with tearful sincerity. "I would never do nothin' to you, Joe."

Joe Di gestured impatiently. "Sure, I know, you have too much respect for me. I heard it all before. I even said it to guys I was gonna clip two minutes later. I'll make all the arrangements now, but nothin' will click until I call in the OK from my house. Okay, kid?"

Lang nodded humbly. "Anything you say. Joe."

He looked hopelessly at Letitia. His mood seemed to have deflated so rapidly. But then she realized he was acting, pretending to believe the old man. It was the same trick he had played on the other two, making them think he could be manipulated.

"Anything you say . . ."

LUBIMOV HAD KNOWN PUTIN

in the KGB. They were stationed together in Dresden in the last days of the Soviet Empire. To him Putin was a drab little paper pusher. He had no idea that their casual acquaintance would make him a millionaire. Lubimov was an elite "operations" man. Fluent in Arabic and Farsi, he had been posted to the military attaché at the embassy in Teheran. He was given the dead end job of liaising with the mullahs around the exiled zealot Ayatollah Khomeini. When the very same mullahs astonished the world by deposing the Shah, he was in the privileged position of being the only Russian they trusted. He became liaison with the Pasdaran, helping them set up their espionage operations in the West. Then he went to Beirut, where he spent eleven years as an adviser to Amal, the Shiite militia under the control of the Iranians. He was there during the civil war, the taking of foreign hostages, the attack on the Marine base, and the Israeli invasion. He was there when Hezbollah, the competing Shiite militia, took three Russians hostage to demonstrate their power. He commanded the operation that systematically assassinated the families of the Hezbollah commanders until the hostages were released. They awarded him the Order of Lenin in a secret ceremony.

In the late '80s Lubimov was made security officer at the Dresden station. Panicky spies were defecting, buying their way to asylum in the West with trunk loads of classified information. It was Lubimov's job to staunch the flow. He needed information on East German employees and was directed to Putin's cramped office in the Commercial Mission.

Putin had a file on every official, embassy employee, spy, and criminal contact in East Germany. Lubimov guessed he was the Russian control of Staasi, the East German intelligence service. He was careful about releasing gems from his archives, but when told that the people were selling secrets his normally expressionless eyes flashed with indignation. "Traitors, eh?"

They would meet occasionally at a safe brothel in Tallinn where the spies could go without fear of being compromised by a Western service. They had a few half-drunk conversations while watching sex shows, but never got friendly. Even in a whorehouse the operations men scorned the "clerks," who had never been in the field. But Lubimov played up to Putin, thanked him profusely for every piece of information, invited him for drinks, showered him with servile flattery in the old Soviet style.

And Putin rewarded his attentions. He opened his files, what he called his "wasp's nest" to Lubimov. It seemed that every prominent person in East Germany had been a secret informant for the Staasi. Friends had denounced friends, brothers had turned in brothers, husbands and wives had routinely informed on one another. In West Germany, thousands of business people, writers, artists, and highly placed government officials had been seduced, bribed, or blackmailed by the Staasi or the KGB.

Putin knew where all the bodies were buried. He saw the archive as a great weapon in the ongoing Soviet struggle with the West.

Lubimov saw it as an information machine that would print money. He copied every file before returning it.

In a matter of months the massive Soviet edifice imploded. The "evil empire" was dead and a score of venal statelets had risen to take its place.

Putin came out of nowhere to prominence as Yelstin's right hand man. The KGB was gone and he was the head of the new intelligence apparatus. He held the key to the dark secrets of seventy-five years of Soviet history.

Lubimov was transferred to Berlin as military attaché to the new Russian Embassy. He began to accumulate his fortune. Working methodically through the files, he visited all the East Germans who had spied or informed for the Russians, told them what he knew, and negotiated the price of his silence.

A Mercedes dealer in Dusseldorf had provided cars to Staasi agents. The man let Lubimov use his export license to ship used Mercedes to Vladivostock. A famous dissident songwriter in East Berlin had been in the employ of the Staasi for twenty years and had provided information that had sent some of his closest friends to prison. The man paid plenty to keep that quiet. The biggest art dealer in Bonn had a "secret collection" of art that had been confiscated from Jews during World War II. The man took him to a subcellar under his gallery. There were Klimts and Kandinskys, Kurt Schwitters, Oskar Kokoschka. Isaac Levitan.

"Pick a painting," the dealer said.

Lubimov laughed. "I'll take them all."

Lubimov frequented a café on the Friedrichstrasse right across from Checkpoint Charlie, the old border crossing between the East and West Berlin. How many times had he smuggled agents past the American GIs? Now the place was a museum.

He liked going on Sunday afternoons when the street was full of tourists. Americans took pictures in front of the kiosk. Germans tried to explain the Cold War to their children. He drank a beer in a café across the street and went over his Swiss bank account.

One Sunday he saw a thickset man with a blonde crew cut

and rimless glasses sitting at an outdoor table. He recognized him from surveillance photos and background checks. It was Cliff Hartung, his opposite number at the American Embassy. Hartung's cover was commander of the Marine security detail, but he was operations officer for the top secret Pentagon unit that the Russians knew all about.

Hartung stared straight ahead as Lubimov passed. He ate a cherry strudel and had two *café royales* with *shlag*, never once looking in Lubimov's direction. All this conspicuous inattention was a signal that he wanted to talk. When he got up, he made a slight gesture for Lubimov to follow him. He walked down the Zimmerstrasse and Lubimov caught up.

"This is a very public place for a contact," he said.

"Nobody's watching," Hartung said. "They're all too busy trying to make deals for themselves." He took an envelope out of his pocket. "Here's a copy of your bank statement in case you misplaced the one you were looking at."

Hartung offered him the envelope. He didn't take it.

"What do you want?" he asked.

Hartung turned down a narrow side street. Lubimov followed him into the shadowy courtyard of an old office building. An old man stood at a window watching.

Hartung faced him, poised on the balls of his feet as if he were about to attack.

"I'm going to make you an offer you can't refuse, Colonel Lubimov." Then relaxed and smiled. "I've always wanted to say that . . ."

"What is this offer?"

"I'll spare you the details for now. The short answer is we want you to come over."

"And why can't I refuse this offer?"

"We know you have access to Staasi files and are using them to blackmail prominent people," Hartung said. "You don't want us to tell your colleagues how much money you've been salting away in that little bank in Basel . . ."

Lubimov was trapped. One of his subjects had obviously informed on him and the Americans had taken it from there. Behind the false smiles and the backslapping, the bad taste and the absurd chauvinism, they were good at their jobs.

"What do I have to do?" Lubimov asked.

"Answer questions. Do a little research in the files. Make contacts for us in a discreet way. Easy stuff for a professional like you."

"And what do I get for this?"

"It's what you don't get, dude. Arrested, tortured, sent to Siberia . . ." Hartung gave him a sly look. "Your new boss, Mr. Putin, is the vindictive type. He wouldn't like to hear that his old buddy is using secret files for less than noble purposes."

Lubimov thought of the brothel in Tallinn. How careful they had been, vetting the girls, sweeping the premises once a week for bugs and cameras. And all the while the Americans had been watching.

Hartung read his mind. "We owned that cathouse and everybody in it. I don't know what made you guys think you could trust a bunch of whores, especially Estonian whores who hated Russians . . ."

So they had been on him since the Tallinn days. They had spent time and money. Maybe they had high hopes he could be a mole inside the FSD bureaucracy. Maybe he had some leverage after all.

"I know Putin well," he said. "I could be a valuable asset to you if you treat me with consideration."

Hartung laughed. "We don't have to be considerate, dawg, we have you by the balls."

So Lubimov went to work for the Americans. Under Yeltsin all of Russia was for sale and Lubimov became a buyer. Hartung was his case officer, giving names and instructions in their weekly meetings. Lubimov bought information on nuclear plants, corrupt officials, government dealings with other countries. He corrupted generals, spies, and bureaucrats, taking commissions from everyone he bribed. The Americans knew he was getting kickbacks and didn't care. Dollars he banked in Switzerland, marks and rubles he turned into gold bullion, diamonds, used cars, negotiable bonds, anything he could convert quickly into cash.

As a boy in Odessa he had grown up in the culture of the black market, the shady deal. He had been taught that life was a struggle in which minimal gain was only achieved by strenuous effort and great risk. But this was Capitalism, the system of right place, right time. The money flooded in with minimal effort and no risk. He watched his bank account grow in amazement. If he, a mere errand boy, was making millions, he could only imagine how much the "oligarchs" were raking in. Billions!

Then it ended as abruptly as it had begun. Yeltsin stepped down and Putin replaced him. The day the news broke, Lubimov met Hartung in a safe house outside Berlin.

"I have to leave the country."

"Don't worry about Putin," Hartung said. "He'll be voted out in the next election."

Lubimov had to laugh. How naïve these Americans were. "Do you know where you are, Major? This isn't America where the loser walks off into the sunset. In Russia no one voluntarily relinquishes power. They either die or they're removed."

"Then we'll remove him."

"Why? To bring democracy to the long-suffering Russian people? Putin has ten thousand former KGB ready to do his bidding. He'll keep order, kill the Chechens, and sell you cheap oil. You'll welcome him with open arms."

"Then he'll be no threat to you," Hartung said.

Lubimov understood. He was performing well. Hartung wanted to keep him in place as long as possible. It was like installing a bug in someone's house and leaving it there until the battery died. He had to convince Hartung to keep him alive.

"Did you listen to the briefings I gave you?" he asked. "Putin is an ideologue, a Communist, who wants to recreate a new Soviet Empire. To him I'm nothing but a traitor. I'll be arrested and tortured into confessing. I'll tell him about you. Your cover will be blown. You'll be expelled from Russia. No more promotions or high level assignments. They'll put you behind a desk in Washington and force you to retire. I'll be in prison and your career will be over . . . Dude."

Hartung thought about it for a moment, then nodded. "Work on your golf game, Colonel. You're leaving tomorrow."

In America, Lubimov entered the wonderful world of Free Enterprise. A simple wire transfer transported all his money from Berlin to Central Park South. Lawyers and accountants appeared magically to help him shield his fortune from the EU taxmen. He bought a "shell" corporation in the Cayman Islands and was able to escape US taxes on money earned out of the country. There was what he called a "wealth club" in the US. You didn't have to be an aristocrat or a member of the *nomenklatura* to join. This was America: all you needed was money, about twenty million. Membership conferred access to sweetheart deals all over the world. He invested in the "carry" trade, borrowing money from Japan at .025 interest and buying New Zealand bonds paying 12.5. He bought oil futures in syndicates put together by producers who controlled production. Every bet was fixed.

In America, anything a rich man bought instantly appreciated in value—real estate, art, antiques, yachts. No matter how much you spent for something it was always worth more the next day.

And there was always someone to buy it.

He set himself up as private investor. Every variety of Russian, Arab, and South Asian hustler washed up at his door with a scheme. He consulted with oil companies on who to bribe in Baku, arranged to ship hundreds of tons of copper to a contact in the Chinese Ministry of Defense.

The money rolled in from all sides.

In America, he wasn't KGB, hated and feared, but a wealthy Russian with a mysterious past. He was courted socially, invited to openings, solicited for charity events. He was asked to lend his Kandinsky, his Levitan, and his Tchelitchev to a traveling exhibition of Modern Russian artists. No one asked how he had come to acquire these masterpieces. It was enough that he was generous with them.

Then, some piece of scum off the street had come into his home and tried to steal something he loved. It had taken days of phone calls and threats to stop him. He had been under their thumb in prison. He could have been terminated at any time. Instead, he had escaped. The whole adventure was inconceivable. This, too, could only have happened in America.

"The purpose of a social order is to protect the powerful," Lubimov said. "In Russia one bullet would have ended this."

Hartung stood at Lubimov's picture window looking out over Central Park, trying to control himself. He felt like saying: if you miss Russia so much why don't you go back? Because they'll throw you in Lubyanka Prison and stick electrodes up your ass!

Instead, he said: "It was a mistake, taking care of the woman. Lang's desire for vengeance seems to have given him supernatural strength. And luck. He's had some pretty miraculous escapes . . ."

"Miraculous?" Lubimov raised an eyebrow. "You believe God is on his side, Major?"

"Like my high school coach used to say: never give your opponent another reason to beat you."

"So, are you saying that I can expect to see him outside my door?"

"It won't get that far. I have two men on him right now . . ."

"Then why not take him out now?" Lubimov asked, incredulous.

"We don't assassinate people on the street."

"I have two Moldovans in Coney Island," Lubimov said. "They can do it for you."

Hartung shook his head with a pained look. "The New York police would not accept a killing in their jurisdiction. Besides, now this girl is involved as well."

"So there will be one less lap dancer in the world."

"We're the good guys," Hartung said. "We try not to kill innocent people."

"You don't do a very good job at it," Lubimov said

Hartung shrugged. "We try, Colonel. We try . . ."

"Sinatra was Playin' The Copa,"

Joe Di said. "That's how long since I been up here . . ."

They had driven up First Avenue to Patsy's in Italian Harlem.

"This joint hasn't changed in forty years," he said. "Seems like the wink of an eye, but it's gotta be forty years."

"Best pizza in town," Lang said. "We used to come all the way up from Forty-eighth and Tenth."

"They made it fresh for Sinatra. I can still taste it." Joe Di licked his lips. "Some nights when the nice people came in to see him, he'd keep the band and the bartenders after hours. Call up here and order forty pies. Jimmy Napoli would send me and Joe Beck to pick 'em up."

"I don't see the great Joe Di as a pizza delivery man," Lang said.

"You kiddin', it was an honor. The chauffeur would drive us uptown in his limo. They'd put the boxes in the limo, we didn't lift a finger."

Lang leaned over the driver's seat and nudged Letitia. "Did you ever hear of the Copa?"

"Only from the song," she said.

"See Joe," he said. "Ancient history."

"Don't I know it. That whole life is gone."

"Shows how big you guys were to get a private concert from the Chairman of the Board."

"He never sang, just drank Jack Daniel's and kibitzed with

143

the guys," Joe Di said. "Then when he got loaded, he'd pick on some poor *gavone,* who had come all the way in from the asshole of Jersey just to see him. He'd make fun of the guy about his suit, his tie, he'd take the pizza outta his hand and tell him 'you're fat enough already.' Everybody would laugh and the poor guy would look like he wanted to go through the floor."

"Did he ever make fun of you?" Lang asked.

"Nah. He knew who I was. He never said nothin' to me."

But he got quiet and Lang knew it was a lie. Looking at the old man in profile he knew that nose hadn't escaped Sinatra's attention.

A stocky old man staggered up the steep metal steps from the cellar, carrying a hundred pound sack of flour on his shoulder. "I remember this guy." Joe Di said. "He was just outta the army, the nephew of the owner, and they gave him a job until he got started . . . So he's still here forty years later, shleppin' dough every day. Betcha he don't even have a piece of the joint."

"At least he knows where he's goin' when he wakes up in the morning," Lang said.

"Yeah, 'cause he's goin' nowhere. These guys . . ." He snorted in contempt and you could just sense him fighting the humiliation of whatever Sinatra had done to him. "Sicilian donkeys. They work every day for a bowl of macaroni. A guy like this lives in same apartment all his life. He's got a wife looks just like him and if she's wearin' pants you can't tell the difference from behind . . ."

With an easy movement, the old man shifted the sack of flour from one shoulder to the next as he opened the door.

"Pretty strong for an old guy," Lang said.

"A donkey," Joe Di said. He coughed and wiped his mouth with a shaky, blue veined hand.

"Think this guy ever met Sinatra, Joe?" Lang asked.

"How should I know?"

"Sinatra would be nice to a guy like this, wouldn't he? He was always nice to the little people. Take a picture with his arm around him, then slip a hundred into his pocket and tell him 'get yourself a plate of chicken chow mein.' The guy would have that picture on his mantelpiece. Every time anybody came in he'd tell 'em all about the day Ole Blue Eyes came to Patsy's . . ."

Joe Di wasn't listening. He was looking down at his slippers, his lips moving, lost in Mafia memories.

When you come to the end you add things up, Lang thought. You're a boss. You got money, power, respect, people shake in their shoes when you walk into a room. And then you see this poor slob. He's working forty years for his family and they still make him bring up the dough from the cellar. But he can hump a hundred-pound sack of flour and you can't even lift yourself out of bed in the morning. He's taking a bite out of a veal cutlet sandwich and you have to swallow three pills and a bowl of oatmeal just to take a crap. He'll go home tonight and watch TV in a warm apartment. You're shivering in your pajamas with a gun to your head and you don't know if you'll make it through the day.

"What do you want on your pie, Joe?" he asked.

Joe Di shook his head slightly and started to say "I can't eat . . . ," but stopped, with a defiant look. "Everything kid. Let's get everything we can get."

"So that's sausage peppers, onions, mushrooms . . . How about you, Letitia? What do you like?"

He could see her watching him in the rearview mirror.

He leaned over the driver's seat. Her eyes were calm, but she was gripping the wheel tightly.

"You gotta get into the spirit of your new reality," he said.

"My new reality is insane," she said.

"How much more insane than dancing naked in a saloon at

145

seven in the morning for an old rabbi?" Lang said. "Workin' for an Albanian thug with two fingers who tries to kill you for no reason. How about the biggest insanity of them all—fightin' roaches in a tenement while you dream about Hollywood stardom."

She raised her hand to quiet him.

"Pepperoni," she said.

"Good choice." He peeled another hundred off Hanif's gold money clip. "Will you do the honors?"

Lang watched her walk into Patsy's. Even in the baggy jeans and Mets jacket he could feel the sinuous movement of her body.

"What am I gonna do with this girl?" he asked.

"You gotta travel light, kid," Joe Di said.

"I could take her with me."

"What for? They got broads in Montreal. Besides, it'll cost you double to get her a passport."

"She's legal. She could use her own."

"Yeah but then they can trace her." Joe Di tapped his forehead. "Don't think with your little head, kid. She's a nice piece of ass, but, let's face it, the best piece of ass in the world is only good for an hour a day. The rest of the time she's just a pain in the ass."

In the end you add it up, Lang thought. There had been kids on his block, just like him. Cramped into small apartments with too many brawling siblings. Drunken red faced dad, long suffering, gray faced mom. The sisters at Immaculate Heart of Mary School smacked all of them with rulers, threatened them with eternal damnation if they didn't do their homework. They were all tough kids, who fought in the street. Angry kids who would take any dare. Snatch a purse in the theater district, fight the bums in the Penn Yards, jump off a roof onto an awning. You had to be careful when you dared somebody because they would say "darers go first" and then you would have to do it. Most of them calmed down as they got older, but he got wilder. Most of them got jobs, got married, moved out. He stayed a thief. He wasn't tougher or meaner or angrier than any of the others. But he had ended up doing bad things. All along the way there had been people who drifted into his life and came to grief.

Letitia came out of Patsy's holding the box gingerly around its edges.

She opened the door. "This thing is heavy."

The pizza box was hot on his lap. The smell filled the car. The cheese was still bubbling around the toppings. Joe Di stuck his head in the box and crowed:

"Look at this, kid. This is what life is all about."

RASSO STARTED MAKING CALLS

in the car as Billy Dario drove him to the hospital. He had to watch what he said. Every phone was tapped. There were guys who were afraid to talk, others who had a bad taste from some beef with him and wouldn't come to the phone. He sat there with his eyeball burning trying to get his message across. Couldn't name names, not even nicknames. Couldn't refer to the "old man" because the Feds would guess it was Joe Di. Couldn't make any reference to a nose, talk about a problem, or say anything about money because that would bring them swooping down. He had already been warned by his lawyers that if he was stopped with more than a few hundred in his pocket they could bring him in on a RICO pinch and then hold him in contempt if he refused to account for the money.

Why not just let the old bastard die? Because there were too many secrets locked up in that shrunken head. Too much money that only he could control with a word or two. Even in this day and age, there were all those union leaders and construction executives and garbage guys and other bosses, who would only obey an order they knew came from Joe Di. He still had the mystique. They loved the myth, the stories about who he had killed, how much money he had made, what cops and politicians he had controlled, what legendary bosses he had "been with." The mob had been history for years, but they still swore by "Joe Di."

Finally, after an "I can't talk to you," a "Tony Rasso? Sorry don't know nobody by that name," and a "what the fuck are you callin' here for?" he figured out a way.

"I had a freak accident, got a piece of glass in my eye," he said to everybody he called. "I'm goin' to the Emergency Room at St. Vincent's. If you know a good eye doctor gimme a call . . ."

It got through. He could tell by the grunts and the quick hang-ups that they understood there was an emergency.

At St. Vincent's, a triage nurse took one look and moved him into an examining room ahead of everyone else. An intern who looked like his fourteen-year-old niece made a face when she saw his eye.

"Can you describe the pain?"

"What kind of stupid question is that?" he snarled.

A surgical resident from the ophthalmology department came in and put cold, practiced hands on his face. "It's an intraocular foreign body. We're gonna have to get it out."

"I got somethin' to take care of, first," he said.

By now there was a group of doctors standing over him. Nurses were peeking into the room.

They know who I am, he thought. They don't know my name, but they know who I am.

"Just gimme somethin' for the pain," he said.

They put a metal shield over the eye and bandage to hold it in place. A nurse swabbed his arm to give him a shot.

"Is this gonna make me dopey?" he asked.

"No more than usual," he heard someone whisper.

"A little disoriented at first," was the official answer.

They gave him a vial of yellow pills. One every four hours.

"I'm not trying to frighten you, but you could lose the eye," someone said.

"I'll be back in the morning," he said.

Only one guy had shown up in the waiting room, Johnny Intranuova, who ran the last after hours gambling joint Joe Di had on the East Side. While Rasso was telling him what had happened, Angie Celeberti, business agent for the Laborers International local, came in and went into a corner with Billy Dario. Then Gino Scipione, who ran shylocking in Brooklyn, and Kenny the Kike, the bookmaker. The joint was starting to look like a sit down. A security guy looked in. Through all his pain Rasso could imagine Joe Di's falsetto sneer: "You had a buncha made guys come to an Emergency Room for a private meeting, you stupid moron?"

Intranuova drew him away from the others. "Can I ask you a rhetorical question?" he said. "What happens if we don't pay off and this guy clips the old man? What happens then?"

Rasso's eye throbbed like it was going to pop out of his head. "A rhetorical question don't get an answer," he said.

"Maybe I meant metaphorical," Intranuova said.

"No you meant just a regular question," Rasso said. "What happens if anything happens to Joe Di? We lose our umbrella that's what happens. We get a new boss and everything gets put back into play again. We'll be startin' from scratch and life won't be any easier. Don't get creative. Just do what I tellya."

They agreed to collect the money and send it through couriers to an electronics store that Scipione had taken over in Brooklyn. They would wrap it in a boom box carton and get one of the Korean girls who worked in the store to taxi it in to Billy Dario's father-in-law's bakery on First Avenue. Billy would stick it in the garbage bag and meet him at the drop.

"What are we gonna do about Jerry Lang?" Scipione asked.

"Let's get the old man back first," Rasso said, "then we'll deal with him."

But he grabbed Billy Dario on the way out. "Go to my house in Fort Lee. The Range Rover's in the garage. In the spare tire compartment, where the jack is, there's a shotgun disassembled.

Bring it into the city. Make sure you bring in both parts of the gun and the box of shells."

Billy Dario shook his head with a worried look. "You want me to go to Jersey at this hour of the day? What if I get stuck in traffic?"

"You won't, you're goin' against the flow."

"What do you want the gun for?"

Rasso felt something oozing down his cheek. He pulled the bandage up and slid his finger under the gauze. It was blood mixed with tears. "Why do you think? A guy sticks my head through a door, snatches my boss, makes me eat shit . . . What do you think I want the gun for, Einstein?"

Every Scam Known to Man

had gone down at the 158th Street parking area. It was the perfect place for a quick transaction and a fast getaway. Drop the thing off, or pick it up. Get back on the West Side Highway, head south, and in ten minutes you're at the Battery Tunnel on your way to Brooklyn. Or you can go the long way, north on the Henry Hudson and across the GW Bridge to Jersey and points south or west. Commuter hornballs from Jersey picked up hookers on Riverside Drive, drove down to the area for a quick park in the dark, and were on their way home in fifteen minutes. People who couldn't be seen together pulled in for private conversations. Bodies were transported in trunks and dumped in the bushes.

At 7:10 Lang had Letitia drive south on the Henry Hudson and pull into a turn off overlooking the parking area.

"Why are we stopping here?" she asked.

"Just to make sure Tony Rasso's not layin' a trap," Lang said. "This is a safe spot. We can see them but they can't see us."

Letitia looked out at the traffic. "Aren't you afraid the police will get suspicious?"

"Good question," Lang said. "Pop the trunk."

He got out and lifted the lid. Hanif was huddled, shaking in the corner. Lang patted his icy forehead. "Don't worry, Mittens, it's almost over . . ."

He jacked the rear fender up just enough to get the tire off the ground and got back into the car. "Any cop drivin' by will keep on goin'. He won't wanna get stuck helpin' some mutt change a tire."

"What if it's a cop who enjoys helping people?" Letitia asked.

"Then I'll shoot him and drive his car off the road." Lang laughed at her stunned expression. "That's what happens when you ask 'what if,' " he said. "Stick to the 'either-or's.' Like either it'll rain today or it won't. Either we'll be layin' on the beach in Maui laughin' about this in a coupla weeks or we won't."

Osler and Stewart drove by in the Tahoe.

Osler called Hartung. "Lang just pulled into a turn off on the Henry Hudson."

"Maybe he has to take a leak," Hartung said.

"I think it's an evasive maneuver," Osler said. "Maybe he pinned the tail. We been watchin' him all day. He's no dope."

Hartung fought off a surge of irritation. The Ten Commandments of Intelligence was taped to the bottom of his desk drawer. The Fourth Commandment was: "Guide the operative step by step through an unfamiliar situation. Reassure, don't criticize."

"Find a spot to stop where you can see, and wait for him to make a move," Hartung said.

"We already passed him," Osler said. "We're at 125th Street and there's no turn off before the exit."

"Double back and get behind him."

"We'll be blind while we're getting back in position. There'll be at least five minutes where he's out of contact. We could lose him."

Hartung looked at the First Commandment: "Believe in the mission and communicate that belief to the operatives." He tried to think of something encouraging to say. The button flashed on his other extension. It was probably Beverly calling with some new problem.

"Major . . ."

Damn! He had gone off into a trance staring at that god-damn blinking light.

"Can you hear me, Major?" Osler asked. "What if we lose him?"

Osler was shifting the blame in case he failed. Rookies risk their necks, veterans cover their asses. "If you lose him, find him, Sergeant Osler," Hartung said, pulling rank to communicate annoyance. "That's why they call it Intelligence."

He stayed on the speaker as Osler sped around Riverside Drive and got back on the highway. Osler drove past the turnoff where the Mercedes was parked.

"He's still there," he said. "Car's jacked up."

"Is he changing the tire?" Hartung asked.

"No. They're just sitting there."

"Maybe he jacked up the car to deflect suspicion," Hartung said. "He's probably meeting someone and they're going to go someplace more private to collect the ransom," he said.

He heard Stewart whisper: "There's a parking lot down there."

"Did I hear parking lot?" he said. "Secluded area? Good place for a meeting?"

Osler took a second to answer. "Sort of, sir."

"One of you will have to recon the lot. Osler, you'd better stay with the car. Let Stewart go. He'll blend in better in that neighborhood."

"Why is that, sir?" Stewart asked with an edge in his voice.

Hartung's other extension started blinking again. It was Beverly again. The hang up and the redial meant a big emergency. "That's Harlem, right, Sergeant Stewart. Sergeant Osler is a big white guy. They'll take him for a cop. As an African-American you will blend in better. No offense intended."

"None taken, sir," Stewart said.

In the back seat of the Mercedes, Joe Di was getting nervous. "You're givin' Tony to seven thirty, right kid?"

"Yeah, yeah, don't worry Joe," Lang said. "I like to show up early for payoffs, just in case somebody's got ideas . . ."

"Tony ain't gonna pull nothin'. I gave him the high sign in the house."

They sat silently in the dark. The smoke from Lang's cigarette swirled around his face.

Joe Di curled up, shivering, in the back seat. "I'm freezin' to death back here."

"It'll be over soon, Joe," Lang said. "Then you'll be in a nice warm car tellin' Tony Rasso what an asshole he is."

"I'll do worse than that."

Lang got a cold slice of pizza out of the box and offered it to Letitia. She shook her head. "It'll make me sick."

He was quiet. She could feel him studying her.

"You're not the stripper type," he said.

"You already told me that," she said. "Strippers have a dog's mentality. I'm more like a cat, you said."

"Okay so I'm repeating myself. I'm a dumb crook with just enough repertoire to talk gullible girls into doin' what's not good for them."

Lang reached over and opened the driver's door. "Get outta here." He gave her Hanif's money clip. "Take it all, I won't need it. Get a cheap room for the night. Tomorrow there won't be any dead Albanians in your apartment. You'll go on with your life like nothin' ever happened."

It was insane. Six hours ago she had been sure she wouldn't survive the day. Now she actually felt rejected.

"You're just letting me go?"

"I don't need you anymore."

"What's going to happen now?" she asked.

"Either I'll get the money or I won't."

"You'll get it kid," Joe Di piped up from the back seat.

"You could stick around for your end," Lang said, "but you don't care that much about money so why take a chance? You're not a real grifter."

Was there the slightest edge of derision in his voice? She felt a twinge of jealousy. I'm in the moment, she thought. I'm auditioning for a part in his crazy world and he's typing me out.

"I guess Gloria would have stuck around," she said.

"You're not Gloria."

Letitia got out of the car into the cold air. Lang slid over behind the wheel, the passing headlights glinting in his gray eyes. "Be careful crossin' the highway. You don't wanna get hit by a car."

"That would be the end of a perfect day," she said.

Did he smile? Was he sad? It was too dark to tell.

"Good luck," she said.

It seemed like a strange thing to say.

through the bushes down the hill toward the parking lot.

Osler was watching a dark figure scamper across the highway.

Hartung had just gotten off the phone with Beverly. Amy was locked in the bathroom, threatening to hurt herself.

Beverly was frantic. "I'm going to call the police to break the door down."

"Try to talk to her, first," he said. "I don't want cops poking around the house."

"Why are you so weird about the police? You're all on the same side."

He had explained this a thousand times. "I'm not supposed to be here. If they get suspicious they could punch me up . . ."

"So you'd rather your daughter slit her wrists, then you blew your precious cover . . ."

His other extension was blinking. That would be Osler or the Voice looking for a progress report.

"Does she have her cell phone?"

"Yes, that's how I've been talking to her."

"Okay, tell her not to do anything, I'll call her in a few minutes."

"Why can't you call her now?"

He knew this would make her crazy. "I've just got to got to deal with this one problem . . ."

"You don't call this a problem? Your daughter could be bleeding to death right now." He cringed. When Beverly got shrill there was no reasoning with her.

"I'll call you right back," he said and punched his blinking extension.

It was Osler. "I think he let the girl go," he said. "I just saw a woman running across the highway."

The girl, the girl . . . It took him a second to refocus. "The stripper?"

"Now there's no collaterals, Major," Osler said. "There's just three bad guys sittin' in a car. Stewart's already there. I can zoom down into that area so fast they won't know what hit 'em. Fifteen seconds of bang bang will cover the fire zone. Pick up Stewart. In thirty we're back on the highway . . . 'Mob boss slain, film at eleven.' "

Osler was out of Delta Force and those guys were trained to resolve problems by killing them. But the Ninth Commandment of Intelligence was "Always look for a reason not to do it," and this was an easy proposal to shoot down. "You're driving away in my car," he said. "Somebody might take down the plate number."

"Okay," Osler said. "We can tip the NYPD now, right?"

"We need a clean phone in case the cops ID the number," Hartung said. "And if we get a curious cop who wants to know what these three guys are doing in a car together, he could go down a long, winding road and find our Russian friend at the end."

"So what do we do?" Osler asked.

"Watch and wait," said Hartung. "This thing might take care of itself."

A metallic silver Chrysler 300 drove down the narrow access road into the parking area. It backed into a dark corner and cut its lights.

In the Mercedes, Lang reached into the back seat and shook

Joe Di. "Hey, Joe, your boy is here?"

Joe Di popped up. "Tony?"

"I think it's him. Chrysler 300?"

Joe Di pressed his nose against the window. "Yeah. New car every year and he wonders why he's got FBI comin' out of his ass."

A moment later a dinged up Crown Victoria rolled down the hill.

"Gypsy cab," Lang said. "The drop car?"

"Billy Dario with the money," Joe said. "See kid, everything's gonna be okay . . ."

The Crown Victoria circled the area.

"He's checkin' to make sure nobody else is around," Lang said.

The Crown Victoria backed into the bushes on the other side of the lot across from the Chrysler and cut its lights. A man emerged, carrying a gym bag.

"Billy Dario, the guy with the ruby pinky ring?" Lang asked. "Yeah."

Lang hefted the Glock. "He's one of the guys who grabbed my old lady, Joe."

Joe Di turned away from the window.

"If he did, he didn't do it on my say so," he said, carefully.

Lang could sense his mind working. *What is this guy really after?*

"He works for you, Joe," he said.

"He works for Tony."

"Tony works for you."

"Tony's got his own things, kid, you know how it is. What I don't know I don't get a piece of."

"Tony wouldn't hold out on you," Lang said.

"He thinks I'm a senile and can't see what's goin' on under my nose. But I happen to know he's got all the dope dealers in

Soho under his protection. He good for five Gs a week on that, which he ain't kickin' back to the higher-ups. I been savin' that little piece of information for a rainy day . . ."

"Somebody reached into jail to kill me, Joe."

"So Tony's takin' contracts, I wouldn't put it past him. He uses this Albanian and other freelancers who he thinks I wouldn't know about. A guy gets so greedy sometimes it makes him stupid."

The dark figure passed the gym bag through the window of the Chrysler and walked back across the lot to the Crown Victoria.

"See he's passin' him your money, kid," Joe said. "That's what you gotta think about. Not who did what to who five years ago . . ."

Billy Dario came out of the Crown Victoria again, this time carrying a black garbage bag.

"Your guy was there when they killed my old lady, Joe," Lang said.

"You lookin' at the ring?" Joe said, talking fast. "There's a schmuck in every club in New York with a ring like that. They wanna tell the world 'I'm a wiseguy. I'm Vito Corleone, I'm Tony Soprano.' Then they wonder why they get popped and have to rat out a whole crew just to keep their fat asses outta jail . . ."

"They killed my old lady and then they came after me, Joe," Lang said.

Joe Di fidgeted in the back. "How long you been in this business? You gonna tell me nobody's got a beef with you?"

"Not bad enough to spend money tryin' to kill me."

"Maybe it's the guy you stole the drawing from, did you ever think of that? Maybe he's a guy like us and wants to get even in the old fashioned way . . ."

Lang remembered the apartment. The high art on the living

room walls didn't go with the low life that was going on in the bedroom with the round bed, black silk sheets, the cognac, the smell of marijuana, the videos . . .

"Your Mr. Tessler would know who this guy was," he said.

Joe Di grabbed his shoulder, eagerly. "Sure he would, he set the score up. After we get your money we'll go talk to him . . ."

He was buying time, hoping to stay alive as long as he could.

Dario dropped the garbage bag into the can and tied the top. He hesitated for a second, his hand on the bag.

"That's the payoff, Joe," Lang said. "So what did he have in the gym bag he passed to the guy in the Chrysler?"

"Maybe some *cannolis*," Joe Di said. "Who knows with these guys . . ."

Lang turned back to the lot. Now that the drop had been made the two cars should have been driving away. But they were parked, lights off in the bushes.

"It's a trap, Joe," Lang said.

Joe Di clutched at his arm, his voice hoarse with fear. "No, kid, they wouldn't take no chances with me in the car."

"I gotta be sure," Lang said. "Stay here for a second."

"Where am I gonna go?"

Lang got out and jacked the tire down. He opened the trunk and waved the Glock over Hanif as if trying to make up his mind. Hanif shook his head frantically. Lang ripped the tape off his mouth.

"I need a favor Mittens," he said, pulling the tape off Hanif's ankles.

Hanif tried to sit up. "I can't move, Jerry."

Lang pulled him out of the trunk. "I wanna show you something."

Hanif's legs buckled. "I'm paralyzed, Jerry. I get these is-chemic strokes . . ."

"Your feet fell asleep." Lang dropped and rubbed his ankles.

"All you gotta do is get your circulation back." He dragged Hanif to the slope overlooking the parking area. "Tony Rasso just dropped off two hundred and fifty Gs for the old man."

Hanif turned with a startled look. "You mean you snatched Joe Di in my car? Shit Jerry, you tryin' to get me killed?"

"I'll keep you outta of it, don't worry," Lang said. He grabbed Hanif's neck and jerked his head around toward the parking lot. "See that trash can? There's a black garbage bag full of money in there. We'll drive down and you get it for me."

Hanif squinted down at the trash can. "Why don't you do it?"

"I gotta stay in the car with the old man. Make sure he don't walk away. I could leave you with him, but then they would think you were in on it. We don't want that, do we?"

Hanif's eyes widened. "No. Shit no." His eyes moved from the can to Lang. "They just left the money like that?"

"Yeah. I told 'em if I seen anybody I'd total the old man."

"Two hundred and fifty Gs?"

"There better be or there'll be two hundred fifty pieces of Joe."

Hanif wheezed and struggled for breath. Then he calmed down and looked shrewdly at Lang. "What happens when you get the money?"

"We'll put Joe in the bridal suite in the trunk. We'll go back to the Casbah. Hang out there until you can get me a clean car. Then I'll get in the wind and you can take Joe back to Tony and be a hero."

An ugly smile spread across Hanif's face. "You're talkin' about big favors here, Jerry. Without me you're screwed."

The worm has turned, Lang thought. All of a sudden he thinks he's got an edge. "I don't know about that," he said. "I could always figure somethin' out."

"Like what? You'd be runnin' around with a bag full of money and no place to go. Cops and Tony Rasso racin' to see who gets you first." Hanif's voice rose with indignation. "You knocked me around and dumped like a sack of shit in that trunk. But now you're screwed without me, Jerry."

Lang pressed the Glock against his head. "Don't press your luck, Mittens."

Hanif shrugged the gun away. "Don't call me Mittens. And don't play psycho because I know you won't shoot your meal ticket."

Lang stepped back. "Okay, what do you want?"

"Ten per cent of the score like always."

"Okay, okay . . ."

"Wait a minute, I'm not done." A pulse fluttered in his throat. "The college girl's gotta go . . . She's a witness."

"To what?" Lang said. "Cops won't know nothin' about this."

"She could get scared and go to them herself. Can you guarantee me she won't?"

"No."

"I can. Tell her you wanna meet her, I'll tell you where, then we don't have to lose sleep."

Lang hesitated.

"I know you got a soft spot for pussy, Jerry," Hanif said, "but we can't let this girl run around knowin' what she knows . . ."

"Okay, okay," Lang said. He pulled the tape off Hanif's wrists. "Can we go now?"

Hanif shook his arms, rubbed his shoulders. "I'm cold, Jerry."

"Okay, okay . . ." Lang jammed the orange Mets cap on Hanif's head. He took off the green parka and helped Hanif into it. "Now, you got the shirt off my back. Anything else you want?"

Hanif hesitated. Lang could read his mind, too. Have I missed anything? Is there any way this guy can get over on me?

Then he nodded.

"Okay, Jerry, let's do this."

Lang gave him the keys. "You drive, okay, I'll stay in the back with Joe. Later you can say I was holdin' him hostage and you saved the day."

Hanif opened the driver's door and slipped in behind the steering wheel. "Hey Boss . . ."

Joe Di sat up, his head jerking like a parakeet from Hanif to Lang. "What's he doin' outta the trunk?"

Hanif started the car. "Been a long day, huh Joe? Don't worry, it'll be over soon."

"TAKE A DRINK, TONY,"

the old timers said. "It'll give you balls."

That was when he was seventeen and they sent him out to "cowboy" with his cousin, Richie. It was how you proved yourself in those days. The bosses picked a neighborhood somewhere in the asshole of Brooklyn and you were supposed to steal a car and stick up every liquor store and gas station you could find.

Neither of them had ever used a gun before, but after a pint of Southern Comfort they were ready to do battle. They hit four spots, in a half hour, Tony going in, Richie keeping the motor running for a quick getaway, then changing places at the next spot. The clerks handed the money over, meekly. It was almost as if they knew this was some kind of ritual and if they played along they'd be okay.

Once you had cowboyed a couple of times the bosses would send you on collections. Richie's father had jukeboxes in some black bars on Fulton Street in Bed Stuy. They would split a fifth of Gordon's vodka and go in for the rent. They always got an argument. "We gave it to the guy last week . . ." "The machine was broken for three days." They'd be surrounded by big black dudes who were fed up paying off the white cops, white numbers runners, white garbage collectors, but the booze gave them just enough attitude to bluff it out and get the money.

In those days, the bosses tested you with harder and harder jobs. It wasn't like you got a raise or a promotion. You just kept hoping a crumb would drop off the table.

Tony was a street fighter, his knuckles pounded smooth in brawls. So when a bum from Bensonhurst was disrespectful to some made guy's daughter in a club on the East Side they sent him and Richie to straighten him out.

They parked across the street from the club and waited for the guy to come out.

"I never hit nobody I wasn't mad at," Tony said.

"Here . . ." Richie handed him a vial of white powder. "This'll make you mad at the world."

Tony was shocked. He had been taught that dope was for quiffs, but here was the son of one of the biggest guys in the family, offering it to him.

It burned his nose and made his eyes water. He choked back a wave of puke, but when it passed he was better than mad, he was invincible. He stuck a sawed off pool cue up his sleeve. "I feel like a pussy waitin' out here," he told his cousin. "Let's go get this asshole."

What happened next made Tony's reputation. He and Richie went into the club and confronted the guy. "Take your beating and we won't hurt you too bad." The guy cursed and went to his pocket. They whipped out the cues, knocked him out. Then they dumped everybody standing at the bar. There were broken ribs and fractured skulls all around. They stepped over groaning bodies and skidded in a pool of blood getting out of there. That had been twenty-two years ago, but people still talked about it.

After that cocaine was Tony's little secret. It made him smart and lucid when he went to talk to the bosses. It made his eyes shine when he was out for the night. There was no better pimp for a certain kind of broad than an eighth of an ounce vial pressed into a hot hand. "Here, doll, go powder your nose."

To deal dope was a death sentence, but everybody had a way of getting it. Tony hooked up with some neighborhood kids who were copping wholesale from the Dominicans in Washington Heights. He lent them money, which he reported as shylock loans to the bosses. Twenty-five Gs got him thirty-seven five three weeks later. Plus a "taste," a sandwich bag filled with a few scoops of white powder. They left it in the toilet paper dispenser in the men's room of a noodle shop on Pell Street in Chinatown. That's how careful he had to be.

Tony would crack the bag as soon as he got into his car. It was right off the boat, 87 percent pure, sometimes 92. Whiter than new snow. Smooth like baby powder. No pebbly lumps. He'd stick his nose in and take a deep breath. It smelled like sunshine and clean laundry. Shovel a little onto his thumbnail for a quick one and one to get his heart beating. Little shot of Courvoisier VSOP out of a silver flask to smooth it out and the lights went on inside his head. Suddenly, everything was clear. If he had a problem he knew how to solve it. Nervous or scared, a couple of toots and he could feel himself floating over his fear until he was way above it. If his mouth was dry and his hands were shaking it was from excitement.

Sober he was a lousy shot; Richie called him "demolition man" because he was always hitting walls. Wired he was even worse, but that made him get closer, right on top of the guy so he couldn't miss.

Wired he got a little confused. Like the time Joe Di gave Richie a hit on Tommy Theobaldo, a made guy from the Bronx. "This is big," he told Tony. "This is a boss."

He and Richie followed Tommy and some young broad to a joint on the Second Avenue. They sat at the bar, drinking Courvoisier and making trips to the bathroom, waiting for the place to empty out. But they got so loaded they decided to do it then and there before they were too wrecked to shoot straight.

They barged into the dining room and opened up. But Tommy Theobaldo had changed tables because his girlfriend didn't want to sit by the kitchen. They ended up blasting a guy in the trimming business who was sneaking a dinner with his secretary. The next day the papers were talking about a gangland hit on a mob connected garment executive.

They were scared and hid out while Richie called his father. The word came back: "Everything's cool, Tommy got the message anyway."

Then they got hysterical laughing thinking about the dead "garmento."

"Poor bastard gets caught cheating, gets clipped for nothing, the papers call him a crook, and all he wanted to do was get a little nookie on the side," Richie said. "Why'd you shoot into the ceiling?"

"I tripped on a pocketbook," Tony said.

"You shoulda seen that broad's face when the plaster fell on her head," Richie said.

They laughed until it hurt.

A few weeks later Joe Di's brother in law died in Sing Sing and everybody had to go to the funeral. Tony remembered at the last minute to buy a Mass card and came late. Richie waved frantically to him as he slipped into the back row. Joe Di was up front in the mourner's pew. He turned, counting the house. The church was SRO, half FBI, half wiseguy, but Tony felt Joe's eyes. The old timers had a way of looking at you. Even across a crowded room you knew you were in trouble.

On the receiving line Vito Mottola, Joe Di's driver, gave him a hard hug and whispered: "Your cousin Richie's on the spot . . ."

Tony didn't dare look toward the street where Richie was waiting, or flinch or argue or show any sign that anything had been said to him.

With all the surveillance, the wiretaps and bugs, they had to find secure ways to give orders. They never said anything directly. You were supposed to understand. And Tony did.

"When?"

"Yesterday."

It's that botched hit, Tony thought, moving down the receiving line. They don't know I was in on it and now they want me to clip him because I'm his friend and they know it will be easy.

When he got to Joe he looked down and mumbled, "I'm sorry for your loss."

"Joe Bird" was a name they had given him when he first came up. Nobody dared call him that, even behind his back, but it popped into your head when you saw him. He had the bright black eyes of a stuffed crow, the famous beak, the big hands coming out like claws at the end of skinny arms. They said he had choked guys to death with one hand and feeling his grip you could believe it. His crew was called the "Four H Club" for "hijacks, heists, hooers, and hits." If you were with him you did the hard work and made the big money. And you had respect wherever you went.

Joe Di squeezed Tony's hand. Pulled him close and blew a hot blast of espresso in his ear.

"Vito talk to you?"

"Yeah . . ."

Joe's grip tightened. "Thanks for comin'."

Outside, Richie was lighting one cigarette from another. "I think I'm okay. He didn't say nothin' to me about that thing. You smell his breath? My old man says he's got an ulcer and everything he eats turns to garbage."

By the time they got to the diner Tony had a plan. "You know that Binelli bird gun I was tellin' you about? I got it yesterday."

Richie lit up. He loved guns. "Let's go try it out."

It was so much easier when the guy trusted you. Now he had to stay with Richie every second to make sure he didn't call his father and tell him, "I'm goin' out shootin' with Tony." They drove all the way into Brooklyn to his house on Avenue X and pulled into the garage. He had the Binelli hidden under a box of old *Hustlers*. It was a sleek, compact shotgun with a wood grained butt and a shiny black barrel.

Richie wanted to go up to his father's place in Rhinebeck, but Tony said that was too far. He did a couple of hits to clear his mind and suggested his uncle's empty house on ten wooded acres up a hill in Mohunk just off the Taconic Parkway. Richie said they should take Tony's car, but it flashed through his mind that he would be driving and Richie holding the gun. What if Joe Di had given Richie a contract on Tony? They did stuff like that, puttin' two guys on each other so they only had to get rid of the winner. So he said he was out of gas and besides, if he got stopped and they found the gun they'd revoke his parole and lock him up again.

Richie hefted the Binelli. "Light . . ."

As the blow kicked in, he was seeing the holes in his plan. Shooting somebody in broad daylight, even in the middle of the woods, was a bad idea. Sure, nobody can see you, but you can't see them either. Some guy could be walking his dog and could be watching you all along. Cops could be waiting at the end of the road.

"Loads real easy," he said. He grabbed the gun. "Gimme, I'll show you."

Everything else he had ever done had been drop the guy where he stood and walk away. But this was his friend, so close they called each other cousin. This was the son of a made guy. He couldn't let any fingers point at him. This time he had to be smart.

Then it hit him. He was in a garage with the door closed. Nobody around.

It must have hit Richie, too, because he backed up, his eyes bulging as Tony slipped a big shell into the gun.

"Wanna hit?" he asked, bending down.

Going to his ankle holster, Tony thought. He whipped and pulled the trigger. The Binelli boomed like a cannon in the small space. It took the top of Richie's shoulder off and knocked him back against his car.

"Tony, please . . ."

Tony slid in another shell. If he talked loud and fast he wouldn't hear him. "Good huntin' gun, Richie. Can't you just see them ducks flappin' out of the tall grass?"

He aimed at Richie's gut. The Binelli bucked and blew a hole in his chest. The car rocked as the pellets went right through him and into the floorboard.

The noise made Tony's ears ring. The neighbors might hear it, but he wasn't worried. This part of Brooklyn had produced hundreds of wiseguys. People minded their own business.

Tony put an old Hustler over Richie's face. Then he raised his pant leg. Richie wore ankle boots to give him a few more inches of height. He kept a .380 automatic in an ankle holster in the boot, but this time all Tony found was a Ziploc bag full of white powder. It smelled fresher than his stash.

"Holdin' out on me, huh?" Tony said. He married Richie's coke with his own. It came to about an ounce.

"Party time," he said. "Only it's a party of one."

After dark Tony tossed Richie into the back seat of his De Ville. His arms were scrawny. He'd been a chunky little dude, hard to take down, but the coke had wasted him. Good thing he had become a shooter; he wouldn't have been much good in a fight.

Tony hated to do it, but he scattered some grains of blow on the back seat so they would think it had been a drug hit. That would shame Richie's father and he wouldn't ask a lot of questions. He drove over to Shore Road, a dark street that ran alongside the Belt Parkway. He parked on the service road and waited for a late night jogger to pass. Then he got out and walked away under the trees on the dark side of the road, cars speeding by on the Parkway.

That had been more than twenty years ago. He had gone through many different kinds of shotguns since then, but hadn't made a friend since Richie. Now he had a new Binelli. It was lighter and sleeker and had a slot on the side where you could use different size shells depending on what you were hunting. It loaded and reloaded really fast, so you could get a bunch of shots off before the birds scattered. The gun lay on the floor under the seat. With his record it was ten years for possession of a firearm if he was stopped.

The Darvocet had taken the pain away, but his eye was throbbing so hard he could see it jumping under the bandage when he looked in the side mirror. He knew even a speck of coke could send him away for life, but he had dropped a gram into a piece of newspaper and folded it like a ravioli.

The gold Mercedes came down the ramp into the parking area. Tony's hands trembled as he opened the package. He could hardly unscrew the flask with gloves on. Lucky there was a chain on the top.

Tony cradled the Binelli and suddenly Richie popped into his head. He could see him clearly, crawling out from under a pile of bodies with a bloody hole in his chest.

"I'm hallucinating," Tony said. His laugh sounded strange in his ears.

A guy got out of the Mercedes and walked under the streetlight to the trash can. Bulky green ski jacket and orange cap. Tony slid two shells into the Binelli and stepped out of the car. It was like the time he had caught the raccoons going through his garbage can. Just for fun he had shouted at them.

"Hey Jerry. Jerry Lang!"

The guy's head came up, just like one of those raccoons.

"Tony," he said.

"Yeah that's right, scumbag . . ." He fired and missed just like with the raccoons. Only they had turned tail and run. This guy froze.

"Tony, wait . . ."

He took a few more steps and fired again. The guy fell and twisted around and tried to crawl. Tony reloaded while he was walking, and fired. The guy went down on his face.

"Fuck you, Jerry!" he shouted.

"Whaddya doin', stupid?"

Joe Di came out of the darkness, shimmering like a ghost in his white bathrobe.

"What are you shootin' him for?"

That cackle. He even sounded like a bird. All these years you took abuse, but this was too much.

"Look what he did to me?"

"He didn't do . . ."

"You call this nothin'? Then fuck you, too."

He fired. The old man blew away like a piece of newspaper on a windy day. He landed flat on his back, his stick of a leg bent under him. Tony fired again. His body jumped.

"Everybody's a jerk, Joe." The scream roared out of his chest. "Nobody can do nothin', but you . . ."

And then the plan lit up in his head. Just tell those assholes that Lang took the payoff and wasted the old man, anyway. They'll be sorry they're out the money, but they'll be happy the old man is finally out of their hair, and I'll have it all.

He pulled the garbage bag out of the can. "Two hundred and fifty Gs, Richie."

He heard a motor screech. It was Billy Dario in the Crown Victoria, so scared that he had turned the key while the engine was running.

Tony snapped a shell into the Binelli. The Crown Victoria

skidded as it pulled out. The back end drifted out. He could see Billy fighting the wheel.

He fired into the windshield. A hole opened up like a sunburst. He stepped around and fired through the driver's window. The glass dropped like a waterfall. Billy was lying on the seat, blood pouring out of his neck.

Tony walked back to the car. Never run away. It draws attention.

For a second it felt like Richie was walking next to him. "Two hundred and fifty Gs," he said as he got into the car. "Biggest payday of my life."

He turned the ignition key calmly. The Chrysler purred like it was going for a drive in the country and accelerated gently.

In the back seat of the Mercedes, Lang ducked under the window as it passed.

The Chrysler picked up speed on the access road and merged onto the highway. Behind the wheel, Tony had the ravioli shaped package on his lap and was dipping his thumb for a quick hit as he drove downtown. He could see the tip of the Binelli sticking out from under the seat.

"If I get pulled over they'll lock me up forever for this, Richie," he said. "I'd get more time for the blow than I would for those three guys."

He whooped with laughter and floored the pedal.

The Chrysler sped past the turnoff where Osler was opening the door of the Tahoe. Stewart scrambled up the hill, his shoes smeared with mud and jumped in, his eyes big.

"This you are not going to believe," he said.

"Some Problems Solve Themselves,"

Hartung said.

He could hear his voice on the speaker in his car and got the feedback in his phone so he was hearing himself three times. "You're sure he's dead."

"The guy took two shotgun blasts to the upper torso, sir," Stewart said. "If that didn't kill him he's bleedin' to death as we speak."

"And you saw the whole thing."

"Front row," Stewart said. "Rasso was out there in the open shootin' and screamin' like a shaheed. Any second I thought he was gonna start screaming *'Allahu Akbat.'* "

"Better get out of there," Hartung said.

"Yes sir," said Osler.

"Take my car. I'll take the van home and bring it back in the morning."

"Yes sir."

They were waiting for a "good job, men." But they had been a little salty with him and if he praised them they might see it as a sign of weakness and get saltier next time. "Command is an art, not a science," his instructor at the War College had said. With these two it might be better to withhold the compliments than dispense them freely.

"Stay on your cells," he said.

"Yes sir."

In an hour Hartung was sitting in traffic on the Williamsburg

Bridge on his way out to Queens. He had been transferred so quickly to this new unit he hadn't had time to find a decent house out of the city. They had put him in a building in Forest Hills where the US mission to the UN kept staff apartments. It was an upscale immigrant neighborhood, mostly Indian, Asian, and Israeli with a few Russians thrown in. Hartung had spent most of his life overseas so he was used to the rudeness, the resentment. But it was infuriating to be snubbed in your own country by foreigners who were raking in the bucks, while you eked along on a major's pay and grudging allotments. In the elevator the men would look him up and down, see American, and pointedly ignore him. Some of the Israelis and the Russians would recognize military and put the whole package together in a heartbeat—American spy. The women were scornful and overdressed, furs and jewelry and trails of scent. Their daughters were carbon copies, same facial expression, even the same intonation in their voices. Hartung had always been amazed at how closely foreign children resembled their parents, while with Americans you never knew who was related to whom. These little girls were women, he could tell the way they checked him out with sidelong looks and fussed with their hair. His gangly little Amy still thought the only difference between boys and girls was that boys could run faster.

Warren was the one they had worried about. He was bookish, undersized, and fanatically non-athletic. It was as if he had looked at his dad, the high school football star, decorated in the Gulf and Afghanistan, and decided he could never measure up so he went the other way. A military town outside of Fort Bragg was not a good place for a kid who couldn't catch. He was tormented by the other boys and disappeared into his computer.

But in Forest Hills he had blossomed. Within days he had found a group of kindred spirits. "Nosepickers Anonymous," Hartung called them. They hardly spoke, just sat silently in front of the TV watching *South Park* reruns or playing "Grand Theft Auto." They would bring in bags of Taco Bell and disappear into Warren's room for hours.

Amy was the problem. They had thought her athletic prowess would help her make friends, but foreigners hated it when an American was better at soccer than they were. In the first game of the season Amy had run from her center forward position all the way down the field and tackled the opposing striker on a breakaway. On the sidelines the parents had gasped at her speed. But the coach, a red-faced Englishman whose dumpy daughter was the goalie, had screamed at her: "You leave your position like that again, young lady, and you'll never play on my team."

Beverly greeted him at the door. He noticed strands of gray in her hair as they walked down the hall to the bathroom.

"What happened?" he asked.

"I told you. The coach benched her for coming late. I told him you'd been held up at work, but he said I should have called and left a message on his voice mail. He's jealous because his fat bitch of a daughter can't play."

There was no light under the bathroom door. "She's sitting in the dark," he whispered and knocked softly. "Amy . . ."

No answer. He took out his phone and punched her number. He heard her ring, the Olympic theme. She picked up. "I don't want to talk, Dad."

"I know that, honey." He held the phone out so Beverly could hear. "I've been calling you for an hour . . ."

"Mom screamed at me. She said I was just trying to get attention."

"People who love you sometimes say things they shouldn't, Amy. Because we're your parents we blame ourselves."

"Well, it's your fault. You made us come here. Nobody wants me here. They hate me." Her sob was so mournful it brought hot tears to his own eyes. "You should hear what they say about the Army in school. That we're torturing people and killing women and children . . ."

Beverly gave him a helpless look. "They don't understand, honey," he said. "We're defending their freedom to say those things about us. Nobody will ever thank us for it . . ." His voice broke. Beverly looked at him in surprise. "Look Amy, your mother and I love you very much and we're really sorry that we can't protect you from the stupid world you have to live in because of my job . . ." He struggled to keep the tears out of his voice. "Please, honey, don't hurt yourself. It's so pointless . . . Please."

The bathroom lock clicked. She was standing there in her soccer uniform, still wearing her cleats and shin guards. She loved those shin guards so much sometimes she wore them to bed. "I'm sorry, Dad."

He knelt to kiss her tearstained cheek. "I'm the one who should apologize. And I can't even promise I'll be around the next time you need me."

"I know."

He walked her down the dark hallway to where Beverly waited. Left the two of them to cry in each other's arms and collapsed on his bed. It was amazing that a guy like him who had pursued women for one thing only, discarding the old and the ugly, dismissing the ones who didn't interest him, should be overwhelmed by such pure tenderness for this little girl. It was a feeling he'd never had for anyone else. He understood what they meant when they said "nothing's too good for my little girl." He wanted things for her that the world couldn't offer.

In a little while Beverly came in. "She's making your favorite turkey quesadilla."

"That's sweet." All of a sudden he was so tired he could hardly lift his head.

He slid his hand an inch along the cover and turned his palm up. She took it. She was always ready to kiss and make up. "You're paying your dues, too," he said. "I know I stuck you in this strange place with a lot of hostile people, too. You can't make friends here, either."

"It's not so bad," she said. "At least I can get into the city."

And get picked up by some random guy, he thought. Eating a sandwich in the park. Looking in shop windows on Fifth Avenue. Sneaking into an afternoon movie. Jeans and a sweat-shirt, hair in a ponytail, minimal make up, but slim and streamlined. Built for speed and that soft Southern twang would be pretty exotic up here. New York was full of men with their afternoons free, actors, bartenders, hustlers . . . spies. He was surprised one of the neighbors hadn't taken a shot. Or had they? Israelis thought they were Romeos. Mossad specialized in sexual exploitation.

She lay down next to him and snuggled under his arm.

"Did you make the world safe for democracy today?"

"Funny you should ask." He fished out his cell phone and called the Voice. Shouldn't be doing this in front of her. She could get the number off his call list. Could give it to her new lover, who could be working for anyone from Islamic Jihad to MI6. The CIA would like to know more about his operation, too. Stranger things had happened. Wives had been seduced and recruited as double agents and stayed with their husbands for years, passing information. In training they hammered it home: Keep your family out of it. The person you know the least is the person you sleep next to.

The Voice picked up on the first ring. "So . . . ?"

He put his hand over Beverly's ear. She smiled and she shook her had as if she could care less.

"To coin a phrase," he said, "Mission Accomplished."

LANG EASED THE GOLD
MERCEDES

around the bodies. The headlights picked up Joe Di on his back, his leg bent under him, a piece of his head caved in from Rasso's second shot. A few feet away Hanif lay, forehead pressed against the ground, one knee drawn up as if he were about crawl away. The Crown Victoria had traveled a few yards after Rasso had fired into it and come to a stop in the bushes where it stood shuddering, black smoke belching out of its tailpipe, while Billy Dario bled to death inside.

Lang drove up the ramp and got onto the highway. It had all been so easy. One move had dictated the next and there had been no resistance. Like everybody was going slow motion, but him.

The element of surprise had been on his side. Those two Albanians thought they had all the time in the world. They had jumped a lot of unsuspecting people, and had lost their edge. Letitia had been the perfect decoy to draw Hanif. Spiro was one of those big guys who had never been tested and turned out to be a punk. Hanif had a gun to his head before he could turn around. Tony Rasso had a bunch of worthless bullies working for him. Joe Di was just a sick old man with no back up.

The green jacket and orange hat were meant to be a distraction. Rasso, in a dark car, blind in one eye, crazed with pain and rage, had taken Hanif for him. Then he had killed Joe Di for the money. And Billy Dario to eliminate a witness. Without knowing it he had gotten even for Lang. Three of the guys who had killed Gloria were dead. Tony was still around, but his guard would be down; he'd be easy.

It was the most elegant score he had ever pulled off and he hadn't planned one moment of it. It had unfolded with dream-like logic all its own. But like a dream it had left him with an incomplete feeling. Why had they killed Gloria in the first place? Why had they come after him?

Even before that there were questions. If they wanted the drawing without paying him, why not just stick him up and take it? Why had they gotten the cops into it? And who was that weird dude with the buzz cut they called Hartung?

Hanif's cell phone vibrated in his pocket. The Caller ID read "Number Unknown." He grumbled an Albanian "hello."

"Lang?"

It was Letitia.

"Can't live without me, huh?"

"Something like that. Remember my two houseguests?"

"Vividly."

"Well, they were still here when I got home . . ."

"Overstayed their welcome, huh? We'll have to do something about that."

"Sorry," she said.

He could see her sitting in that room with those two stiffs on the floor.

"It's okay," he said. "I didn't have nothin' better to do tonight."

"I Smelled Them,"

Letitia said. "Even before I put the light on I knew they were there."

"Spiro's probably in Macedonia by now," Lang said. "I guess he knew Hanif was history so why do his dirty work."

She was sitting at the kitchen counter, a handkerchief doused with perfume pressed to her nose.

Lang lit a cigarette. "You start with two guys who don't take showers or brush their teeth. Add a little vodka and garlic, scare 'em so bad they crap their pants, then cut their guts out, you're gonna raise a pretty good stink."

Letitia didn't laugh or make a face. Gloria would have said something about his stupid jokes.

"What happened after I left?" she asked.

"Rasso killed everybody, Hanif, Joe Di, and one of his own guys. It was like a movie."

Her hand started shaking. He put his arms around her and let her shake against him.

"You're in shock," he said, "but that's good."

"Why?"

"Because if you weren't you'd be the coldest bitch in the history of the world."

"Did you get the money?"

"Rasso took it."

"You didn't care about it anyway. Hanif would have given you everything he had."

"Yeah, but I wanted to bang that fat girl called revenge . . ."

"If you had taken Hanif's money you'd be on your way right now," she said.

"To where?" he asked. "To do what?"

Her shaking subsided. She looked at him like she was just beginning to understand.

"Is that Chinese restaurant downstairs any good?" he asked. "I haven't had pork fried rice in five years."

"I Blame it on that Chocolate Donut,"

Lang said.

Letitia gulped her lukewarm tea and tried not to look at the array of dishes he had ordered.

"Blame what?"

"My downfall." He broke open an egg roll and squeezed a ribbon of mustard into it. "Ever wonder what was in these things? You never see nothin' you recognize." He held the egg roll up to a passing waiter. "Hey, what's in this?"

The waiter ignored him.

Lang laughed. "He don't know, either."

It seemed so normal. The clatter of plates, the customers, absorbed in their conversations.

Lang spooned a mountain of saffron rice into his bowl and looked at it fondly. "See, my mom worked nights and holidays and didn't have time to cook. My old man was a drinker so food was just a waste of space to him . . ." He paused with a spare rib poised. "You okay?"

She leaned over the table with a vehement whisper. "There are two dead bodies in my apartment and you're talking about chocolate donuts."

"There's a connection, believe me. See on Sundays after Mass my mother would take us to the Market Diner for the dinner special. Pork chops or veal cutlet with mashed potatoes and succotash." He offered her half an egg roll. "You better eat somethin'."

She pushed it away. "I don't like Chinese food."

"You see that's what I'm sayin'. It's like jail. You eat what you don't like or you don't eat."

"You're not making any sense," she said.

"That was the choice. There was Jello or rice pudding for dessert. I hated them, but you had to pick one because it was the dessert special, anything else was extra. It was like you got one Coke with the meal and you had to make it last. So my mom sends me to the cashier to get cigarettes and I see they got donuts in one of them serving stands on the counter. Plastic cover on it, people standin' around. In the time it took the cashier to get the cigarettes off the shelf behind her, I snaked that sucker right out so fast nobody saw me. Then I wolfed it down and wiped the chocolate off my mouth before I got back to the table. The perfect crime . . . I'm eight years old, see, and now I know: if you want somethin' you gotta steal it . . ."

"Why are you telling me the story of your life?"

"Just makin' small talk." He reached across and touched her cheek. "You got a dimple, I didn't know that . . ."

"You honestly believe that if your mother had paid extra for a chocolate donut Archie and Malik would be alive today," she said.

"I don't know about those guys, they were doomed from birth. But I wouldn't have killed 'em. I wouldn't be sittin' here."

"What would you be doing?"

"Maybe I would have married the first girl who gave me a smile. I'd be workin' for UPS, runnin' home to play catch with my kids before it got dark. Somethin' like that. Listen . . ." He leaned over the table, whispering earnestly. "There were kids on my block who are dentists today, CPAs, even a priest, and they were ten times worse than me. Beatin' up the PR kids, four, five on one. Settin' fire to the winos at the Port Authority. Gang bangin' a halfwit girl, who didn't know no better. I never did nothin' like that and never would. But I turn out to be the bad guy and they're all good Republicans livin' in Jersey. There's gotta be a reason for this."

"My family never ate together, either," she said. "My dad was in the navy. He left early and had breakfast at the base."

"Did your mom cook?" Lang asked.

"She clipped recipes out of magazine, but never made them," she said. "We had Carnation Instant Breakfast, frozen waffles . . . My mom never cooked while my dad was away on sea duty. We had takeout or we went to the Chilis . . ."

"Maybe that's why you're here."

"No," she said. "Every service family ate that way . . . Almost every family broke up . . . I'm here because I wanted to be an actress. Every bad thing that has happened to me happened because I wanted to act."

Lang nodded. "God punishes artists because they make graven images. A counterfeiter at Allenwood told me that."

She told him about the overheated classroom where she had played Juliet in the third-grade play. About her little Romeo blinking and awkward in his tights. Her costume, one of her mom's cut-down white silk slips, a red bow in her hair. She told him how the class had giggled and her Romeo turned away, red faced, from her ardent gaze as she recited: "Romeo, Romeo / Wherefore art thou Romeo / Deny thy father and refuse thy name / Or, if thou wilt not, be but sworn my love, / And I'll no longer be Capulet."

"What did you look like?"

"I was a gawky eight year old with braces. I hunched over because I was taller than everyone else and my mom was always telling me to stand up straight. But that day she hugged me. 'My little movie star.' All the other moms were saying, 'Isn't she adorable?' In the car I announced 'I'm going to be an actress.' They all laughed and it made me cry. 'I am, you'll see.' "

"They thought you'd grow out of it . . ."

"I didn't," she said. "I was in everything. *Bye Bye Birdie, Our Town*. When I was in seventh grade they were doing *Grease*, but they wouldn't let me try out because I was taller than the male lead. In high school I tried to join the drama club, but I was on the basketball team and had a conflict. So my parents made me quit."

"Can't blame 'em. It's a tough way to make a living."

"My mom said I was too skinny and my nose was crooked and besides you needed connections to get anywhere. And what would happen if I didn't make it? What would I do then?"

"How about your dad?"

"He had moved out and was living on the base. He wanted me to keep playing ball so I'd get a scholarship. He said all actresses were sluts."

"Doesn't make them bad people."

"He said every girl you saw on TV had prostituted herself to get a part. And no daughter of his would ever do that."

Lang got busy with his food. "He was wrong about that."

She stared at him. I won't say anything until he looks at me. But he kept his head in his plate and finally she couldn't stand it.

"What's that supposed to mean?"

"You needed more money to pay for your classes so you went to work for Hanif."

"Right . . . Okay . . ."

"And then after a coupla days you had to hump somebody . . ."

He said it in an offhand way like it was the most natural thing in the world, but she could still feel the blood rushing to her face.

"You know everything, don't you?"

"I know what goes on in greaseball strip joints. You gotta go

187

home with one guy and then they leave you alone after that. If you don't they all jump you and you lose your job to boot." He finally looked up. "So who was it?"

"That's none of your . . ."

Lang silenced her impatiently. "I got a reason for this . . . Who'd you go home with?"

"Spiro," she said staring hard. If he even cracks a smile I'll smash a glass in his face.

He just nodded. "Spiro, huh? He was the official bronco buster."

"You knew I had done this from the moment you saw me," she said. "Why do you bring it up now?"

"How was it?" he asked.

"It was pathetic, okay?"

After work Spiro had taken her to the Athena on Eighth Avenue for baklava. He had shaved all his chins and she could smell his cologne across the table. They had gone to a room in the Holiday Inn on Fifty-seventh. He took off his clothes in the dark. It was over almost before it started.

"He was shy like he didn't really want to be there," she said. "Like they were making him do it."

"Well, I'm glad it was him and not Archie or Malik."

"Why?"

Lang went back to his fried rice. "Because we're gonna have to chop Archie and Malik into little pieces."

"You Got a Yellow Pages?"

Lang was sitting on the couch, staring at Archie's body.

"You need a corpse removal service?" Letitia asked. She had tried to open a window, but it wouldn't budge and the effort had made her giddy.

"I'm looking for a hardware store," he said. "We're gonna need tools, a hacksaw, some sharp knives. Maybe a restaurant supply house for a meat cleaver . . ."

"No need to elaborate," she said.

She went online and found ten hardware stores up and down the West Side.

Lang made a shopping list. "I'll have to buy a different tool in each store. Hammer, chisel, hacksaw . . . Chainsaw is too noisy. We'll need plastic sheeting to put under the bodies so the blood doesn't get on the floor. And alotta black garbage bags . . ."

Letitia's leg started to shake. She clutched at it with both hands, but it wouldn't stop.

"This is the only way," Lang said.

"I know . . ."

"You're not gonna do the surgery," he said. "You won't even be here."

He took her into the bedroom and closed the door.

"The smell's coming through the walls," she said. "It's inside my head."

189

Lang sat next to her on the bed. "You got something nice to wear?"

"Why?"

"I'll get rid of these two guys for you, but you gotta do something for me."

He looked through her closet and came out with a light blue jacket with VIXENS in gold lettering on the back. "What's this?"

"My high school basketball team. The boys were the Portsmouth Red Foxes . . ."

"Good, it'll look vintage. Put on a pair of slacks that shows your ass."

"What am I going to do?"

"Play two scenes," he said. "You're an actress, you can do it."

"This is different."

"It's the same. The trick is to make them wanna believe you. Like, you go into a fancy store, playin' rich ditz. They wanna believe you 'cause they wanna make a sale. You'll need something expensive. I'll leave you money. Buy yourself a Prada bag, and a cool watch like an old Piaget. You can always sell rich with accessories."

"Working with props," she said.

"Yeah props. Go over to Thirty-six Central Park South, okay. It's an old building across from the park. Find out who lives on the twelfth floor. I need a name and any other information you can get without comin' on too nosy."

"How do I that?" she asked.

"Play it by ear. You can make believe you heard the place was for sale and would like to see it. Then the doorman'll ask the manager, 'Is Mr. Whatshisface sellin' his apartment?' You can also go in like you're looking for your friend Eloise on the twelfth floor and they tell you who really lives there. Once you get there you'll figure it out . . ."

"Then what?" she asked.

"Then you go down to Twenty-seventh and Fifth, Tessler's Rare Coins and Jewelry. Little corner store. Tessler's gotta be at least in his sixties. Flirt with him, tell him you're gonna bring your husband down to buy a ring. He'll wanna believe that."

"Then what?"

"You'll come up here to your nice clean apartment, okay. The place'll smell like the Botanical Gardens. We'll go to Tessler's. You'll walk me in and point him out. Then you'll turn around and go out into the sunshine and this time your nightmare will really be over."

Lang looked through her closet and came out with a pair of white jeans. "Your ass must look great in these . . ."

"What are you going to do with Tessler?" she asked.

"I'm gonna ask him what happened to that Levitan he was willing to pay a hundred K for."

"You think he killed Gloria?"

"I'll ask him about that, too. He'll say no, of course. And then I'll have a decision to make." He showed her a black halter-top covered with sequins. "What's this masterpiece?"

"Wardrobe from a show I did," she said. "I don't know if I want to help you kill somebody."

"I don't wanna chop those guys up either," he said.

He threw the sequined top on the bed. "This is so ugly it's gotta be cool. Anyway, it'll show your abs . . ."

"I thought you said revenge wasn't what it was cracked up to be," she said.

"It's not, but I want it anyway," Lang said.

"Wham Bam with Native Women Don't Count,"

an old hand had once told Hartung

"Native women aren't cheating."

"Try telling that to my wife," he had said.

It was an unspoken rule. You were away from home for months at a time. The work was stressful. You needed release. It was recreation pure and simple, like having a drink or playing a round of golf.

White women were off limits. You got some slack for the Eastern European prostitutes, but they were only "technically white," as the old hand explained. It was the coworkers you had to avoid, the secretaries at the embassies, the college girls at the NGOs, the nurses, the military personnel, who were younger, prettier, and more vulnerable than ever. If they were married it only took one drink to find out how unhappy they were. If they were single they were desperate for a life, any life, even a life they could have just long enough to make themselves miserable and alone again.

After 9/11 it became harder to observe the rule. In Indonesia, Sri Lanka, and Central Asia Americans were strongly advised not to hit the streets looking for fun. In the Middle East and most of Africa they were under curfew when they were off duty. They found themselves thrust together with their female colleagues. There were barbecues, holiday parties; every base or embassy compound had a rec area where the booze flowed freely. There wasn't much to do but watch videos, drink, and pair off.

Life was intense. Men made rash promises to shortcut the seduction. Women thought they were in love with a guy just because he had an armored Suburban.

Hartung stayed clear. He had heard stories of hysterical scenes, e-mails and midnight phone calls to spouses in the States. There had been suicides complete with incriminating notes cc'ing superiors.

In Kandahar he was "adviser" to a local warlord. The guy would give him the name of somebody he wanted dead and he would bounce it up to the higher levels. When the approval came back down, which it almost always did, he would take a squad and hit the guy's house.

A Thai woman who owned a restaurant in Kabul sent her waitresses to Kandahar once a week for the foreign personnel. They weren't natives, but they were foreigners, so Hartung could stretch the rule in good conscience.

He was in Kandahar for nine months straight with no time for leave. When they went into Iraq they gave him a few weeks to wait out the military phase. Then sent him to Mosul.

They made him the chief bodyguard to a Kurdish politician. It was the same detail, going after "troublemakers"—Turkish spies, ex-Baathists, Iranian agents, anyone who was a problem for his guy.

A British guy who ran a security service started sending Turkish girls in from Kurdistan to work as "receptionists" in his office. He'd shuttle them back and forth across the border. But one Thursday his convoy was held up on the highway, the drivers killed, and the women taken off never to be heard from again.

The Kurds stepped into the breach with cases of Scotch and Arab prostitutes. One night there was a girl in his room. She wouldn't drink the liquor. She kept covering her face. He spoke to her in guidebook Arabic and she replied in faltering English. Her brother was in prison, she said. The Kurds told her they would torture him if she didn't do what they said. Now she would never have a husband. Her father would kill her if he found out . . .

Hartung was sick. He gave her money and sent her home. After that he drank himself into oblivion every night and left the girls alone.

The night had gone well. Amy had gone to bed, sniffling and holding his hand as she drifted off. He came out of her room to find Beverly waiting for him on the couch with a bottle of wine. There was a feeling of serenity in the air. He'd been a caring dad and she appreciated it. The love they shared for their little girl brought them together again. She put her head on his lap. He stroked her hair. They walked hand in hand into the bedroom.

He lay in bed, waiting for her to come out of the bathroom. She wore one of his tee shirts and on nights when they were going to make love she would pull it over her head before she got into bed. He loved to watch her body emerge. She was one of those women who looked better undressed than dressed. "My little secret," he had called her in their courting days. Their first night out they went skinny-dipping on the Outer Banks. She ran, laughing, into the surf, shedding her bikini top and bottom, with him following, amazed at how much more beautiful she was without these tiny strips of cloth. They went behind a dune and made love, salty and sandy and not caring. Then there had been that drab garden apartment in Columbus when he was stationed at Fort Benning. On that lumpy bed, his feet hanging over the end, they had perfected a kind of dance, which ended with her exultant sobs.

Even now he could feel that warmth rising through him as she slid into bed. As he felt under her thigh to the smooth curve of her buttock, she pressed into him, brushing her lips against his nipples. What a surprise it had been that first time after years of anxious or unresponsive or frenzied females to kiss this tall, quiet girl, who he had seen on the fringes of the crowd at a pep rally. No twisting reluctance, no tongue thrust frantically. Just warm lips and gentle pressure as she wrapped her arms around him. How odd to move so precisely yet with such urgency. How amazing to be so calm in the midst of volcanic excitement.

What a surprise it would be for any man to discover this woman. To think he was in for a quick matinee like all the others and then see this goddess emerge.

This wasn't a wham bam. No man would walk away from this. If there had been somebody while he was away the guy would still be around.

He had read that every new lover changed a person's behavior in bed in subtle ways. So after that, while they were making love he would go through the motions and watch her for a telltale sign, a move, a sound, anything that would show she had been with someone else.

And as he cupped her face in his hands he caught a questioning look. Did she sense his distraction? Was she watching him as well?

A red light flashed like an ambulance on the walls. It was his cell phone on mute.

Beverly clutched at him. "Let it take a message."

He rolled off her. "Can't. Too much goin' on."

It was the Voice. "Wake up sleepyhead. Lang is alive."

"No way. My boys saw him get it."

"We got the body count from our sources," the Voice said. "There' a Joe Di Corso, a Billy Dario, and a Hanif Gallega. No

Jerry Lang . . ."

Hartung felt a hollow ache in his chest. Why had he bragged? Why had he said "Mission Accomplished"?

"I don't know how that could have happened."

"Of course you don't know. You weren't there."

"I was monitoring the operation. I was in constant touch . . ."

"Well somewhere along the way he evaded. You'd better get your ass out in the field and find out where he is."

"He's could be halfway to Florida by now," Hartung said.

"Probably is. But we have to stay with our Russian friend until we get a twenty on him. That means you, personally, on the line until this thing is over."

"Okay," Hartung said.

"Okay doesn't live here anymore, soldier. I want a 'Yes sir' and a repeat of my order."

He could see it all going into the shitter, his promotion, his raise. They'd transfer him out of this unit to the worst detail they could find, training rebels in Darfur, backstopping the militias in Ethiopia or the Congo. His family would be fractured again, just when it was starting to come together.

"Yes sir," he said. "I'll stay out there until this thing is over."

"I can't see you, boy," the Voice said, "but I sure as shit hope you're saluting."

"I Can't Close My Eyes,"

Letitia said. "I keep seeing Archie and Malik."

"They'll go away," Lang said. He turned off the light. "Pleasant dreams . . ."

She panicked. "Where are you going?"

"Just to watch TV."

"Don't leave me."

He hesitated in the doorway. Behind him she could see Archie's head on the living room floor.

"Okay." He lay down next to her. "Damn narrow bed for a grown woman," he said.

Every man who had seen it had made a comment. "A nun's pallet," Barry, the young playwright had called it before he passed out on it . . . "Looks like my baby sister's bed," Eloy had said.

"Sixty-seven dollars plus mattress at the Salvation Army Warehouse," she said. "I didn't think about having company when I bought it."

"That's the difference between boys and girls," Lang said. "A guy would get a double bed for all the women he was sure he was gonna have . . ."

She felt his shoulder in her back and inched over to the edge.

"You don't want me to leave, but you don't want me touch you either," he said.

"Can you try not to?"

He slid over. "We could put a sword between us." He lit a

197

cigarette. "I know we didn't have sex, but can I smoke anyway?"

"Sure."

Wisps of smoke floated in the darkness. Like when she would awaken to see her dad in her bedroom doorway, his cigarette glowing.

"Goodnight baby," he would say.

It was the deep freeze after the blizzard. The snow had melted and then frozen into jagged pieces of black ice. The wind was shrieking, through every corner of the house. There was no place to hide. Mom was hunched at the kitchen table, blue fingers sticking out of torn mittens.

Letitia tried to scrunch up into a tiny ball, but couldn't get warm. Then she was awake. The night was crinkling to gray around the edges. She was on top of the bed, shivering in her clothes. Lang was gone.

Has he done it already?

She got up and went into the living room. Archie and Malik were still there. Their faces were still as stone. They seemed deader than yesterday.

Lang had left Hanif's recharged phone and gold money clip on the kitchen counter with a note:

"Use this . . . Call me on Malik's phone . . . Don't forget. We don't want a record of any calls to or from your number. Get Prada bag, Gucci shades, old Piaget. 36 Central Park South. Who lives on the twelfth floor?—Tessler's Rare Coins and Antique Jewelry. 27th and Fifth. Get good look at Tessler. Tell him you'll be back with your hubby . . . Call when you're done . . ."

She looked at the clothes he had laid out. Combine that with expensive accessories and you got rock star or punk heiress. She put her team jacket on and looked in the mirror. A slight droop in the shoulders, a petulant, impatient look. A very rich, very spoiled very entitled girl out shopping because she was bored and had nothing else to do.

"I can play that," she said.

"You're Messin' with My Pension,"

Hartung said. "You're takin' the food out of my babies' mouths."

He had set the meeting with Osler and Stewart at a dingy bar on Eighth Avenue, down the street from the Fourteenth precinct. It was a cop hangout. Nobody would look twice at three big, surly guys growling at each other in a booth.

Stewart spoke slowly. "I saw the guy get outta the car," he said. "Then I saw him take two point-blank hits with a shotgun."

Hartung leaned in closer. "You got sand on the brain, Sergeant. You think the only slick guys are the ones with towels on their heads."

"I'm tellin' you what I saw," Stewart said.

"No, you're not. You saw a guy in green jacket with an orange beanie. It was a Decoy 101. Lang stuck the jacket on Gallega so Rasso would think it was him."

Osler moved his head into the force field between the two men. He liked Stewart and didn't want to have to break in a new partner. "That must have happened while we were repositioning, Major. You remember I told you we had momentarily lost contact."

"I remember you overshot the target, if that's what you're referring to, Sergeant."

"Any quick action on our part would have aroused suspicion . . ."

Hartung glared him into silence.

Never get into arguments with subordinates.

"Just 'cause you're not in uniform, doesn't mean you're not in the Army, Sergeant," he said. "In the Army we shut up when our superiors are addressing us, right?"

Those were strong words to use with combat vets. Stewart stirred angrily, but Osler gave him a quick, cautioning look. This detail was too good to blow. "Right sir," he said without a trace of defiance.

Hartung leaned in even closer. "So here's the deal. Acting on information supplied by you, I made certain claims which turned out to be wrong and bought me a reaming from my superior. So now because shit flows downhill I'm givin' you worse than he gave me. And I promise you if I get kicked off this detail I'll kick you off, too, and bust you down a rank while I'm at it. And wherever they send me I'll make sure you go someplace worse."

"That would be only fair, sir," Osler said.

"So here's the deal," Hartung said, then winced inwardly. He was repeating himself, a sign of agitation. "I have no idea what Lang is up to or where he's going, but we have to make sure our asset is secure, so Stewart you sit on his house and Osler you sit on him. This is surveillance, not security, okay. We don't want to alarm anybody."

"How about his wife?" Osler asked.

"She's his problem."

"How about Lang?"

"He's toast," Hartung said.

"So it's shoot on sight?"

"Won't be that easy. Find him first. Then I'll figure out a way to fry him."

"ACTING IS MERELY DECEPTION,"

Jamie always said.

Letitia put on the costume Lang had laid out for her. She took a cab uptown to Bergdorf's. Hanif's clip was thick with hundred dollar bills, more than enough for a shopping spree. The morning had turned sunny and the breeze was warm on Fifth Avenue.

The security guys jumped out to open the door for her. The sleek old salesladies checked her out with forced smiles. They didn't like the punk heiress look, but they could smell big sales. Lang had chosen brilliantly.

She bought the dark glasses first. They were a great prop and could hide a multitude of wardrobe sins. The Gucci logo was too prominent for her. She liked the Chanels, discreet with super opaque lenses.

The Pradas all seemed plain so she bought a Judith Lieber, encrusted with jewels, for thirty-two hundred. "If my mom can have one so can I," she ad-libbed. The saleslady, stiff Botox smile, pearls over a black dress, had seen it all. But her eyes popped when Letitia snapped the bills off Hanif's clip the way she had seen Lang do it. The tea room wasn't open yet, but the saleslady got her an espresso and two chocolate biscotti. Then she offered her card. "Call me next time you come in and I'll have everything ready for you . . ."

She walked to Tiffany's and looked at watches. They were all wrong, but she saw a nice ivory pin in the shape of an elephant, adorned with diamonds and emeralds, for twenty-nine hundred.

"The elephant is considered good luck by the Chinese," the salesman said.

"I didn't know they even had elephants in China," she said, all wide eyed and drug-deb dumb.

"Love the jacket," the salesman said. "Did you get it on St. Mark's Place?"

"Flea market on Sixth," she said. "There's an old hippie lady with a few racks of vintage clothes."

She marveled at the way the lines flowed out of her without any conscious thought. It was as Jamie had said: "Once you know who you are you can never say or do the wrong thing."

The doorman whistled a cab for her and she took it downtown to a watch store she had often passed on Prince Street. She picked out an old Movado with a gold band, eleven hundred dollars. The salesman was a blonde Swede with a ski tan. He told her the story of his life in a minute and gave her his card.

"What's the big deal about Swedish massages?" she asked.

"My Swedish is the biggest and the best," he said.

He watched from the window as she hailed a cab.

Tessler's was a small dark store on the corner of Fifth and Twenty-seventh. A tattered green awning flapped against the store window. The gold lettering, TESSLER'S RARE COINS, ANTIQUE JEWELRY was faded. She could see the display of coins in the window, but could barely make out the man standing behind the counter inside.

The place had a sinister vibe, but she was so deep into her character she entered without fear. The man had disappeared when the doorbell jingled. She wandered around in the dim light looking in the cases. Was he watching, waiting for her to go away?

She stood over a case, looking at a tray of old rings until he came out. He was in his sixties, sagging jowls and sad, brown, basset hound eyes. He had a shock of white hair, lovingly coifed. Dark suit, white shirt, red tie—did he get dressed up like this every day? The diamond on his pinky and the gold bracelet peeking out from under his cuff hinted at a kind of dangerous vanity.

Letitia could feel him sizing her up, taking in the bag and the pin. She looked impatiently at the Movado so he'd catch that, too.

"See something that interests you?" His European accent had been worn smooth by years in New York. She'd heard it before on an old woman who altered dresses in a dry cleaner's, an ancient lawyer in a musty office who had hired her to put his files on computer.

She pointed to a ring with large blue stone in a gold setting.

"Too big," he said. "It's for an old woman who needs something to distract from her wrinkles. You want something understated to call attention to your beauty."

"What do you suggest?" she asked.

He took her hand like he was about to kiss it and grazed a manicured nail against her palm. Just like that black guy outside Joe Di's house, only his technique sent a chill right up her arm to her neck.

"A beautiful hand like this with such long, graceful fingers should be shown unadorned," he said. He pressed her third finger, ever so lightly.

"Newly wed?"

"Yes. How'd you know?"

"The ring hasn't had the chance to leave its imprint on the finger," he said. "To brand you forever so even when you take it off people can see that you're enslaved . . ." He took a gold band braided with diamonds and sapphires out of the case. "Now this is nineteenth-century, eighteen carat . . ."

She played along. "This is much nicer than the one my

husband bought me."

"Perhaps a bit more imaginative. Lovers lose inspiration when they become husbands." He took out a string of pearls on a gold chain. His accent got more pleasant the more you heard it. "I always tell my customers that jewelry is not to be admired for itself. It is meant to enhance the beauty of its wearer."

He stepped around behind her. His breath was warm and antiseptic. Had he taken a few gulps of mouthwash in that back room?

He clasped the pearl necklace behind her neck and held up a mirror. "I could put this piece on an ordinary woman and it would look like costume jewelry." He had that old world charm working full blast. She wondered how many women had gone into that back room with him. Even if you weren't fooled the act was so good you were curious to see what happened next. "May I take a wild guess?" he said. "You're an actress."

She was astonished for a moment, but then realized it was the seducer's no lose line. If he was right, he was a mind reader; if he was wrong, he was forgiven.

"How did you know?"

"You've got that glow, that certain kind of magnetism."

She pouted. "I wish the casting agents agreed with you."

"Oh they will," he said. "Every artist needs a break, you know. My son's a producer. Ethan Tessler, ever hear of him?"

"No."

"He's very successful."

"I'm sure he is, if he's anything like you."

"Oh, he's nothing like me, thank goodness. He's in town casting a new film. Would you like to meet him?"

"I'd love to," she said. "I'd love to buy this necklace, too. Can I bring my husband back in a few hours?"

Tessler smiled. "If I haven't sold it by then."

She took his hand this time and squeezed it lightly. "Oh please don't. I promise I'll get him to buy it no matter how much it is."

He smiled. "It is sixteen five, but I'll give it to him for thirteen cash."

"He'll like that."

"I thought he would. I'll put it away for you. You'll buy it today, tomorrow I'll take you over to meet my son." He seemed genuinely happy. "We will share that rarest of things, my dear, a truly reciprocal relationship . . ."

Tessler offered to call a car service, but Letitia decided she didn't want him to know where she was going. She stood on Fifth Avenue, arm raised, hand limply summoning a taxi like she had seen so many spoiled rich ladies do. In second three cabs appeared and raced, tires screeching, to get to her.

Sixth Avenue was clogged with uptown traffic. The meter flopped and the driver swore in something guttural, but she relaxed and played with her new toys. It was nice, for once, not to care about money.

Outside Thirty-six Central Park South she tried to pay with a hundred.

"I cannot make change of this," the driver said, thrusting it back at her.

The doorman, a thick, pasty Irish guy with beady bloodshot eyes, came from out of nowhere and snatched the bill in a thick, freckled hand. "So the lady gets a free ride."

The driver looked from her to the doorman to the building and appealed to her. "You have nothing smaller? I will have no change . . ."

"Go to a bank and break it, pal, what's the big deal?" the doorman said. He watched as the driver counted out seventy-eight dollars in change, then grabbed the change and gave him the bill. "Don't tip him," he said, as the driver sped away, shaking his fist out of the window. "Gotta teach these guys a lesson." His hard look melted into a servile smile. "Can I help you?"

"I'm supposed to meet Johanna Edelstein from William May Real Estate?" she said, raising her voice interrogatively like a spoiled little rich girl. "She's going to show me the apartment on the twelfth floor?"

He led her into the alcove where an old, bald version of himself was standing at a desk. "They sellin' on twelve?"

The old guy looked hurt. "Nobody told me nothin' about it." He picked up the house phone and looked at her from under his glasses. "Whom shall I say is calling?"

"I'm supposed to meet Joanna Edelstein from William May?" Johanna Edelstein, a chubby girl with a nest of zits, had been the manager of her high school basketball team. The name had just popped into her head, but it was perfect.

The old guy hung up the house phone. "Nobody home."

"You sure you got the right apartment, Miss?" the young one asked. He was so solicitous, but he was the same kind of guy who threw balled up dollar bills at her in the Casbah and cursed her out when she wouldn't sit with him.

She pretended to consult a piece of paper. "Their name is Slater."

He shook his head. "No Slater here. Twelfth floor is Mr. . . ."

"Mrs. Lubimov," the old guy said. "Just the person we've been looking for."

A blonde in a black leather jacket brushed by in a cloud of gardenia.

"This young lady is here to see your apartment."

The blonde looked her up and down with cold blue eyes.

"You leavin' us, Mrs. Lubimov?"

"Not that I know of. But my husband's full of surprises."

Letitia played young and flustered. "Maybe it's a mistake. They said the owner's name was Slater . . ."

"You sure it's Central Park South, not West?" the blonde said.

There was her exit line. She looked down at the address and forced a blush. "Oh God, I think it was West." She turned to the blonde. "I'm so sorry."

"No problem." The blonde got into the elevator. "Good luck, honey," she said as the door slid closed.

The doorman walked her to the street and pointed out Central Park West. "It's around Sixty-fourth I think. Can I get you a cab?"

"No thanks, I'll walk." She wiggled her ass to give him something to think about. Her mouth was dry, her heart pounding as if she'd just come off stage. Her hand trembled as she picked up Hanif's phone.

Lang answered guardedly.

"It's me," she said, trying to keep the excitement out of her voice.

"Did you get everything?"

"Everything."

"Then you can come home," he said. "All is forgiven."

She crossed the street, dizzy with elation.

A cab came speeding up as if on cue. She was going downtown, but she told the driver, "Seventy-seventh and Central Park West," just in case they were still watching from the building. It was a chess game. You had to anticipate.

On the park bench, a homeless black man watched her cab turn uptown and punched out a number.

In his office, Hartung answered. "What's up?"

"Lang's girl just came out of our boy's building," Stewart said.

"The stripper? What the hell's she doin' there?"

"She went in, talked to the doorman, and came out."

"Lang?"

"No sign of him."

"Hold on," Hartung said. He called Osler. "What's up?"

"Lubimov is at One Fifteen Gold Street, his broker's I guess. Corner office, I can see him talking to two guys."

"How'd he get there, cab it?"

"Town Car. Two guys who can hardly fit in the front seat."

"Those are his Moldavians," Hartung said. "He wants his own guys backing him up." He got back on the line with Stewart. "If Lang shows just call me and I'll be right up."

"Yes sir . . ."

Hartung slammed down the phone and punched up Lang's file for the hundredth time in two days.

What the hell was this guy up to?

FIVE BLACK GARBAGE BAGS

stood in a row along Letitia's living room wall, neatly fastened with yellow ties.

Lang was on his knees in his underwear scrubbing the floor with Comet, a cigarette dangling between his lips. He was dead white. The streaks of blood on his arms, legs, and face were like Indian war paint.

"I tried to do it with their clothes on," he said, "but that just made it harder. It got easier as I got into it, but I had to put bags over the heads . . ."

She raised her hand to stop him. "I get it . . ." She had stopped for donuts, and showed him the bag. "I have no idea why I did this."

"Maybe later," he said.

"The room looks so clean."

"I did it in the bathtub," he said. "Put the plastic sheeting under them and dragged them in."

She waited for the revulsion, the nausea, the guilt.

"My God, I don't feel anything."

"You should feel happy. It could be us in those bags."

"The smell is gone," she said.

"The bags are deodorized. I sprayed some Glade around just to make sure . . ." He jumped up as she headed for the bathroom. "Don't go in there yet."

"I'll be okay," she said.

The tiles were streaked with blood. There were pink stains on the shower curtain. A collection of hacksaws, knives, and cleavers were submerged in the bloody bath water. Shreds of bone and flesh floated on top. Strands of black hair were plastered to the sides of the tub.

The room started to spin. Then she felt Lang's hand on her elbow. She caught a quick glimpse of herself in the bloody mirror. "It looks like I have freckles."

"I'll take a shower and clean the bathroom," Lang said. "It'll be like nothin' ever happened."

"I forgot what I came in for," she told him. She looked at his baggy gray jockey shorts. "Is that what they give you in prison?"

"Sexy huh? Let's get outta here."

"Wait." She opened the medicine chest and took out some moisturizer. "This is what I wanted."

"Can't have too much moisturizer," he said.

"Am I making sense?" she asked.

"No. C'mon . . ." He walked her back into the living room and sat her down on the couch. "See, I told you to eat last night. It finally caught up to you."

A sob welled up inside of her. "Oh yeah," she said, between choked breaths, "it has nothing to do with dead guys in garbage bags in my living room or bloody butcher knives in my bathtub. If I had only eaten that egg roll everything would be just fine."

"Don't crumble on me," he said. "Tell me who lives on Central Park South?"

She held her breath and bit down on her lower lip. "A man named Lubimov," she said. "While I was there his wife came in, a very chic blonde."

"What about Tessler?"

"He's an old European man, kind of a lecher. I picked out a pearl necklace and he said he would hold it . . ."

"Was he suspicious of you?"

"Not at all."

"He could have sniffed you out. He makes a call and I walk in to a jackpot."

"Excuse me," she said, annoyed at his lack of confidence. "Not only is he not suspicious, he's totally captivated."

"I didn't mean to offend you."

"He told me about his son the Hollywood producer. He wants to arrange a meeting."

Lang got up and stretched. He was very trim, funny she hadn't noticed it before. His arms were cut and he had thick tendons on his biceps. She'd heard that men worked out compulsively in prison.

"Do you realize that yesterday at about the same time I was taking a shower to wash these guys' blood off me?" he said. "Now I'm gonna take a shower to wash the same guys' blood off me again. It's like that movie, *Groundhog Day*."

His ass was really tight in those stupid jockeys. He had a kind of natural swagger that women would find attractive. Men, too, in prison where there were no women. It was hard to imagine him having sex with a man, even in jail. Maybe he had just let the effeminate ones do things to him.

He turned at the entrance to the bedroom as if he sensed she'd been thinking about him.

"I'm gonna put some clothes on," he said.

The TV remote was on the table by the couch, undisturbed by all the frantic activity that had taken place around it. The TV was tuned to *Headline News,* the last thing she had watched before going to work yesterday morning.

"A Mafia Don was gunned down gangland style in a parking area off the West Side Highway in New York late last night."

Lang came out of the bedroom in a black silk shirt and black pants. "What do you think of the wardrobe?" He put on a black raw silk sports jacket. "Kinda like standard New York, one style fits all . . ."

He came closer.

"I can hear you janglin' . . ."

"What does that mean?"

"Your nerves are goin' jingle jangle. I didn't kill those guys if that's what you're thinkin'. It was Tony Rasso."

"Why would he do it?"

"I put Hanif in that green jacket with the orange beanie. He must have thought Hanif was me . . ."

"Because you planned it that way."

"I didn't plan it," he said. "It might have been in the back of my mind . . ."

"So why did Tony kill the old man?"

"The money. He must have realized he could kill them and take the money and blame me."

"You arranged that, too," she said.

"I'm not that good. This thing has its own logic."

They switched to a live report from the parking area and a reporter chirped about the "grisly scene" with the shrouded bodies in the background.

"I hope they don't do a live report outside of Tessler's store tomorrow," she said.

"That'll be up to him," Lang said.

"He's just a horny old man, who likes to brag about his son," she said. "What do you want with him?"

"I want an answer. This was a simple score. Steal the drawing, get the payoff. But then it got weird. There were cops, but also wiseguys. Gloria was killed. They tried to kill me. Maybe Tessler can tell me why . . ."

"And you don't have some clever plan to kill him."

"Can't get answers from a corpse," he said.

"What will happen when you get your answer?" she asked.

He looked surprised, as if he hadn't thought about it.

"I guess it depends on the answer."

IF THE STRIPPER WASN'T A HOSTAGE,

she was an accomplice, Hartung decided. Lang worked with women, that was his MO. Even when he broke out of jail and was on the run he stopped to get a woman to help him.

To do what?

Did he want to steal the drawing again? Did he think that it would finance his life on the run? Or was it something deeper and more dangerous? Did he want revenge?

It was just a hunch, but Hartung had no place else to go so he drove to the girl's building and parked across the street. He had barely turned off the engine when the two of them came out of the building . . .

Gotcha.

The girl stayed in the doorway, shoulders hunched, shivering although it wasn't that cold. Lang, all in black and looking like the coolest dude in the world, put two fingers in his mouth and gave out with a piercing whistle like his football coach or the tough old drill sergeants in basic or his dad calling him in for supper . . . Only the coolest dudes could whistle like that.

Gotcha cool dude.

Hartung punched up Osler. "Where is our friend?"

"Still talking to his brokers."

A cab raced up. Lang and the girl got in. He swung out behind them. "I got Lang and the girl."

He tried to keep the excitement out of his voice, but Osler got the message.

"You gonna need my special skills?"

"Not right away. I've got one more call to make."

He punched off and hit the number. This just might work after all.

"Hey Tony, Got a Minute?"

That was what Steve had said the first time. That was his little joke. Tony knew what he wanted and didn't call back, but he kept leaving messages.

Hey Tony, let's go for coffee.

Tony had stashed the money in a box of briquettes in the garage and went straight to the hospital. He showed his insurance card from the Laborer's Union and they put him in an examination room.

Hey Tony, I know you're there.

An eye surgeon had shown up barking orders. "Elevate his head, give him drops to dilate the pupils." A nurse took his temperature and blood pressure. He heard her whispering. Next thing he felt two fingers spreading his nostrils. They were looking up his nose. He pushed them away. "Hey, the thing's in my eye, not my nose."

"We're going to give you a special anesthetic called saxamethonium, Mr. Rasso," the surgeon said "We just want to make sure it doesn't conflict with any medication you might already have in your system."

"Is it gonna knock me out?" he asked.

"It'll numb the area and make it easier to work on the eye," the doctor said. "You see you have what we call an intraocular foreign body causing a laceration in your eyeball. Once we get it out, you'll be fine. I wouldn't advise any strenuous activity for the few days. Don't even blow your nose . . ."

There was a smothered giggle. Then the nurse swabbed his arm. "Just a little preoperative relaxant, Mr. Rasso," the doctor said.

Hey Tony, you still owe me that favor.

He had met Steve in the summer of '06. He had gotten a call from Lenny Burns, a shylock in South Beach. There was a Venezuelan guy who needed five hundred Gs which he would pay back in a month.

"I think it's a coke deal," Lenny said. "When they want that much that fast down here, that's what it usually means. He'll pay us a point a week and six for five on the principal. If this goes good this guy will come back for more."

"What kind of collateral we talkin' about?"

"Guy owns four Laundromats, coin ops. Two in North Miami, one in Delray Beach, one in Boca."

Laundromats were a cash business. No checks, no credit cards. You could "bust them out," take cash then declare bankruptcy. You could launder money as well, put cash from other deals through them. There were a lot of things you could do with Laundromats.

"I'll be down in a few days," Tony said.

First, he had to clear it with Joe Di. He went up to the house on Thirty-first. The old man was trying to eat a *zeppole*, getting powdered sugar all over his bathrobe.

"Lenny thinks the guy's doin' a drug deal, huh?"

"That's what goes on down there," Tony said. "He thinks this guy can be a regular customer."

"So this bum turns the five hundred Gs we give him into three million and gives us back six hundred at the end of the month and we're supposed to kiss his ass?"

"It's a good return."

Joe Di looked at him with contempt. "Lemme teach you somethin' about this business. If you're dealin' with a nine to five schmuck this is a good return because the schmuck is just lookin' to keep his head above water and you can't get blood from a stone. But this coke dealer is on our side of the fence. He's gotta come in like a man and say 'I'm workin' on a deal. You finance it and we'll go fifty-fifty partners?' "

"This guy's not with us, Joe," Tony said.

"Hey Stupidhead!" Tony flinched as Joe Di raised a gnarled hand. "Everybody's with us until we tell 'em different. So here's what you're gonna do. Front these guys the money and then hire some local cowboys to stick him up. Then he can't make his deal, can't pay the loan. We get our money back and his fuckin' Laundromats."

Tony sat there thinking: this old bastard can't eat, can't drink, can't fuck, and can't shit, but he hasn't lost his taste for money.

He was on the go for the next twelve hours, picking up the cash from the two other "partners" in Brooklyn and explaining the deal a hundred times over. He went through a gram and was cracking another one when he and Billy Dario put the money into the trunk of a rented Caddy and headed south on I-95. Driving in shifts, they made it to Miami in twenty-two hours flat.

The blow had put a jagged edge around his exhaustion. He lay in the hotel room with the AC blasting. Just as he was starting to drift off, the phone rang.

It was Lenny Burns. "I thought I'd give you a coupla hours to relax. Little dinner?"

He couldn't say no. A shower and a gram later he was down in the lobby. Lenny Burns was really Larry Bonpierno from Howard Beach, gold Rolex, eggplant tan, desperate to please. He was officially "with" the Gambinos, but Joe Di laid off his big loans and he was happy to take the short end.

They went to Perinos. Larry had arranged the full "boss" treatment. Corner table, bows and fervent handshakes, "it's an honor to meet you Mr. Rasso." Free cocktails and "try the grouper, Mr. Rasso."

He had a few drinks to take that jagged edge off, then made a trip to the bathroom to put it back on again. He ordered a huge meal and couldn't touch it. He knew Larry was onto him and didn't care.

After dinner they went to the China Club. It was just after midnight and the place was starting to heat up. Lenny walked him to the front of the line and the bouncers lifted the velvet rope and stepped aside. They went to a booth in the back. Two girls, one dark, one blonde, showed up. "May we join you?"

Tony checked his stash. There wasn't enough to share. "Can you ladies give us a minute?"

With the music banging and people whirling by on the dance floor, he laid out the plan.

Lenny listened with a pained look. "Jeez Tony, it's a simple loan. The guy's good for it and he'll come back for more. And if he can't pay us back we get his Laundromats."

"That's not the way the old man wants to do it."

"I'm gonna have to reach out to find two heist guys."

"Can't you use your collectors?"

"No, I got bouncers, concrete workers, two guys on the Miami U scout squad. They don't do ripoffs."

"You'll find somebody."

"Yeah, but . . ." Lenny took a desperation shot. "Think I'll just pass on the deal, Tony okay?"

Tony could almost feel for him, going along just fine and suddenly his balls were in a vice.

"You know you can't do that, Lenny."

"But the guy'll know he was set up. I'll never be able to lend another nickel in this town again. He might even come after me."

"What can I tellya Lenny? The old man's got a hair up his

ass about this."

After that the party was over. Lenny drove Tony back to the hotel.

"So you'll take care of this, right Lenny?"

"I'll take care of it," Lenny said and drove away.

In the short walk through the muggy air he felt the sweat boiling out of him. The frigid AC in the hotel lobby just made him feel clammy. He could hardly stand on his feet, but he knew he wouldn't be able to sleep once he lay down.

He opened the door. In the dim light of the wall sconce he could see a big black guy sitting on his bed.

"Been out clubbin', Tony?"

The black guy made him think ripoff, but then a big white guy slipped in behind him.

Cops!

They were too trim to be detectives, more like motorcycle cops. But it didn't read right. Cops worked themselves up for a shakedown. They gave you that mad dog look, tried to scare you. These guys were calm. The white guy had a mocking look like it was all a big joke. "Put your hands against the wall, Tony, and take the position."

"Can I see some ID?" he asked.

"We don't gotta show you no stinkin' badges," the white guy said with a phony Mexican accent and they both laughed.

"You have no right to search me without probable cause," Tony said.

The white guy patted Tony down and found his eighth of an ounce vial. Then pulled the gram out of his sock. "Lucky for you this isn't a bust, Tony. We're not cops."

"Who are you?"

"Did you ever hear of Big Brother?"

The black guy got up. "That's me, Big Brother . . ."

"We're like you guys," the white guy said. "Like the Mafia."

"Only we're the sho 'nuf Mafia," the black guy said. "We run everything."

"FBI?" he asked.

"Let's take a ride, Tony," the white guy said. "Our boss wants to see you."

It wasn't a hit, or he'd be dead already. It wasn't a bust or he'd already be in cuffs. He didn't care, anyway. He just needed a one and one.

"Can I have my shit back?" he asked.

The white guy flipped him his vial. "Knock yourself out."

They drove across the Harbor Bridge in a Sebring convertible—"Nice car for a rental, huh Tony?"—and walked him into a dental building that was closed for the evening.

A big guy with a blonde crew cut and rimless glasses was in the waiting room. "Hey Tony, got a minute? I'm Hartung."

"Yeah, yeah, what's your real name?"

He laughed. "Can't put anything over on you, Tony. Just call me Steve . . ."

They sat him in a dentist chair and stood over him. He tried to stare back, but he was too tired and too confused.

"We know who you are, Tony, and we don't care," Steve said. "It's bad luck for you that our paths had to cross, but it's good that it happened here away from the city. Because nobody can ever know about our deal. If Joe Di or Hanif ever find out, we're gonna get the word out that you've been talking to the Feds. You won't last too long after that."

Suddenly, he needed a cigarette. He patted his pockets, looking for the pack.

"Go ahead and load up if you want to, Tony," Steve, said.

"Just want a cigarette."

The white guy gave him one. He held it with trembling hands as Steve guy lit it for him.

"We know you're settin' up a burglary on Central Park South, Tony."

He froze for a second. What were they talking about? Then it came into his head. The drawing. The Russian . . .

"The guy who owns it is kinda like a friend of ours," Steve said. "He's a very important man and we don't want anybody messin' with him. But at the same time we don't want anybody to know we're lookin' out for him. Can you help us out here?"

"Yeah, we'll call the thing off," he said.

"Thanks, but it's not that easy. Mr. Tessler wants his drawing. Joe Di wants his hundred thousand. They're gonna wanna know why this thing isn't happening."

It's a sign of weakness to ask a question that won't be answered, but he couldn't help himself.

"How do you know all this?"

"We know everything, Tony. The trick is to accomplish this without making some very paranoid people even more paranoid. I'm talking about Joe Di. He's a hard man to fool, isn't he?"

"He don't trust nobody if that's what you mean."

"That's what I mean. So we were thinking we let the burglary take place, okay. Then we bust them at the drop. This way everybody will think the police were tipped off."

"Okay, so I'll tell you where the drop is and you tell the cops."

"We can't do that," Steve said. "We're a secret organization." He turned to the big white guy in annoyance. "Didn't you tell him?"

"I told him we were secret, just like the Mafia."

Steve turned back to him. "We're so secret we don't even know who we are. But we know we can get away with murder, Tony. Especially if we're killin' a wiseguy."

All of a sudden the coke, the *agita,* the lack of sleep all came together and he couldn't breathe. Then his nose started to bleed.

"High blood pressure," he told them. "I'm on blood thinners."

They stuck a wad of cotton up his nose and let him lie on the couch in the waiting room. After a few minutes they brought him back to Steve.

"Did you have any bright ideas while you were recuperating, Tony?" he asked.

"I know a cop," he said. "I can tip him. He'll be waitin' at the drop. He'll bust Jerry and return the painting."

Steve gave him a cigarette. "This cop a good friend of yours, Tony? Has he done special things for you?"

"He's a cop. He'll do anything for money."

"Okay, we're on the right track. 'Cause we want Jerry Lang to be killed resisting arrest."

Jerry the Actor, he thought.

"Jerry's done a lotta things for me."

"Here today, gone tomorrow," Steve said. "He won't feel a thing."

"It'll cost money."

"That's your problem," Steve said. "This party's on you, Tony."

"What do I get for it?"

"It's what you don't get." Steve waved a big .45 in his face. "Okay, Tony?"

He had no choice. "Okay . . ."

When he got back to the city he contacted Gene Donofrio, his connection in the Organized Crime Squad. Gene was Billy Dario's cousin and was their pipeline into the Task Force, keeping them up to date on every move the government was making.

They made a plan. Gene would claim he got an anonymous call about the burglary. That he arrested Lang in the hotel room, Lang resisted, and he killed him in the struggle. Gene would get the money and brownie points for a headline collar.

Tony told Steve the plan.

"Elegant," Steve said.

Then the roof started falling in. In the afternoon he got a call from the house on Thirty-first. Joe Di's cackle came over the phone. "Come up here, genius."

Joe's sister May met opened the door for him. "What happened, Tony? He's really mad."

In the kitchen Joe Di was pouring coffee with a palsied hand. "Did you take care of that thing in Miami like I told you?"

"Yeah. Just like you told me."

"You fuckin' jerk!" Joe Di lunged and threw the cup at him. "Can't you do anything right?"

He stood there, scalding coffee dripping down his face, thinking how he could snap this little prick like a twig.

Foam bubbled out of the corners of Joe Di's mouth. "Your fuckin' guy down there hired two niggers from Liberty City to stick up that coke dealer. The guy had a bodyguard and fought back. They shot him and took off with the money . . ."

"So we're out the five hundred Gs."

"We're not out nothin', *stunada*. You are." Joe Di jabbed him in the chest with a crooked finger. "That loan has been transferred to you. You owe us five hundred Gs plus points. You got friends in this family. They're givin' you a break at a point a week. I woulda put you on two points to teach you a lesson. Next time I tellya to button somethin' you button it personally until it's done. You understand?"

A point was five Gs. With the 20 percent interest he'd probably end up going for half a mil before the loan was paid off. He'd be in hock to this little prick forever.

"I understand," he said.

That night another sweet plan went bust. Jerry Lang, a nonviolent burglar, shot one of the toughest cops in the city with his own gun. This was something nobody could have foreseen.

In the morning, Steve and his boys were waiting for him at the end of his driveway.

"Close but no cigar, Tony."

"Not a problem," he said. "We'll get this guy as soon as he comes outta jail."

"A lotta bad things can happen in seven years. We want him gone now."

Pleading never worked, but he couldn't help it. He couldn't even keep his voice from cracking. "C'mon guys, gimme a break. You know how tough this is gonna be? . . ."

"People die in the can every day. You got guys inside who'll kill for a carton of cigarettes." Steve squeezed his shoulder. "You can do it, Tony. Tell me you can do it."

Setting up a jailhouse hit meant reaching out to guys inside, spreading money around to guards, trusting people who had nothing to lose. At any moment somebody could trade him for a better deal.

But he had no choice.

"I can do it," he said.

That had been a year and a half ago. First, there had been ten Gs to the Mexican Mafia to set Lang's cell on fire. Then ten to the old lifer who needed a copay for his old jailhouse boyfriend's chemotherapy. Then twenty to the family man who would do anything to get the money for his daughter's tuition. Seven Gs to guards and friends inside made forty-seven. Three tries, and Jerry Lang was still alive . . .

Then, two days ago, Hanif called.

"Guess who just walked into my joint . . . Jerry Lang."

He didn't ask how or what or why. He slammed his fist on the table. "Squash him. Now!"

But Jerry Lang was still around.

The nurse put a shield over his other eye. The anesthetic spread in a warm wave through his body. He drifted, weightless, in the soothing darkness. This is how you die. They dope you up until it's over. Over the years with all the guys he had clipped he had gotten to thinking: is death such a punishment? Most of these poor slobs were strung out or in hock or trying to get away with some scam or another. They were miserable and scared and pissed off and at the end of their run anyway. So what if one night a guy popped up with a gun and BOOM! it was over?

The pain went away. It was like his eyeball had been taken out of his head and he could feel someone polishing it. A few more pricks of the needle and he could float away into outer space. Instead, they were bringing him back to the mother ship. He could see the lights, hear the voices.

"Let me go," somebody said. It was his voice, but it sounded like it was coming from another room.

"Just rest for awhile, Mr. Rasso," someone said. "Let the anesthetic wear off. The doctor will take one more look at you and then you'll be able to go home."

A cool hand took the shield off his other eye. A piece of glass glittered in a pair of tweezers.

"A few days' rest," they told him. "Don't move your head a lot. No exercise and no strenuous activity. Try not to sneeze or blow your nose . . ."

"Yeah, you told me that already."

He sat in the lobby waiting for Billy to bring the car around, but then he realized there was no Billy anymore.

There were four new messages on his cell phone. He listened to the last one.

"Hope you're dead, Tony. At this point that's your only excuse."

He called the number. Steve answered.

"Where have you been?"

"I had to have surgery."

"Get that glass out of your eye?"

How did they know that? Had they been tailing him all along?

"We've found Jerry Lang, Tony. And now we want to close the deal. You take care of this for us and we're even."

He could have used Billy for this, but Billy was gone.

"Okay," he said, "lemme reach out."

"It's gotta be today."

"I don't have anybody right now."

"Then you do it yourself."

"I don't do that kinda work anymore," he said.

"You do for us. To us you're just a grunt, Tony."

Panic flooded through him. "I just had surgery. I'm weak, I gotta rest . . ."

"Don't worry, we'll make it real easy for you. Piece of cake, Tony."

It was Pure Theater.

Tessler had come out of his back room smiling broadly, playing the benign merchant, as Letitia and Lang entered the store. "I was just thinking about you."

Lang played the indulgent husband with a slight midwestern twang. "I tried to talk her out of it, but she has to have that ring."

"And it has to have her," Tessler said, opening the display case. "I know that somewhere along the way a woman very much like your wife owned this piece. I can almost feel her spirit urging her to buy it . . ."

Lang held the ring up to the light and squinted with one eye closed. "And I can hear her husband's spirit saying, 'Give this man a discount.' "

Tessler's laugh seemed genuine. "You know I think I can, too."

Lang turned to Letitia. "Better go meet your mom, honey . . ."

She had been so absorbed she had forgotten the plan they had made in the taxi. She would walk Lang into the store, then say she had to meet her mother and leave. Later, he would come up and help her move the garbage bags out of her apartment.

Now he was looking pointedly at her. "If you're late, your mom will blame me." She offered her face for a peck on the cheek. "Don't let him talk you out of it, Mr. Tessler," she said.

"My husband's a very good salesman."

"I'll be steadfast, my dear," Tessler said.

The door tinkled behind her. She blinked in the sudden brightness and raised a limp hand for a taxi, then turned back. Through the store window she could see Tessler crawling at Lang's feet like a man looking for a lost contact lens.

The door tinkled as she ran back in.

"What are you doing? You said you weren't going to kill him."

Lang grabbed Tessler by the hair and pulled his head up. "Does he look dead to you?"

Tessler gagged. Blood poured out of his mouth onto his silk shirt.

"I asked him nice," Lang said, "but he got an attitude. Told me he didn't know nobody named Joe Di and to get out of his store before he called the cops . . ."

"Take the jewelry," Tessler gasped. "Take everything . . ."

Lang kicked him in the back, slamming him down to the floor. "Who makes this knock off crap for you, Tessler, some junkie in Greenpoint? Where's the real swag?"

Tessler gestured to the back room. "Office . . . Office . . ."

Lang pushed Letitia toward the door. "Lock it as long as you're here." He grabbed Tessler by the collar and dragged him into the back room. There was a desk with a tensor lamp and a jeweler's glass. A large round vault was built into the wall. It was unlocked. Lang pulled it open.

"This the real stuff, the stuff you fence?"

"Take it, take it," Tessler said.

"I'm not takin' anything out of the vault." Lang horsed Tessler up by the back of his pants. "I'm puttin' somethin' in. You."

Tessler went yellow under his tan. "For God's sake, what do you want from me?"

"Remember that Levitan . . . ?" He shook Tessler. "Don't tell me you don't."

"I do, of course I do."

"Who were you stealin' it for?"

"No one."

"See what I mean about these guys? Lyin' to the very end . . ."

"It's true," Tessler said with such surprising force that Lang let him go.

Tessler staggered back and drew himself up. Through the pain and terror a glimmer of defiance showed through.

"I was stealing it for myself," he said. "That drawing is mine."

"PROVE THE DRAWING IS YOURS

and I'll let you live," Lang said.

He stood over Tessler with Malik's .25, suddenly crude and impatient.

Tessler nodded as if he expected no better treatment. He took an old photo album out of his desk. "These pictures will establish my chain of title," he said.

He showed them a crumbling sepia tone in an oval frame: a thickly bearded man in a black suit, standing stiffly behind a stoutish, cross-eyed woman in a high-necked dress, luxuriant dark hair piled high in a bun on her head. Two little boys in short pants and Fauntleroy collars stood on either side of her, their hands resting lightly on her lap.

"My great grandfather," he said. "He made syrups and soda water on commission from the tsar himself. He had a special residence permit to live in Saint Petersburg."

He turned to another photo. A group of young men at a picnic in a meadow, empty bottles and the remains of a meal on blankets behind them.

"The famous Moscow Art Academy." He pointed to young man with a pointed beard and curled mustachios in the center. "My grandfather," he said. "A dilettante, just like the sons of the rich today. He thought he wanted to be an artist, but look who he had to compete with . . ." He pointed to the other young men. "Nesterov, Korovin, Polenov . . . And here"—he pointed to an older man with a long stemmed clay pipe—"Sarasov, the master . . ."

Lang shook his head. "Sorry pal, after Da Vinci I draw a blank."

"The leading members of the Russian landscape school," Tessler said. "They built their movement around Tolstoy's credo: 'The basis of human happiness is to be together with nature, to see it and talk to it . . .' "

Letitia thought of the rats on her grandfather's farm, the stink of the chicken coop. The little girl who had to milk an old cow in an icy barn, her fingers freezing together.

Tessler handed Lang a magnifying glass. "There is Isaac Levitan."

Lang bent for a closer look, then looked up in surprise. "The face in the drawing."

He offered the magnifying glass to Letitia. She saw a slight bearded young man with a pensive smile.

"Levitan was the star of the academy, but more than that, a sweet man who everybody admired. My grandfather couldn't paint, but he had a natural talent for retail. He opened a gallery in Moscow and marketed his friends as painters of the holy Russian soil, the holy Russian peasant. He invented a business. But my father made it an institution."

Tessler turned the page to a photo of a beardless young dandy in a rakish pose with two young women. "He was a merchant with the temperament and the vices of an artist." Tessler spoke to Letitia as if he sensed Lang wouldn't understand. "He became the darling of the Moscow demimonde. After the Bolsheviks took over he escaped with his White Russian friends to Berlin." He turned to a photo of the same young man in a gallery lined with paintings. "Berlin, 1923" was printed in faded ink. "My father had a good eye. He took up the modernists. Those are Kandinskys and Kokoschkas and Schwitters on those walls, along with everything else."

Tessler unfolded a newspaper clipping, a photo of a nightclub. Several men were toasting a naked young woman, while another drew on a tablecloth. "My father always spoke with great nostalgia about his time in Berlin."

"Correct me if I'm wrong," Lang said, "but I thought you folks didn't too well in Germany . . ."

"Nineteen thirty-three was like an earthquake to them. They were too wrapped up in their little world to see it coming." Tessler unfolded a faded document. "This may be the most valuable thing I own." It had an official-looking stamp with "KAUFVERLAG" in bold black letters.

"What's that mean?" Lang asked.

"Bill of sale," Tessler said. "My father waited until 1937, hoping that his beloved Berlin would return to its senses. Then one day he had a visitor, a fat man in a chauffeured Daimler. He was told his art was decadent and would no longer be permitted to be shown. It was now the property of the Reich. He was given a bill of sale and three hundred and fifty marks, which happened to be the exact price of two tickets to Vienna. Recognize this signature?" They looked on the bottom of the page. "Hermann Goering" was written in a spidery hand.

"Do you know what I could get for this?" Tessler said. "There are so many wealthy collectors of Nazi memorabilia, I could hold an auction on eBay. Instead, I'll leave it for my grandchildren if I ever have them." He pointed to a list . . . "Goering was very efficient. He compiled a catalogue of the art they were taking. Do you see this item?"

Halfway down the list was the name Itzhak Levitan.

"That's the drawing you stole from that esteemed looter of confiscated art and newest paid-up member of New York society, Mr. Alexander Lubimov," Tessler said.

"How did Lubimov get the drawing?" Letitia asked.

"There's no time for more life stories," Lang said.

"What is your name, dear?" Tessler asked.

"Letitia."

"Lovely old English name. You might want to hear this," he said to Lang. "It might help you decide what to do next."

Lang shrugged. "Five minutes."

Tessler turned to Letitia.

"My parents arrived in Vienna with the equivalent of seven dollars in their pockets. That's where little Willi—that's me— was born. Then in thirty-eight Hitler marches into Austria and my father begs handouts from the Austrian dealers he had done business with and goes to Paris. In thirty-nine when Hitler conquers Poland, he manages somehow to get me on a boat to England with other little children. I am put in school in Leeds where I am taught English and impeccable British manners.

"In nineteen forty my mother sees a newsreel of Hitler driving through Paris and decides that he has been pursuing her personally from country to country and he'll stop the killing once she is dead. To save the world and especially her little Willi, she drinks carbolic acid.

"My father survives the war thanks to the kindness of his friends in the art world. They shuttle him from basement to attic, from barn to forest hovel. Do you have a cigarette?"

Lang held out the pack. Tessler lit the cigarette and held it between his thumb and forefinger European style.

"In nineteen forty-six, I am an eight year old English boy playing rugby with my school mates. I see the headmaster with a skinny ragamuffin of a man. 'This is your father,' he says. The ragamuffin, smelling of detergent and cheap tobacco, wraps his bony arms around me, speaking in the language of our enemies, the Germans. That night he takes me away. I cry so piteously in the train that people think I'm being kidnapped. Next day we're on a ship. I'm sick for seven days. Then the Statue of Liberty. We go to a room in Washington Heights with dark wooden furniture and a window shade always drawn. I share a bed with him, living with the odor of sweat and Lucky Strikes . . ."

Tessler appealed to Letitia. "People should know of these things, shouldn't they? I tell my son: This is the movie you should make."

Lang reached over and tapped Tessler's watch. "Cut to the chase, Willi."

Tessler took a deep drag of his cigarette. "My father started selling heirlooms for the refugees. Old silver, jewelry, whatever they had managed to smuggle out of Germany with them. He opened this store. We had a life.

"I became some kind of an American. but he never did. He never remarried. Never made friends. His free time was devoted to recovering the paintings the Nazis had stolen. He filed suit in the US and Germany. Every summer we went to Europe to all the galleries and museums. He hired detectives. They told him: 'The paintings are in the Eastern Zone. The Russians have them. You'll never see them.' "

Lang drummed his fingers on the desk. "Okay Willi, that's Papa. What about you? How did you fall into a life of crime?"

Tessler gave Letitia a quick, anxious look. "What happened to me would take more than five minutes to tell."

"C'mon, Willi, tell us how you got bent," Lang said. "Was it drugs or little girls? Little boys, maybe."

"Why are you doing this?" Letitia asked. This man seemed so harmless. Of all the monsters she had seen in the last few days she couldn't understand why Lang was picking a fight with him.

"Maybe I'm jealous," Lang said "You're gettin' all teary over Willi's bio and you just write me off as a mutt from Tenth Avenue who steals 'cause he doesn't know no better." He looked at the items in the vault. "Is all this swag, Willi?"

"My private trade," Tessler said, carefully. "Consignments,

estate purchases . . ."

"Very smooth Willi. You've got the young lady sold, right Letitia?"

"I believe him," Letitia said. "I think people should know what happened."

Tessler turned to her, silently grateful. "After my father died, I dropped his lawsuits. But that list was burned in my memory. One day I'm reading about a certain Russian millionaire, private investor Alexander Lubimov, who is loaning a priceless drawing to a traveling exhibition of Russian art.

"The work he is loaning is *Self Portrait* by Isaac Levitan." Tessler stopped and shook his head. "I read it three times before it registered. I was sitting here alone as I often do. And I started to laugh. This Russian thug had my father's drawing and I was going to get it back. And he would never know why . . . I called Joe Di . . ."

"And he called Tony Rasso who called Hanif who called me," Lang said. "And I stole the drawing for you."

"You were the famous burglar," Tessler said. "They said you would find a way to get it."

"Don't schmooze me, Willi," Lang said. "This was an easy score, too easy. It was a trap."

Tessler gestured as if it were self-evident. "Somebody informed on you."

"It wasn't the cops. Maybe Hanif or Joe Di tryin' to get the drawing for themselves."

Tessler shook his head with certainty. "No, they wouldn't know where to fence the painting. It's a special market. The buyers use middle men like me." He thought for a moment. "Maybe Lubimov. He's a powerful man with powerful friends. He would want to send a message . . ."

Lang nodded as if it were slowly dawning on him. "Yes, he would if he was that kind of guy."

"A Russian suddenly appears in New York with millions of dollars he says he made in used cars and Moscow real estate," Tessler said. "What kind of guy do you think he is?"

"Yeah," Lang said. "So he finds out about the score. He reaches out for a bought cop and busts it up. He gets his drawing back, but that's not enough. He kills my partner and tries to kill me so people will know not to mess with him in the future."

Lang nodded at Letitia. "Yeah. It was probably the Russian."

"TWENTY-FIVE THOUSAND FOR THE LEVITAN,"

Tessler said.

"No deal, Willi," Lang said. "I'm gonna make Mr. Lubimov get on his knees and eat that drawing, frame and all."

Tessler upped it to thirty-five, then fifty, but Lang waved him off. No wisecracks, just a cold turndown.

Tessler got panicky.

"You can't destroy a work of art."

"Hey, some people like to look at art, some people like to steal it. I'll show my appreciation by shovin' it down that Russian's throat."

By now Letitia understood his style. He was negotiating.

"A hundred thousand," Tessler said.

Lang took a tiny silk bag out of the vault. Inside was a gold Rolex.

"Get this on consignment, Willi?" he asked.

"It's an original," Tessler said. "Sixty-five years old. There's a dealer in San Francisco who'll give you fourteen, fifteen thousand without an owner's certificate. That plus the hundred can get you very far away."

"Will it get me to Mars?" Lang asked. " 'Cause that's how far I'll have to go."

"If you don't care about the money think of the young lady," Tessler said.

Lang offered Letitia the watch. She shook her head.

"Only if you give him his drawing?" she said.

Lang slapped the watch into her palm. "I know this woman for one day and already she's givin' me orders." He closed her hand around the watch. "Okay, a hundred thousand."

Tessler got a prayerful look. "Can you get it?"

"For a hundred Gs," Lang said.

"Yes, yes, get it." Tessler gave him a business card and gave one to Letitia. "I'm always on my cell . . ."

"We'll call you an hour before we come," Lang said. "Have the money ready."

"I'm familiar with these transactions," Tessler said.

He stopped them at the door. "Wait." He took the ring Letitia had admired out of the case and slipped it on her finger.

"I can't," she said.

"Please take it, my dear," Tessler said. "If you do this . . ." Tears rose in his eyes . . . "You have no idea how much this means to me."

"I can tell you to the penny how much it means, Willi," Lang said. He took Letitia by the arm. "Let's go."

In the street, she pulled away. "What's the matter with you?"

"You believed that crap, didn't you?"

"Why shouldn't I? He had the old family photos, those painters . . ."

"He coulda got them at any antique store. It coulda been any family or any buncha guys. You don't know what those Russian painters looked like."

"But one of them was Isaac Levitan, you said so yourself."

"I just wanted to see where he was goin'. It's an old con. He shows you a blurry photo. Could be any skinny kid with a beard. He convinces you it's Levitan 'cause he has all this other stuff to back it up . . ."

"What about the bill of sale with Hermann Goering's signature?"

"The same guy who made him all that phony jewelry coulda

made that, too. The story adds to the price of the drawing. If he's willin' to go a hundred Gs he must have a buyer on the hook for a coupla mil."

"He says he's not going to sell it."

Lang threw back his head and gave out with a despairing bark of a laugh. "Alice in Wonderland over here. You fell down a hole into a world of lies. The only way you'll make it out is by not buyin' into anything anybody says."

"Including you?"

"Especially me. I been in that world all my life. There was only one person who told me the truth and I got her killed."

A taxi sped by, trying to make the light. Lang whistled and it screeched to a halt.

"Watch what'll happen when we get it. Your poor persecuted friend will try to give us twenty cents on the dollar."

Across the street, Hartung swung out into traffic and followed the taxi down Fifth Avenue. He called Osler.

"Where's Lubimov?"

"On his way uptown," Osler said.

"Okay drop him, we know where he's gonna end up. Go down to Cornelia Street. Mr. Tony Rasso will be waiting on the corner. Bring him up to Lubimov's."

"Then what?"

"I don't know yet. I'll tell you when you get there."

"This Time You Don't
Turn Back,"

Lang said. "Even if World War Three breaks out you keep goin'."

They had gotten out of the cab on Sixth Avenue and were walking along the park side.

"What are you going to do?" Letitia asked.

"We're talkin' about you now. You're gonna stroll into the lobby and tell 'em 'This is my husband, here to see the apartment on the twelfth floor.' As soon as the doorman picks up the house phone you hit the street and fast . . ."

"They won't let you go up," she said.

"I'm not gonna ask permission."

His face was set, his eyes looking ahead to what was about to happen.

"What are you going to do when you get there?" she asked.

"Get the Levitan and some answers."

"But you have the answer. It was Hanif."

"Mittens was a pimp, he couldn't mastermind dirty cops and stings and jailhouse hits. It had to be this Russian."

Letitia felt a falling sensation in the pit of her stomach.

"I'm not going to help you do this, Lang."

He opened his jacket. Malik's gun was in his belt. "Then those two poor doormen will have a real problem."

"You'll have to hold them hostage, or worse. More people will die."

He shrugged. "That Russian's a hood. He'll deserve what he gets."

241

"What about his wife?"

"She shoulda known better than to marry him."

"And you?"

"Me? You worryin' about me now?"

"Somebody's going to get hurt."

"Just make sure it's not you. You keep walkin' all the way to the Ninth Avenue. Take a cab downtown. Tonight, I'll show up with a hundred Gs for you . . ."

"I don't want the money. Don't do this for me."

"I'm doin' this 'cause I got nothin' else to do, you understand." He pointed as the passersby, walking by quickly, heads down, eyes averted. "These people all got someplace to go. What am I gonna do, sleep in the park and wait for the cops to get me?"

Over his shoulder, Letitia saw Mrs. Lubimov come out of the building. A black BMW 765i had pulled up. The parking attendant jumped out and held the door, while she fiddled in her purse for a tip.

Lang followed her eyes. Then turned back with a wild look.

"You know who that is?"

"Mrs. Lubimov," she said.

"It is, huh? Okay, go home now. I'll see you later."

He turned and dashed out into oncoming traffic.

Letitia ran out after him.

"Lang!"

Why did I tell him?

Horns blared. Lang leapt onto the hood of a cab and rolled over onto the street. The driver jumped out, turban fluttering, fists clenched.

"Leave her alone," Letitia called.

Lang turned back with a jubilant laugh.

"No way!"

★ ★ ★ ★ ★

Hartung had followed the taxi uptown and slid in behind a tour bus. He watched Lang race across the street and force his way into the BMW, pushing the blonde over to the passenger's side.

He could see Stewart jumping off the park bench. He punched him up. Saw him stop and reach for the phone.

"Lang just grabbed Lubimov's wife," Stewart said.

"I know. I'm sitting here behind the bus. Sit down, there's nothing we can do."

Now the girl ran up. Lang lowered the window. It looked as if she were trying to talk him out of something. He pushed her away, but she grabbed the door handle. He started the car, but she grasped the side mirror with two hands and slid a few feet before he stopped the car.

The girl opened the rear door and dove into the back seat. Lang floored it into a screeching U-turn. Cars on Central Park South braked hard, squealing and sliding, smoke snaking off their rear tires. The BMW came so close, Hartung could see their faces. Mrs. Lubimov, rigid behind dark glasses; the girl leaning over the back seat, talking urgently. And Lang hunched over wheel with that dazed smile you got in combat when you knew you had to do something crazy to save yourself.

He heard a beep. It was another call. Maybe the Voice.

"I'll stay with them," he told Stewart. "Contact Osler and tell him to squat by the house and keep Rasso with him."

He disconnected. The call was gone, but there was a text message.

"Good news. The coach called. Wants Amy for the big match. She's thrilled."

He stared at it for a second, thinking it was some kind of code like the ones they used in NATO countries where they knew their phones were monitored. Then he realized it was from Beverly. Amy was back on the team. He messaged back.

"Great news."

Then followed the BMW up Central Park West.

In the BMW Lang turned to Letitia. "You're a glutton for punishment, kid. Why didn't you just take off like I told ya?"

His laugh was light without the angry edge. He seemed elated. The blonde sat motionless.

"I know your plan," Letitia said.

"Oh yeah, then tell me 'cause I'm stumped."

"You'll tell Lubimov you'll exchange his wife for the Levitan. But it will just be a way to get him out in the open somewhere. It'll be the same thing you did with Hanif and Joe Di. Only this time it will be innocent people."

"Innocent huh?" Lang made a left on Seventy-seventh. A group of Catholic schoolgirls in middy skirts and blouses was walking double file into the Museum of Natural History. "That's innocent," he said. "And don't check them out in five years."

"You know what I mean."

Lang turned down Columbus. "This Russian has a stolen painting. How is he innocent?"

"He may not know it's stolen," Letitia said. "He might have bought it from a dealer. If Tessler made up the whole story like you said, he could be the legitimate owner."

"You're a smart girl, throwing my scenario back in my face. But what if Tessler is tellin' the truth like you said? That means the Russian is a crook with an apartment full of looted art. If his world comes down on him too bad, that's the chance he took."

"Okay, but his wife is still innocent."

"Eureka, a meter," Lang said. He pulled in front of a meter on Columbus. The blonde sat still as if she were waiting for something to happen. He lifted off her sunglasses.

"Those eyes still glitter like sun on the sea," he said.

The blonde stared at him impassively.

"I know," he said. "You hate it when I get philosophical."

He took her chin gently and turned her face toward Letitia. "Letitia Hastings, meet Gloria Pavlich."

"They're Parked,"

Hartung said.

He had pulled in front of a hydrant across the street and raised his hood, as if he were overheated.

Stewart conferenced him into Osler.

"Where are you?"

"Coming up Eighth Avenue," Osler said. "I should be there in a few minutes."

"Okay, here's the deal," Hartung said. "Lang grabbed Mrs. Lubimov. They're in a black oh-five BMW with diplo plates on the west side of Columbus between Seventy-sixth and Seventy-seventh. The stripper tried to stop it and he took her with him. I assume he's trying to raise money like he did last night with Joe Di. We can't even think about doing anything until he gets away from the ladies."

"Mr. Rasso wants a word," Osler said.

Rasso came on, hoarse and strained.

"You want me to shoot a guy on the street?"

"I thought we already had this conversation, Tony . . ."

Rasso's voice cracked. "I'm warnin' you: If I get caught, I'll give you up."

He was melting down fast. This was no time for threats.

"Tony, wake up," Hartung said. "You've got zero leverage here. The trick is do it and get away with it. And you will. Any situation we put you into we'll get you out of. That's a promise."

★   ★   ★   ★   ★

In the BMW, Lang offered Gloria a cigarette.

"Gave it up," she said.

"Bet your boyfriend smokes."

"Like a chimney . . . And he's my husband."

Lang lit up. He was using the cigarette as a prop to hide his hurt, but it wasn't working. For the first time Letitia could read his mood.

"The Beemer a wedding present?" he asked.

"I like jewelry, you know that," Gloria said. "Anyway, I wanted a Ferrari, but Sasha said it wasn't practical in the city, shifting gears and all."

"You coulda bought an automatic."

"Sasha said putting an automatic in a Ferrari would be a sin."

Lang reached over and opened the glove compartment.

"There's nothin' in there," Gloria said.

"I'm a thief," he said. "I go through drawers, I open doors." He felt under the seat. "Decided to tough it out, huh?"

"Would it do any good if I got down on my knees and said I was sorry."

"Are you sorry?"

"I'm sorry about the way it happened." Her eyes dropped and she blinked as he opened the compartment between the seats. He pushed down and the bottom panel flipped open, revealing a small black revolver. He lifted it out.

"I didn't know that was there," Gloria said.

"Doesn't matter," Lang said. He put the revolver back without unloading it and closed the panel. He lit another cigarette. He didn't seem to know what to do.

"Letitia's my new leading lady," he said.

Gloria didn't take her eyes off Lang. "Kinda young."

"I picked her up at the Casbah," Lang said. He was trying to get her to look at Letitia, but she wouldn't do it. "She's real good, Gloria."

"She's got a good teacher."

"She could be better than you, but she doesn't have enough grifter in her. For her it's slummin', for you it was steppin' up."

Gloria looked at her manicure. "I've got a lunch date, Jerry."

"Yeah okay," Lang said.

Gloria picked a speck off her slacks. "You know I hate when you look at me like that."

"Like what?"

"Like you were tryin' to figure me out."

"Does Sasha look at you like that?"

"All men do. They're never happy unless they know what you're thinking . . ."

"You didn't have to set me up," Lang said.

"I wasn't going to," Gloria said. "I was gonna leave you after this last score."

"Why? I said I was gonna quit."

"Maybe for a few months, maybe even a year. But then something would have come up that was too good to turn down. You're an outlaw, Jerry. There was no future with you."

"I could have changed," Lang said.

Gloria went on as if she hadn't heard him. "Life with you was too stressful. What if one day Rasso decides you're holdin' out and puts out a contract on you? You always said he was paranoid from all that coke. You always said Hanif would clip you for a dollar."

"I was right about that," Lang said.

"What if you got caught in the act and had to hurt somebody? Then you'd be on the lam and out of business. Or if somebody gave you up to get a better deal for themselves? That was your worst nightmare."

"And you made it come true," Lang said.

She ignored him, intent on her side of the story. "Or if you just ran out of luck and get busted for no good reason? The cops would pile every unsolved burglary they had on your plate and you'd do ten, twelve years for low. Then you'd come out all broken down and sit in a bar telling war stories for the rest of your life."

"You really thought it all out," Lang said.

Gloria went on. "Where was I in this picture? I do ten years, come out a middle-aged hag who lost her looks. I'm lucky if I can peddle my ass at the Port Authority."

Lang shook his head, stubbornly. "It didn't have to be that way."

Finally, Gloria seemed to hear him. "Do you know one grifter who died of a ripe old age in a house in the country surrounded by his grandchildren? What's that fish that runs into the water and drowns?"

"How can a fish drown?" Lang said.

"Lemmings," Letitia said. "They're not fish, they're rats."

Gloria looked at Letitia as if she had forgotten she was there. "That's all you guys. You stay in the life even though you know it will kill you in the end."

Lang closed his eyes. "Okay, Gloria, I'm a lemming with nothin' goin' for me, but you still didn't have to give me up."

"It was your fault, Jerry," she said. "Remember how you used to tell me to scope a place out before a score?"

"Never go in anywhere cold," Lang said.

"I took your advice like I always did. Four days before the thing. I went up to the building on Central Park South for a quick look . . . Remember how you used to say, 'Be careful, even in a big city like New York you can meet yourself coming around the corner?' " Gloria's hands fluttered up from her lap and her voice rose. "I used to think that was more of your grifter crap, but it happened Jerry . . ." She took a breath and tried to lower her tone, but she was excited and the street crept back into her voice "All of a sudden there's these two big Russian guys on me, sweatin' bullets. 'You come with us,' they say.

"I learned when I was a kid if you can smell a guy's sweat he's gonna do somethin' crazy. They took me across the street into the buildin', right past Frick and Frack in the lobby, grinnin' and winkin' like I'm some hooker goin' up for a quickie.

"They take me up to this big floor through on the twelfth floor and I realize this is the place we're gonna hit. It looks like a showroom, Louis Quatorze furniture, crystal chandeliers, but the art is modern and all the pictures have lights over them so I guess they're expensive.

"There's a guy lookin' through a telescope at the window. He turns around and guess who it is, Jerry."

Lang shrugged and shook his head. "How should I know?"

"That Russian guy we beat for the diamonds in Vegas."

Lang looked stricken. "The guy at the Bellagio. The guy we hustled for the diamonds . . ."

"The same Sasha, you believe that? He was lookin' through his telescope and saw me down in the street. Sent his goons to get me. It was like you said, I met myself comin' around the corner."

Lang got that faraway look again. He seemed to be talking to himself. "So the whole thing ends up bein' one score too many."

"Like you said, a loser always presses his luck."

"I didn't think I was talkin' about myself," Lang said.

"So Sasha drags me into the bedroom," Gloria said. "He says, 'Take off your clothes.' He's got this gleam in his eye like he's really gonna humiliate me, but to me it's like yawn yawn I'm gonna drop my pants for another bozo. Then he pushes me down on the bed. 'You promised me something in Vegas, now I'm going to take it,' he says. He's all hot and brutal, but for me it's like another slob I gotta put up with for a coupla minutes."

She looked at Letitia for the first time. "No big deal, right honey?"

"She doesn't know what you're talkin' about," Lang said.

"Oh yes I do," Letitia said.

Gloria smiled and turned just enough to include her. "See he had watched me long enough to know that I was scopin' the building. So he wanted to know what's up."

"And you told him," Lang said.

"I had to."

"You wanted to," Lang said with sudden bitterness. "You were gonna cut me loose, you said so yourself. And now you fall into a guy in a floor through with a park view and the first thing he wants to do is jump you, so you know he's your bitch . . ."

"Didn't you always tell me 'If the thing goes south, take off and don't look back'?"

"Don't keep throwin' my words back at me. I never would have sold you out."

"I know that," Gloria said. "You're a much better person than I am." It didn't seem to bother her to admit it. "But I was lookin' to save myself just like you always told me to do so I told him everything."

A slight smile flitted around the corner of her mouth as she remembered. "You shoulda seen him, he was freaked. He kept shakin' his head, 'The Levitan, why the Levitan?' He walked me around the apartment. He was like, 'This is a Klimt, a Kandinsky, a Kokoschka, Schwitters, Balthus. You know how much these are worth?' I didn't know what he was talkin' about."

"But you do now," Lang said.

"Art is his passion," she said. "I've been to all the museums, all the dealers—they roll out the red carpet for him."

"You hit the big time," Lang said.

"They wouldn't even look at me first time a round. They thought I was just another bimbo." She wiggled the finger with the diamond engagement ring and the gold wedding band. "But when they saw these they put me on the mailing list. I get my own Christmas gifts now."

Lang winced. "Just the facts, Gloria . . ."

"Sorry Jerry," she said. "Anyways, he walked me into the little hallway and showed me the Levitan. He's like, 'This is my favorite piece, why do they want this?' He knew this was a personal thing that had somethin' to do with his past life. He got real agitated. Wanted to know who the buyer was. I told him Tony Rasso, but he said, 'No, he's just the middle man.' He was pacin' back and forth. His two boys watched his every move, their eyes followin' him like dogs."

Lang seemed to lose interest in the story. "You really fell into somethin', with this guy," he said.

Gloria's voice dropped to an awed whisper. "He's big, Jerry. He was a Russian spy and he made a deal with the US. He knows Putin. And big guys in Washington. I hear him on the phone droppin' names. He makes millions in oil contracts. He always seems to know when there's gonna be a blip in the price. He's hooked up with some secret agency, bigger than the CIA. He's got his own minder, some army guy who he can call any time day or night and the guy'll do anything he says. He's always goin' somewhere, Baku, Tashkent, all over Asia. Sometimes he takes me. You should see the dinners with his friends in London and Paris and Hong Kong. Private rooms in the best places. Champagne and caviar . . . They're mean lookin' bastards, his boys. They show up with the slut of the month, little tarts who sit like statues afraid to open their mouths."

"And what are you?" Lang asked.

"I'm his wife. He takes me by the arm, opens doors for me. I'm respected. His boys jump up when I come into the room."

Lang got an ugly look. "You think he don't go for the local talent when you're not around?"

"Sure he does, he's a man," Gloria said. She looked at Letitia for confirmation. "But I make him get checked out when he comes home. He don't get a handshake without a doctor's note."

Lang looked out of the window. "My radar's goin' off. Somebody's around."

"Don't worry, I don't have bodyguards," Gloria said. "Hartung doesn't care what happens to me."

Lang's head jerked around. "Who?"

"Major Hartung. That's the guy I was tellin' you about. He was the first guy Sasha called."

"What does this Hartung look like?" Jerry asked.

"Army guy. Big, blonde buzz cut, tough guy."

"He was in the hotel room that night."

Gloria nodded. "That was him. He planned the whole thing."

Lang shook his head with a baffled look. "You mean we had the feds on our case?"

"Bigger than the feds, Jerry. They do what they want, nobody says boo. In the whole city you couldn't have picked a worse guy to rob than Sasha."

"Yeah, I'm startin' to get it," Lang said. "They set up this sting. And you helped them."

Gloria nodded in a matter of fact way. "That's right. Hartung showed up so fast it was like he'd been waitin' downstairs. Sasha made me tell him the whole thing all over again. This guy's a hick, Jerry. He sat there lookin' at me like I was the biggest piece of garbage in the world. Then he and Sasha went into another room.

"A coupla minutes later the Russians come and got me. Hartung did the talking. 'How long you been with this guy Lang?' he asks, sayin' your name like it was another word for dog shit. So I tell him five years. He comes and stands over me. 'Then it's time for a change, wouldn't you say?' He's lookin' hard at me and I realize if I blow this answer I'm dead. So I tell him,

'Yeah it's time for a change.'

"Then Sasha took over. Very smooth, holdin' my hand. First he tells me he's some kinda spy for the government and his identity can't be revealed. Then he says I have to do what they tell me or Hartung will kill you and me in a heartbeat."

Lang shot another suspicious look out of the window. Letitia followed his eyes to a black Tahoe across the street with its hood up. A man was fiddling with the radiator cap, his face hidden.

"What was the plan?" Lang asked.

"To let the burglary go down. Bust you at the drop. Make it look like somebody had snitched."

"And you went along with this," Lang said. "You came home to me and never said nothin' about it. You lied to me for a week."

"Four days . . . And I didn't lie. I just didn't tell you."

"We hung out like always. You slept with me." Lang looked at her in wonderment. "I'm the king of paranoia and I never copped to it."

"I'm good at hidin' my feelings."

"Did you hide them with me, Gloria? All the time we were together."

Gloria gestured at Letitia. "I feel funny talkin' about this in front of her."

"Your boy said he would go easy on me, didn't he?"

"He said he could get you a deal," Gloria said. "He would let you plead to a lesser charge."

"They tried to kill me, Gloria," Lang said.

"That got all messed up, Jerry. They thought you'd cave when you saw they had me, but instead you went crazy and shot that cop."

"Is that what your boy told you, Gloria?"

She stared hard at him. "You wanna stop calling him my boy."

"They were gonna say I was shot resisting arrest. That didn't work so they tried to kill me in jail."

Gloria's eyes narrowed. "Who did?"

"Sasha did. Your little bitch had a scheme on the side like all little bitches. I knew who he really was, a greaseball peddlin' swag in Vegas. I could make trouble."

Gloria shook her head, doggedly. "Sasha wouldn't do that."

"Ask him, you'll know if he's lyin'. They made four tries on me . . ."

Gloria put her hand over her eyes. "He promised he wouldn't hurt you."

He pulled her hand away. Tears glistened on her lashes.

"I thought you were dead," Lang said.

"I didn't know . . ."

"You coulda come visit me."

"He would never have let me."

"C'mon, you can do anything you want with this guy."

"Okay, okay, I didn't wanna see you. I was done with that dumb nickel dime life."

"Can't blame you for that," Lang said. "You like this guy better than me."

Gloria took a deep, trembling breath. "He's good to me, Jerry."

"Who wouldn't be?"

"He married me, without a prenup."

"He don't need one. If you get outta line he'll get his army buddy to clip you."

"He's good to my mother," Gloria said, as if that were ultimate proof. "He bought her a condo in Boca. She sits around the pool bragging about her rich son-in-law. He flies her up for Thanksgiving and Christmas, gives her charge cards . . ."

Lang raised his hands in mock surrender. "Good to your mother, huh. That's the cheapest trick in the book." He looked out of the window again and turned to Letitia with a smile. "See that guy across the street? He's been workin' on his car for a long time." He patted her hand. "What are you holdin' onto?"

Letitia realized she'd been squeezing the seat so tightly her knuckles were white.

"Relax," Lang said. "We're gonna get a payday out of this if it kills me." He fished a cell phone out of Gloria's purse. "Get Sasha on the phone. We'll see how much he really loves you."

Gloria punched out a number and handed the phone to Lang.

"Hey Sasha, this is Jerry Lang," he said. "What's up?"

"You Bumbler!

In any decent country you'd be shot for incompetence."

Lubimov had called Hartung, screaming curses in Russian before he calmed down enough to insult him in English.

Hartung stayed cool. When the client loses it you go to the other extreme. "We're bringing the situation under control, Colonel," he said.

"Under control? He took my wife right out from under your nose."

"I know, I was right behind him when he did it."

"Then why didn't you stop him?"

It was déjà vu all over again. Smart as he was there were things about America Lubimov couldn't get through his head.

"As I've told you before, the streets belong to the local police here. They don't answer to us. Besides, as you know, our group is not supposed to exist and we certainly can't trust the New York cops to keep our secret."

Lubimov's voice broke in anguish. "But how could this have happened?"

This guy could have any woman he wanted, but he was in love with a thieving little whore who had robbed him once and had been planning to do it again. He had taken her into his life, but he had to lie in bed next to her wondering when she would betray him again. Hartung remembered the psych warfare instructor at Bragg, who used to tap his teeth with a pencil when he lectured. "Sexual obsession is a powerful tool," he said.

"Use it, but don't try to understand it." Now after the insults and the threats he realized Lubimov was in his power. The consequences of failure were much greater for him. He would lose his wife, while Hartung was only facing demotion and transfer. The master had to placate the servant.

"It was a series of uncanny coincidences, Colonel," Hartung said.

"Yes." Lubimov sighed wistfully. "In the old system such men as Lang were not permitted to exist. Stalin had a saying, 'A person, a problem, no person, no problem.' "

"Lang is a very resourceful criminal," Hartung said. "But he's cornered now. His luck has run out."

"Forgive my impatience, Major," Lubimov said in a plaintive tone.

"Perfectly understandable," Hartung said.

"Do you have any idea where they might be?"

"I'm across the street from them right now. I'm looking right at Lang."

Lubimov's voice rose urgently. "Then you can kill him now."

"Can't use a sniper scope on Columbus Avenue. If I rush the car, the bullet might go through him and hit her or a passerby. Or he could see me and kill her on the spot . . ."

"Alright, alright," Lubimov said in agony. "Do you have a plan?"

"A plan and a back up," Hartung said. The back up part was a lie, but you always said you had one. "What does he want from you?"

"The Levitan," Lubimov said. "He wants to trade it for Gloria."

"Okay, how'd you leave it?"

"He's going to call in five minutes."

The BMW slid away from the curb.

"Okay, he's on his way," Hartung said. He slammed the hood

down and jumped into the Tahoe. "Cooperate. Give him whatever he wants any way he wants it."

"Be careful, Major," Lubimov said.

"Always . . ." Hartung disconnected and pulled out. There was no time for subtlety. You need alternating vehicles for surveillance like this, but he didn't have them. It would be a little easier on a broad boulevard with a lot of intervening traffic. Most targets checked directly behind them in their rear view mirrors to see if they were being followed. If you stayed parallel they might not pick up the tail.

Hartung called Stewart. "He's going back down Columbus toward the building. What are you carrying?"

"The Beretta nine," Stewart said.

That gun was specially made for the military. The bullets had distinctive markings. It was one in a million that NYPD Forensics would put them through the ATF database, but he couldn't take the chance.

Hartung conferenced in to Osler. He had a Beretta as well. "Weren't you issued a street gun?" Hartung asked.

"I put in a requisition last year, sir. Never got it."

Hartung pushed a spring under the glove compartment. There was an old Army .45 on clamps. The guys at Ordnance had told him New York bad guys bought Army surplus weapons in South Carolina. But still, an old .45 on a crowded street in the hands of a hysterical wiseguy with one good eye, who probably hadn't fired anything in years. Christ!

The BMW merged onto Broadway.

"Watch out for the black BMW," Hartung said. "Stewart, put yourself directly across the street. Osler, east of it. You each know what you have to do."

They both chimed in. "Yes sir."

"THERE'S A BROKEN HEART
FOR EVERY LIGHT

on Broadway," Lang said. "Ever hear that saying, Letitia?"

"No," Letitia said.

"It's a good thing to know for someone contemplating a career on the legitimate stage," he said.

Gloria looked at him, suspiciously. "You're in a good mood all of a sudden."

"I feel a lot better after our little talk." He fiddled with the side mirror. "You see that black Tahoe, Letitia?"

She had been watching it all along. "It's a few cars behind us on the other side of the street."

"Good eyes," Lang said. "This girl's a quick study like you, Gloria. Gimme six months with her and we'd be set for the rest of our lives. I'm tellin' ya there's more money in this city than there ever was. More stuff to steal and easier, too, with all these security guys and alarm systems. What did I always tellya, Gloria?"

Gloria brushed at his words like pesky flies. "Did you mean what you said before, Jerry?"

"Y' mean about shooting you and putting the gun in my mouth? I think I did. I guess we'll have to wait and see if Sasha and his boys get paramilitary . . ."

"They won't," Gloria said.

"Letitia has to do her job, too."

"I will," Letitia said.

"Oh I know you will. That's the difference between Letitia

and us, Gloria. If the shoe was on the other foot, if I let you outta this car and told you if you don't bring me that Levitan I'll kill Letitia, what would you do?"

"I'd take off and wouldn't look back," Gloria said. "Just like you taught me."

Lang went around Columbus Circle. "But I'm lettin' Letitia out and tellin' her, 'If you don't bring me that Levitan I'll kill Gloria' and she's gonna do it. Letitia's got a conscience. She thinks she'll be haunted the rest of her life if she lets us die to save herself. She don't know that you can do something really bad and live with it. Even if you killed four hundred crippled children you can convince yourself that they deserved it."

Gloria squinted at Lang like she was trying to read a distant sign. "Why are you talking so much, Jerry?"

"I got a captive audience," Lang said with a laugh. "See, in the joint everybody talks at once, you can't get a word in edgewise. I never met so many smart guys in one place in my life. Everybody in jail's a genius, just ask 'em . . ."

He pulled in front of a hydrant on Central Park South a few doors down from the building. He turned as the black Tahoe zoomed past. "There's our friend, Major Hartung."

In the Tahoe, Hartung scanned the street for an empty space. He had started making a list when he got to New York, THINGS THEY DON'T TEACH YOU IN SPY SCHOOL. Now he had a new entry: What to do when you can't find a place to park. Every hydrant, bus stop, and drop off zone was taken. Limos and delivery trucks were double-parked. There were NYPD vehicles stationed at the main entrance to Central Park; a U-turn would bring them down on him.

What you do is travel with a back up driver so he can take the car while you get out and work on foot. But with a small squad it means sacrificing coverage of another area. You can also use a car with phony plates that can be towed without being traced back to you. Everything will end up costing money.

Hartung saw Stewart on the park side lining up across from the BMW. Further down he passed Osler and Rasso in the van. He pulled up alongside.

"I'm going to have to go around the block and come up behind Lang," he said into the phone. "I'll be out of contact for awhile." He rolled his passenger window down, leaned over, and handed the .45 to Osler. How to pass a weapon on a crowded street. More THINGS THEY DON'T TEACH YOU IN SPY SCHOOL. The trick was to carry the weapon in a fast food bag so it wouldn't attract attention.

A taxi horn blared behind him. He stuck his hand out of the window and gave the driver the finger to look like a normal New Yorker.

In the van, Osler pulled back the slide of the .45 and took a bullet out of the chamber. He slipped out the magazine and handed the empty gun to Rasso.

"Fuckin' elephant gun," Rasso said.

"Don't worry, you'll be right in his face," Osler said. "You gotta hold it with two hands to steady it."

"I know how to shoot," Rasso said.

"You need full arm extension," Osler said. He took the gun back and demonstrated.

A man in a tuxedo carrying a cello case passed and looked in for a moment, then hurried on, head down.

"You aim right along the sight," Osler said. "The gun's gonna jump so you shoot low to compensate. Don't try to take his head off or you'll blow out a penthouse window. Aim for his balls and you'll get him right in the gut Squeeze twice. One one thousand . . . two."

"I wanna talk to Steve," Rasso said. Osler got Hartung on the phone.

"I'm stuck at a light on Seventh and Fifty-seventh," Hartung said.

Osler switched on the speaker. "Mr. Rasso has a few questions about his assignment . . ."

Rasso cut in. "Shoot a guy on a crowded street in the middle of the day? Is this your brilliant strategy?"

"That part sucks," Hartung said. "But here's the brilliant part. If you flake out at the last second, Mr. X sitting next to you and his African-American friend Mr. Y will kill you on the spot and then collect a medal at City Hall for stopping a Mafia captain with a .45 and a pocket full of cocaine from kidnapping the wife of a prominent philanthropist. So it's a win-win for us."

"What about me?" Rasso said.

"You're still boxed. But if you do your job right we'll get you out in one piece. I'm gonna try to make this light. Reveal the rest of the brilliant plan, Mr. X."

Osler switched off the speaker. "You drill this guy, hop back in the car, and we'll hang a screamin' huey before anybody knows what happened," he said. "We'll shoot up Central Park West and across town on the Sixty-fifth Street transverse. You jump out on Fifth, catch a cab home in time to watch it on the news . . ."

"Yeah, yeah," Rasso said. He felt in his pocket. "Can I take a pick me up?"

"Try one of mine." Osler handed him a little green capsule.

"What's this?"

"We call it a 'go' pill. Makes your cocaine look like aspirin."

Rasso swallowed the pill. "How long before it kicks in?"

"It just did," Osler said.

Rasso blinked and shuddered. "Is this what they give you guys in Iraq?"

"Pilots on long flights," Osler said. "Delta ops who have to stay sharp for forty-eight hours without sleep . . ."

"Shit!" Rasso laughed crazily. "It's the Indy 500 . . ."

"That's the ramp," Osler said. "It'll smooth down to a low roar."

"Shit!" Rasso rocked back and forth.

"They don't pay us a lot, but they give us fun toys," Osler said.

Rasso leaned in with a confidential whisper. "You could make a fortune on this, kid. I know people in Holly wood who'd pay a grand a pill."

"It's not for the riff raff, Tony," Osler said. "We keep it in the family."

"One of these days one of your family is gonna put it out on the street."

"Never happen, Tony. We're a tight group."

"Tight group huh?" Rasso looked at him with disdain, his arrogance restored by the little green pill. "You guys are a pisser."

"I Just had a Vision,"

Lang said. He turned to Letitia, his eyes shining. "You're opening on Broadway. Somethin' real heavy like Shakespeare, but
they're puttin' it on anyway 'cause you're a big star and they
know people will come. Gloria, you're front row center. When
Letitia comes out on stage to a round of applause you two
make eye contact and there's this little nod like, 'Would anyone
believe how we know each other?' "

"Where are you while this is goin' on?" Gloria asked.

"I'm on Maui sellin' wind up hula dolls. That's the happy
ending to this little drama."

He reached around and opened the back door. "You know
what to do."

"Get the drawing and leave," Letitia said. "Don't talk or
answer any questions. Make a left out of the building and walk
toward Columbus Circle. Don't look back no matter what happens."

"Go," Lang said. "I'll see you later."

Letitia's legs wobbled as she hit the sidewalk. The young
doorman held the door for her.

"Back again?"

"Yes," she said, "this is the apartment I was supposed to see
after all."

He followed her in. "Mrs. Lubimov just left."

"Mr. Lubimov is expecting me," she said.

The two doormen exchanged knowing looks. Frick and

Frack, she thought, just like Gloria had said.

"Who shall I say is calling again?" the old one asked.

"Mrs. Lang," she said.

"Mrs. Lang's here," he said into the house phone and then gave her the deadpan look. "Go right up, they're waiting."

The young guy pushed the button for her. The elevator creaked and wobbled up to the twelfth floor. The door opened onto a bald, sallow man with weary eyes in a soiled white shirt and black suit pants. He walked her through a vestibule into a large living room. A young guy with massive arms bulging out of a tank top was sitting on a white couch channel surfing on plasma TV. He looked at her, then went back to the remote.

"Is this Mrs. Lang?"

A dark haired man in a blue silk shirt, beige slacks, and Gucci loafers came down the hallway carrying a Petrossian shopping bag. His eyes were unreadable behind tinted glasses.

"New York seems to have an inexhaustible supply of beautiful young women who will do anything for money," he said. "Or is it just Mr. Lang?"

Letitia thought of something Jamie had said in acting class. "Never play Irony. Play what it is trying to hide."

Lubimov was trying to hide fear. He knew better than to let his hands shake or his voice crack, but the unconvincing irony gave it away.

"Tell Mr. Lang he is being watched," he said.

She nodded.

"Tell him if anything happens to Gloria I will personally hunt him down and cut his balls off . . ."

She nodded.

Lubimov handed her the shopping bag. Inside was a drawing of a young man with a wispy beard.

He spat out something in Russian. The gray-faced man rang for the elevator.

"Good bye, Mrs. Lang," Lubimov said.

She rode down with an old lady in a mink coat and cloche hat with two rouge spots on her weathered cheeks. The young doorman jumped when he saw her. "Your car's here, Mrs. Herman."

"Thanks Johnny," she croaked.

Letitia walked toward Columbus Circle. The black Tahoe nosed next to a fire hydrant. She could see the big blonde guy talking into a cell phone.

She walked on without turning back.

LANG SAW LETITIA

come out of the building.

"Done," he said to Gloria.

"You takin' the car?" she asked.

"Nah, I'll be better off walkin' in this traffic." He opened the door. "You gonna have kids with Sasha?"

Gloria made a face. "You kiddin'?"

"Give you a little extra leverage."

"He could care less. He's got two daughters in Moscow he never sees."

"What are you gonna do when he dumps you?"

"I'll get a settlement. Plus he gives me my own money so I won't bug him. I got a broker to buy bonds just like you used to do. I'm up to four hundred thousand."

"Unearned income," Lang said. "That's what I was shootin' for."

He looked in the rearview mirror. Letitia was almost out of sight. "Funny the way things twist and turn. I went crazy when I thought you were dead. Stayed up nights plannin' how I was gonna get even. But that turned out good. You need something to keep you focused in the joint, otherwise you start goin' to war over dirty looks."

"So I guess it would have been better for you if I really was dead," Gloria said.

"No. Because I was blamin' myself. Night after night I went over everything I'd ever done. I realized I had messed up a lotta

268

people. I didn't mean to, but I did. I felt real bad because about you because I . . ."

Gloria turned away. "Don't say it Jerry."

"Okay, I won't," Lang said. "I thought you woulda been better off if you had never met me. But now I see it was good that we hooked up. Because you never would of met Sasha."

Gloria looked out of the window. "What's goin' on, Jerry? What are you lookin' at?"

Lang got out of the car and leaned in the window. "Stay in the car for awhile," he said.

"When should I get out?"

"You'll know when," Lang said, and closed the door.

"LET'S EXECUTE CORRECTLY,"

Hartung said into the phone "Lang just hit the sidewalk and is coming toward me."

Hartung got out of the Tahoe. He was hoping Lang would see him and turn to run away. If not he would have to call out his name and take some overt action which might draw the attention of potential witnesses.

Lang sauntered past the building as if he didn't have a care in the world. Hartung moved directly in front of him, trying to get into his eye line. Lang looked everywhere, but in his direction.

Is this dude playing with me?

"Hey Jerry," he called.

Lang saw him and stopped.

Hartung beckoned.

Lang shook his head and turned walking quickly in the other direction.

"He's coming your way," Hartung said.

In the van, Osler slipped the clip into the .45 and handed it to Rasso. "Keep him on your left so you can see out of your good eye," he said.

"Relax kid, I've done this a coupla times," Rasso said. The pill had made him aggressive. He shrugged out of his jacket. "Start the motor now and keep it runnin'. I don't want you to get nervous and stall out."

Osler started the motor. He concentrated on the side mirror. As soon as Lang came into view he nudged Rasso. "Go Tony." "Too soon," Rasso said. "Gotta be sure he's so close he's got no place to run." He gave it another long second. "Now," he said. He got out of the van and threw his jacket over his arm, hiding the gun.

Across the street, Stewart saw Rasso moving toward Lang.

A little Latina cop, maybe five two and looking like she was weighed down by all her equipment, came walking by.

"Yo officer," Stewart shouted, pointing across the street, "there's a guy with a gun over there. The guy with the jacket over his arm."

The cop looked and walked across the street, reaching for her walkie.

On the street Tony moved along the parked cars until Lang was almost on top of him. Then he stepped out.

"Jerry."

Lang walked toward him, spreading his arms as if for a hug. "Tony . . . So you're the one."

Tony pulled the jacket off. His hand was steady, everything was clear. He aimed low and squeezed. BLAM! The street went quiet like everybody was taking a breath. Lang doubled over.

Tony counted one one thousand and BLAM!

Lang jerked. He fell on his back and rolled onto his stomach, clawing at the sidewalk.

The explosion faded out of Tony's ears and he heard the screams of the passersby. He ran out into the street. The van was pulling away.

"Hey."

It picked up speed. The guy was ditching him.

"You motherfucker!" He fired, shattering the back window.

He fired again, tearing a hole in the tailgate.

"Freeze!"

He turned slowly. The motor whirred in his head like a gun on a turret.

A little lady cop was on one knee in the middle of the street, gun pointed at him. Before he could raise his arm he took a blow to the chest like a horse had kicked him. He went "whoof" and tried to catch his breath. Then another kick. The gun flew out of his hands. He watched it climb in the air, turning over and over. He never saw it come down.

A crowd gathered around Lang. Everybody was on a cell phones calling 911. In seconds sirens were shrieking. The cops ran up and cleared the area. "Keep movin' please . . . Give him some air." Lang was holding his stomach with one hand, while the other clawed at the sidewalk like he was trying to scale a wall.

"Oh my God, he's trying to talk," a woman said.

MOM WOKE JERRY

early in the morning. "We're goin' to visit Uncle Jimmy at the beach." The thought of a whole day away from his boys on the street was agony to him, but he had to go because Uncle Jimmy was rich and Mom wanted to stay in good with him.

Mom gave him a strawberry Pop Tart and an ice cold Carnation Instant Breakfast. They met Grandma on Forty-ninth and Seventh. Grandma and Mom lit Newports—"Better have one for the road"—before they went down to the subway. They took the A train to 116th Street in Rockaway. When they got out, Grandma smoked another cigarette while Mom went to the phone. In a few minutes Aunt Grace pulled up in a white Chrysler Imperial. She turned up the AC. Mom and Grandma sank gratefully into the back seat—"What a treat"—but Jerry caught a blast of frigid air right in the face.

Uncle Jimmy lived in a big white house on the beach block in Belle Harbor, the fancy part of Rockaway. They had a lot of dark furniture and a big TV. Uncle Jimmy was watching the news and hardly moved when they came in. "Hey Mom, hey Sis. Hey big guy. What are you feedin' this kid, he's big as a house."

"He's gonna be twelve next week, Jimmy," Mom said.

Aunt Grace brought out her special chocolate chip cookies. They were always raw in the middle and Jerry was feeling sick from the hot subway ride and the freezing trip in Aunt Grace's car. "Don't worry, I can always whip up another batch," Aunt

Grace said. Mom glared at him so he took another.

Mom wanted to take him to the rides at Rockaway Playland, but Uncle Jimmy said "the niggers take it over on the weekends" so they walked down to the beach. Jerry carried Aunt Grace's umbrella and the beach chairs. When they got to the beach he had to take his sneakers off so they wouldn't bring sand back into the house. His bare feet were burning, but he had to help put up the umbrella and the chairs before he could run down to the cool wet part by the shore.

He had a sharp pain in the pit of his stomach, but knew Mom would get mad if he told her.

Two guys were throwing a Spaldeen around with their sons. They started a game of running bases. "C'mon kid, you wanna play?"

The kids played running bases in the schoolyard and Jerry was real good at it. The guys couldn't tag him out. They laughed about it at first. Then one of them ran out and grabbed him, squeezing his shoulders while the other slammed a hard tag on his head.

"Let's play errors," they shouted and started throwing high pops to the kids. First one to miss would be out. But after Jerry caught a few they stopped throwing them to him and he walked away, tears burning in his eyes. By the time he got back to the blanket his stomach hurt so bad he could hardly stand up.

"Look, there's your cousin Agnes," Grandma said.

A novice nun dressed in a gray habit with a white collar was trudging through the sand toward them, her white face framed like a cameo by the cowl.

"Hi Aunt Maureen, hiya Grandma." She kissed Mom and Grandma.

"Say hi to your Cousin Agnes, Jerry," Mom said.

"He doesn't recognize me," Agnes said. "He hasn't seen me since I went into the convent. I used to take care of you

Christmas and Easter, Jerry. We'd eat Oreos and watch TV, while the grown ups got drunk, remember?"

"What's the matter with you anyway?" Mom asked sharply.

The pain was so bad he felt like crying. "My stomach hurts."

"Do you have to go the bathroom, sweetie?" Aunt Grace asked. "Go back to the house. Uncle Jimmy will let you in."

"Dad'll never hear the bell," Agnes said. "I'll take him. C'mon, Jerry . . ."

Her hand was cool and dry. "Put your sneakers on. Don't worry, Mom, we'll clean them out before we go into the house . . . My dad hates sand," she explained to him. "Even if you get a little in the car he goes crazy." She laughed. "I don't know why he moved to the beach."

She held his hand as they walked down the street. It was embarrassing, but he didn't know anybody around there so it was okay. "I'm at Saint Joseph's now in a medical order," she said. "I hope to be a nurse in an African mission . . ." She laughed and tousled his hair. "Is it okay if I practice on you?"

In the house, Uncle Jimmy was watching the Yankee game.

"Jerry's got a stomachache," Agnes said.

"Give him a shot of Coke syrup and a coupla Tums," Uncle Jimmy said.

Agnes took him upstairs to her room. There was a cross with Jesus writhing over her bed. "Now you know how our Lord felt," she said. "Thank God it's only a gas bubble, he had something a lot worse."

Was she joking? It was a sin to make light of the Crucifixion.

"Let's get your shirt off," she said, slipping it over his head. She poked his chest. "See how the skin goes white and then red. That means you've got a burn. We got you out of the sun just in time."

She took off her cowl and shook out her long blonde hair. "There, do you recognize me now?"

She made him lie on his stomach. The sheets were cool and had a fresh lemony smell. She leaned over him, pressing down on his shoulder blades. "Gas is trapped in your stomach right up to your esophagus," she said. "We just have to push it down and out."

Her hands were strong and she pressed deeply. He felt funny about this nun touching him, but she was a nurse so it had to be okay. He closed his eyes. It was so quiet he could hear the murmur of the TV downstairs. The springs creaked. The air conditioner hummed.

She worked her way down his back, pushing harder and harder. He tried not to grunt, afraid that if he made a noise she would stop.

She pulled his trunks down under the small of his back. Her nails grazed his buttocks. He shuddered. His dick started creeping up along his stomach.

Agnes ran her nails up his back and traced "Jerry" under his shoulder blade.

"What did I write?"

"Jerry," he said. His dick was throbbing so hard he could hear it in his head. He prayed she wouldn't notice.

Now she traced, "Agnes . . ."

"What does that say?"

"Agnes . . ."

She leaned down, her breath warm in his ear. "How do you feel now, Jerry?"

The little Latina cop looked up at her sergeant. "That's weird. I asked him how he felt. 'Real good Agnes,' he said."

"Famous last words," the sergeant said. He took a few shots with his camera phone for his private collection of homicide scenes.

A blonde stopped at the edge of the crowd. "Let's keep it

movin' folks," the sergeant said. Everybody walked on, but the blonde stood there staring fixedly at the wounded man.

"He's gone, Sarge," the Latina cop said.

A doorman brought out a black garbage bag and they covered Lang's face.

When the sergeant turned the blonde was gone.

"THE OPERATION WAS A SUCCESS,"

Hartung said. "The patients died."

"Has it hit the news yet?" the Voice asked.

"I'm watching it on my cell phone," Hartung said. "They broke in with a bulletin. Wait'll they find out it's a Mafia captain and an escaped convict. They'll go nuts."

Was he hearing things or did the Voice actually chuckle?

"Have you checked in with our Russian friend?"

"No hurry. He'll just say we should have taken care of this two years ago."

"Right . . ." There was a silence and Hartung knew the Voice was struggling with a compliment.

"Your men did well," he said.

Hartung kept his tone calm like this was just another day at the office, but he was exulting inside. "This was a good training run for them," he said.

"Well, it certainly was textbook," the Voice said. "The perfect way to execute a complicated operation without leaving a fingerprint."

"We were lucky," Hartung said.

Another silence.

He's trying to figure out how he can coattail my success.

"Could you break this operation down into components and make a case study out of it?" the Voice asked.

"I think so," Hartung said.

"Okay because I'm going to recommend that you go TDY to

the War College. You could lecture and work up a research paper. You'd get a bird on your shoulder . . ."

In the Army no one ever did anything for you unless they got something out of it. If Hartung got a promotion the Voice would get one too, maybe from colonel to general, which was the hardest jump to make.

"It will be a chance to get your kids out of the city," the Voice said.

"Actually, they're doing pretty well here," Hartung said.

"Really . . ." The Voice was sensing resistance. "How about your wife? Isn't she kind of a fish out of water?"

"She likes all the different restaurants, the things to do. Once you've been in New York for a while it's hard to go anywhere else."

There was another silence.

He's looking for a button to push.

"You know from a career point of view it's best to make hay while the sun shines," the Voice said. "If you stay on I can't promise you the promotion, plus there's always the risk you'll mess up the next operation and all your good work will be forgotten."

"I'll take that chance," Hartung said. "I'm committed to the mission."

It was the no lose line. The higher ups knew it was a lie, but they didn't dare contradict it.

"Frankly, I didn't think you'd get addicted to New York." The Voice wasn't happy. The Voice was a sore loser. "But if it's what you want. I'll extend you another twenty-six months at this post before you come up for review. That is, if you don't fuck up before then."

"Thank you sir, I'll try not to," Hartung said.

He got Osler and Stewart on a conference call.

"You guys celebrating?"

"I'm kinda tired, sir," Osler said. "Think I'll just grab a burger and go home."

"I'm gonna see my aunt in Queens, sir," Stewart said.

Smart veterans, they kept it correct around their commander.

"The boss says you did good work," Hartung said. "Coming from him that's the Medal of Honor."

"Thank you for communicating that sir," Osler said.

"I'm stickin' around for another two years, but I can get you guys transferred if you want out of New York."

"Not me sir," Osler said. "I'm still committed to the mission."

"Me too, sir," Stewart said.

They knew better than to say they were happy in the city because the Army never kept you in a detail you liked. So they used the same no lose line.

"Okay, then you're stuck with me," Hartung said.

"Looking forward to it, sir."

Now it was Hartung's turn to chuckle.

Yeah, right.

Letitia Heard the Shots,

but kept walking.

On Ninth Avenue people stopped to watch the police cars shriek and weave through traffic onto Fifty-seventh Street.

Her apartment was quiet. The five black garbage bags in the afternoon shadows could have been full of laundry or canned goods for the Thanksgiving food drive they used to have at school every year.

Every station was running the story. CNN and Fox had helicopters hovering over the park showing traffic snarled, police stringing yellow crime scene ribbon across the street to the park side and forcing westbound cars to turn back. The body in the street was covered with a gray horse blanket. The body on the sidewalk had a black garbage bag over its head.

"That makes six black garbage bags," she said. Her voice sounded harsh in her ears.

She found Tessler's card and called his cell.

"Are you alright?" he asked. "Those two men . . ."

"Nothing to do with us," she said.

"You have the Levitan?"

"You have the money?"

"Tomorrow morning."

"I'll call you," she said.

She clicked around the channels. Watched the anchors with their grave expressions. The same cops, the same two bodies in different angles.

She had that wedding ring that Tessler had given her. She stared at that until she didn't know what it was anymore.

Her hands and fingers didn't seem connected.

She went into the bathroom. Lang had cleaned the bathtub and stacked the knives and cleavers in a gleaming pile by the toilet. She looked at her face in the medicine cabinet mirror.

"Who am I?" she said.

Then she lay down on the couch and waited for night to fall.

HARTUNG WENT SHOPPING

on Queens Boulevard. His last stop was the florist where he bought a dozen red roses.

Beverly was in the kitchen, poring over a cookbook. He swooped in and kissed her on the neck.

"You're home early."

"Boring day." He sniffed. "Place smells like an opium den."

"I started that ethnic cooking class at the Jewish Center today," she said. "I've been experimenting with curry . . . That okay?"

"As long as you wear a sari. But first, sound Assembly."

"Yes sir." Beverly gave him a left-handed salute. "Kids," she called. "Your father wants to talk to you."

Amy bounded out of her room and jumped into his arms. "Hey, Daddy, did Mom tell you?"

"Yeah, the coach came to his senses."

"You know that Russian girl, Alana . . ."

"I thought she hated you, Amy," Hartung said.

"That was yesterday," Beverly said. "Today Amy's the most popular girl in town. Alana's dad called the coach and insisted that they make her a striker."

Warren came out of his room, eyes bloodshot, lips greasy from chips. He gave Hartung that "this better be worth it" look.

"I got some news today," Hartung said. "They're extending my tour in New York. We'll be here for another twenty-six months."

Warren jumped and clapped like he used to when he was a happy toddler, running on chubby legs to his dad.

"Sweet! Yes!"

But Beverly was suspicious.

"What's the catch?"

Hartung draped his arm around her. "Stop being such an Army wife. This is all upside."

He handed out the presents. Warren got a boxed set of *Matrix* DVDs and a Texas Hold 'em computer game.

"Sweet Dad, really sweet," he said.

He gave Amy a pair of shin guards, super lightweight, and a Mia Hamm poster. She smiled, but he could see she was disappointed.

Beverly squeezed his hand. "Hate to tell you, Dad, but she's at the age where she'd rather have David Beckham in her room."

"Not my little girl."

Warren had run back to his computer. "Gotta get back on."

His room smelled of stale food and dirty socks. Books, magazines, DVDs, and CDs were thick on the floor.

"We're tracking that shooting," Warren said.

"The one that tied up traffic all over the city?" Hartung asked.

"Yeah, it's big. A Mafia guy named Tony Rasso shot this guy Jerry Lang who just broke out of jail a couple of days ago."

Hartung was surprised the names had gotten out so fast.

"How do you know that? I didn't hear it on the news."

Warren got a secretive look. "Can't tell you, Dad, it's confidential."

Beverly poked him. "Getting a taste of your own medicine."

"You can trust me, Warren," Hartung said lightly. "I've got a security clearance."

Warren beamed. "Well, me and my friend Avigdor in 3A hacked into the Manhattan South Homicide Bureau. Now we can read their emails."

The nosepickers will definitely inherit the earth.

"That's amazing," Hartung said. "How'd you do it?"

"Well, first we went on the their web page and got the names of all the detectives in the squad," Warren said. "Then we Googled them and used this software to get their Socials. When you have the Social you can get the address, date of birth, home phone, and dates of birth. You collect a database of numbers. You input them until you come up with their passwords . . ."

"You did all that on your little computer?" Hartung asked.

Warren's eyes narrowed. He lowered his head like a turtle retreating into its shell. "Mom said you'd get me a G5 with a Tiger."

Beverly pulled him out of the room. "Let's keep the good feelings going. We'll talk about this tomorrow."

Warren's door slammed shut as they walked down the hall.

"That was a short ceasefire," Hartung said.

"He thinks you trapped him," Beverly said.

"The kid can hack into the Homicide Bureau with a four hundred dollar Dell," Hartung said. "What's he going to do with a G5, launch a satellite?"

"I don't know and I don't care. I've had enough of that genius for one day." She tugged on his arm and pouted. "Where's my present?"

"Aren't I enough?"

He had left the roses and a bottle of Veuve Cliquot outside in the hall. Now he opened the door and produced them with a flourish.

"Ooh, champagne," Beverly said. She nuzzled the roses. "What's the occasion?"

"I think I'm getting a bump up to lieutenant colonel."

"My hero." Beverly had way of leaning into him that felt like her body was merging into his. "You deserve a special commendation."

She unbuttoned his shirt. "I was thinking about you today."

"See a Brad Pitt movie?"

"I was thinking about how great you were with Amy last night. And how hard you try with Warren."

"Can't we do something about his room?"

"Forget his room for a second."

She kissed his nipple, rubbing her lips gently against it until he felt a chill in the small of his back.

"The champagne's gonna get warm," he said.

"We'll put it on ice."

She hooked her fingers into his belt and led him into the bedroom. "C'mon big boy . . ."

"Maybe we should wait until the kids are asleep."

She closed the door "They won't bother us."

She dropped to her knees and pulled his zipper down with her teeth.

"There are girls making five thousand dollars an hour in Vegas who can't do that," he said.

"Let's go to Vegas," she whispered. "You can be my pimp."

She pulled his pants down and slid her tongue up his thigh, squeezing his buttocks gently.

I'm gonna go off like a smart bomb. Gotta hold back.

He thought of Lubimov in that big apartment pleading through a locked bedroom door for forgiveness. And here he was getting a blowjob just for being a good dad.

Oh God, I'm goin'.

Beverly held his balls like she was trying to guess their weight. His knees shook like jelly.

I wonder if those nosepickers can hack into the NYPD Terrorist Squad.

The Bang Woke Letitia.

It was a steel security gate hitting the pavement. The Hunan Taste was closing for the night. The light went out and the sidewalk went dark. She watched the weary Chinese walk off in different directions.

It was midnight. There were no bars or late night restaurants on the block. The street was as quiet as it would ever be.

She needed two hands for each bag. One seemed to have both heads in it. She dragged them out one by one onto the landing. Could leave them under the stairs for the super to take out in the morning, but if they opened and the contents spilled out the cops would know that the bodies came from the building.

Lang had thought of that. Lang thought of everything.

She moved the bags one by one, bouncing them down the stairs and praying they wouldn't rip. She opened the front door a slit and peeked out. A few people were walking by, but this was New York, there was always somebody on the street. They wouldn't look twice at a girl throwing garbage on the restaurant pile. It was illegal, but everybody did it.

Lang's words came back to her.

That's what I like about this neighborhood. Everybody's an accomplice.

Couldn't be tentative, had to treat garbage like garbage, not human remains. She half carried, half dragged, the bags out one at a time. Fish heads and spare rib bones protruded from the bags.

Hunan trash and human trash.

Five trips and it was over.

Her apartment was now exactly as she had left it two mornings before. There was no sense of spirits hovering.

After all, what kind of world would it be if God let pricks like this come back and haunt you? Lang had said.

On TV they were showing a surveillance photo of Tony Rasso. Then Lang's prison ID shot. "Police still haven't established a motive," they said.

She lay back and closed her eyes. *I'll rest for a second.*

She awoke to the sound of the garbage truck revving in the street. The vintage Movado said four thirty. She had been asleep for five hours. The TV was still showing the same photos.

She went to the window and watched them throw the bags into the wheezing hopper of the truck. In a few hours Archie and Malik would be towed out on a barge and dumped in the middle of the ocean. The bags would open. Their limbs and heads would float free. Grotesque deepwater creatures would swim up, eyes bulging, lips working, and nibble at them until they came apart and their eyeballs settled on the bottom.

No one would ever know what happened to them.

She stared at Lang's picture on the TV.

"We got away with it, Lang," she said.

The clock radio was blaring "Baby Love" by Diana Ross and the Supremes. It was nine a.m.

She was in bed, undressed, minty tang of toothpaste in her mouth, with no idea how she had gotten there.

Tessler's number was on the bed table where she must have put it. Couldn't use her phone, her number would come up on the Caller ID. She could see Lang nodding approvingly. "Smar girl."

She found Hanif's cell phone and called Tessler.

"Good morning, my dear. Sorry about your friend."

"Do you have the money?"

"Yes. When are you coming?"

"I'll call you."

"I'll be waiting."

It was hard to get into the tub, even when she had satisfied herself that there wasn't a speck of blood or a wisp of hair. She took a shower in her sneakers and washed her feet in the sink.

She thought of Gloria looking coolly at her nails and saying, "I have a lunch date." That was the attitude she needed.

I'll be Gloria for this.

She found a pair of black slacks and a white blouse. Her hair was too short. She had cut it in a fit of self loathing. But it would grow back.

It was hard to get Gloria's makeup right. Add some texture to the eyebrows to bring out the green in her eyes. A little slash of color to emphasize the cheekbones.

Gloria's act was even tougher. The young woman who'd seen it all. Sexy but bored. Powerless yet empowered. Totally ruthless.

She looked at the Levitan to get into the mood. A young man with a shy smile who had dashed off a little self portrait on a rainy day. She could almost hear him saying, "Is all this fuss about me?"

She took a cab to Twenty-eighth and walked down Fifth Avenue to Twenty-seventh across the street from Tessler's store. She had been sympathetic the day before, but today she didn't trust him. He knew Lang was dead and she was alone. The city was full of cut-rate killers. There was no shortage of meat cleavers and black garbage bags and plenty of room on the ocean

...oor for two more eyeballs. It would be easy to get the Levitan without paying.

If I go into that store I'll never come out.

The street was crowded with people mulling their own dark secrets. Nobody would notice two people exchanging bags.

She went into an Old Navy and checked the Petrossian bag. Then called Tessler on Hanif's phone.

"Come into the store, my dear," he said. "We can have privacy."

"We don't need privacy," she said. "You come to me."

A moment later he was crossing the street, all in black like Lang had been yesterday. Did he think she would like him better if he changed styles?

Everybody is somebody else today.

Tessler saw she was empty-handed. "Did you bring it?"

"I checked it at the Old Navy," she said, showing him the ticket.

"Needless precaution. I'm not going to grab it and run away."

He handed her a Starbucks bag that still smelled of coffee. There were two envelopes in it, one crammed with bills.

"That doesn't look like a hundred thousand," she said.

"Let me explain, my dear," Tessler said. "I was operating on short notice and could only get twenty-six thousand in cash."

Lang had called it.

He'll try to give you twenty cents on the dollar.

"In the other envelope you'll find a cashier's check for seventy-four thousand," Tessler said.

She shook her head.

"The check is good, I promise," he said. "Just take it up to Bank Leumi on Forty-fifth. Ask for Mr. Gideon. He's expecting you. He'll give you the cash."

She could almost hear Lang.

There won't be a Mr. Gideon.

"A hundred thousand," she said, "or I sell the drawing b[a]
to Mr. Lubimov. And tell him you're the one who's been tryin[g]
to steal it."

Tessler gave her quick, appraising look, then smiled graciously
like a good loser. "Gambit refused. I'll be right back." He turned
and hurried across the street, dodging traffic with surprising
agility.

She browsed an antique store window. Tiffany lamps, Art
Nouveau chairs, cloisonné boxes, cameo frames, cigarette
cases—antiques bric-a-brac painstakingly arranged. How much
of it was phony? Or swag.

"Swag," she said. The word had a knowing ring. She liked
the sound and said it again. "Swag."

In the window she saw Tessler running back. Now he had a
Lufthansa overnight bag.

"It's all there," he said, breathlessly.

"If it isn't I'll call Lubimov," she said.

She went back into Old Navy. The security guy had been
watching them. He peeked into the Petrossian bag as he handed
it back. If it had been a small package he would have thought it
was dope, but he lost interest when he saw the drawing.

Tessler was waiting at the curb. She opened the bag and gave
him a quick look. His lips trembled. "Yes . . ." He kept nodding the way people do when they're fighting tears. "After all
these years. Yes . . ." He pointed over his shoulder. "My father
is in the store, watching. He always stood at the window as if he
were waiting. Now he has what he was waiting for . . ."

It was a great speech. The ghost of a wronged man finds
justice at last. But was it true? Lang had said, you have to make
them want to believe you. And she didn't want to believe Tessler
anymore.

They exchanged bags. Without a word she turned to go.

"Wait," Tessler said. "I hate to leave a pretty girl with a bad pression. I know that Jerry Lang told you I was just a thief and a liar like him, but here's one thing I was telling the truth about." He fished in his pocket and handed her a business card with an address scribbled on the back. "My son Elliot, the producer. He'll be expecting you."

"For what?"

"For a part in his new film. Elliot is a much better crook than any of us. You can't go to jail for a bad movie and you can make more money than we ever do."

"Aren't you afraid I'll tell him about you?" she asked.

"A little. But that just adds to the intrigue, don't you think?"

He laughed and blew a cloud of Binaca in her face. "My son will love you and just think of the fun whenever we meet. We'll be like adulterous lovers sharing our own exquisite secret."

His grip was strong. Her hand was swallowed up in his. He stroked her wrist.

"Deception is so such sweeter when you have someone to share it with," he said.

THEY'RE ALL CLONES,

she thought.

The casting office was a replica of every casting office she had ever been to. It was in the same seedy midtown building where the same Deco elevator opened onto the same old men in overcoats and fedoras that seemed to have stepped out of the same time warp. The same slovenly doorman made her sign in the same smudgy register. The same janitor lurked with rapist eyes by the stairs. The same reception room was full of the same young actresses, long legs, plastic boobs, perfect makeup. They looked alike, sounded alike, and gossiped about the same people. They all the wanted the same thing and would do the same thing to get it. The gatekeeper who greeted each of them like old friends looked like every receptionist in every casting office in the universe. Like all the rest of them he would pretend not to know her although she had been there twenty times before and would tell her with crocodile regret that "we only see people with agent's submissions."

How could these people ever have intimidated her? Gloria was so strong in her she felt she could crush their pâpier-maché world between her fingers. The actresses tried to ignore her, but she could feel their eyes as she went to the desk. The gatekeeper made his clone speech.

"Do you have a resume?"

"No . . ."

"Did your agent call?"

"Don't have one."

"Sorry, but we only see . . ."

"Letitia Hastings?"

He picked up the phone with an icy look. "Letitia Hastings for Elliot . . ." Then his jaw dropped, his eyebrows arched, and he was her new best friend. "You can go right in, Letitia. Straight down the hall. Last office on your left. Can I get you something to drink? Coffee, water?"

She paused at the door. "Coffeewater," she said with a sweet smile. "That doesn't sound very appetizing . . ."

She walked down a hallway lined with movie posters. A burst of laughter came from the corner office.

"You realize you're enabling your father's sex life by seeing this girl, Elliot."

"Oh God, don't use my father and sex in the same sentence."

The man who had said that, tiny and gym trim, head shaven with a diamond in his ear, rose from behind a desk with startled eyes.

"Miss Hastings?"

"Yes." She towered over him. His hand was small, the grip uncertain. A scruffy little man with a scraggly beard and a Harvard Crew shirt was smirking in the corner. A stubby woman whose feet hardly reached the floor muttered into a cell phone and glared with unconcealed hostility.

It was a world of dwarfs. Why had she ever been frightened?

"I'm Elliot Tessler," the bald man said. He introduced the other two as if she should know who they were. She smiled sweetly as if she didn't.

"My father says you're quite the actress," Elliot said.

"How could he know, he's never seen me work," she said.

He was definitely taken aback. "But he said you were good friends."

"Oh I guess he wanted to make sure you saw me," she said. "I just met him in his store yesterday." She showed him the ring. "He sold me this. Beautiful, isn't it?"

"Yes . . ." He had the look of a man being swept out to sea. "Well, are you an actress?"

"Oh yes and I'd so love to be in your movie, Mr. Tessler, because I'm such a big fan of your work." She batted her eyelashes in burlesque flirtation. "How many times have you heard that today?"

He laughed. "Too many times." He was captivated. It was so easy it almost wasn't worth doing.

"Rhoda," Elliot said sharply. The stubby lady dropped her cell phone with an inquiring look at the smirking midget in the corner. "Can you give Miss Hastings the sides."

Rhoda handed her two script pages with a desperate smile, trying to figure out what had just happened.

"Have you seen *Nanoworld*?" Elliot asked.

"I'm probably the only one in the world who hasn't," she said.

"You and my father," Elliot said. "Any way, this is the sequel, *Revolt of the Nanoids*. You play a Succubot."

"Succubot?" she asked. "Is this porn?"

"No," Elliot said and turned pointedly to the smirking midget. "But we might have to change the character name . . . A succubot is a robot created cell by cell by a master nanotechnologist to seduce and manipulate men."

"Your life story, Letitia," the smirking midget said.

"Only in my case it was my mother who taught me," she said.

"Well let's see how good a job she did," Elliot said. "In this scene a man has been warned about you, but you overcome his resistance and seduce him," Elliot said. "Do you need a few minutes to study it?"

"You've told me all I need to know," she said.

He was flattered. A flush spread over his bald head. "You can read with me if you want."

"I want," she said. She put the Lufthansa bag down and stood over him. It was Lap Dance 101. In New York you were forbidden by law to touch the client so you simulated. It was what Gloria had done to hundreds of men before she met Lang. Letitia read the silly dialogue and simulated.

When she finished there was silence in the room. Elliot looked up at her with a mute plea. I surrender. Please don't make me suffer too much.

"You didn't act like a robot," the smirking midget said.

"A perfect machine designed by a genius wouldn't act like a machine," she said.

"She's right," Elliot said. "I wish you had given that note to the fifty girls we've already seen, Rhoda. Do you have an agent, Letitia?"

"Your dad?"

" 'Fraid not." He walked her to the door. Behind his back, the smirking midget and the hostile dwarf were exchanging puzzled looks.

"Oh wait a minute . . ." She had forgotten the Lufthansa bag.

"Gym stuff?" the smirking midget asked now, deciding to be friendly.

"Stolen art," she said. "My day job."

"I think you might be able to quit it, Letitia," Elliot Tessler said.

In the time it took her to walk down the hall the vibe had swept the office. The actresses knew they had lost out. The gatekeeper was scribbling madly.

"Letitia . . ." He handed her a message slip. "This is Claire Alpert with CAA. She's in town and Elliot wants you to call

her." He scribbled some more. "This is the Gansevoort ⸱
where you're having drinks with Claire at seven. Elliot's g⸱
to come along if that's okay."

She stepped out of the building and real world roared up a⸱
her. A news dealer was wearing fingerless mittens like Hanif.
The headline in the *Post* said: MAFIA DON KILLS ESCAPED
CON. There was a picture of Rasso and next to it Lang's prison
ID. It was the only picture she would ever have of him. She
bought ten copies.

She was on Ninth Avenue, not far from her apartment. Lang
had been raised in this neighborhood. There was an old donut
store where he might have hung out. She could see him as a kid
buying a chocolate donut for some little girl from the block.
How many of those girls had secretly loved him? All these years
later how many lay next to their husbands and still thought
about him?

I'll think about him.

She went in and got a bear claw with a large coffee. Two
sugars and a shot of milk. She sat at a cracked Formica table.
Lang had sat there and looked out at the street.

Hanif's phone was still on so she decided to make one more
call. It could be risky, the call could be traced. She took a bite
of the bear claw and dialed the number.

A familiar voice answered and she felt Gloria melting away.
She was Letitia again, the little girl who wanted to be Juliet.

"Hey Mom, guess what," she said, "I just got a part in a
movie."

ABOUT THE AUTHOR

Born in the Bronx and raised in Brooklyn, **Heywood Gould** got his start as a reporter for the *NY Post* when it was still known as a "pinko rag." Later he financed years of rejection with the usual colorful jobs—cabdriver, mortician's assistant, industrial floor waxer, bartender, and screenwriter. He has written twelve books and nine screenplays, among them *Boys from Brazil*, *Fort Apache the Bronx*, and *Cocktail*. He currently lives in Santa Monica, California.